Austral Skies
A Romance of Wings and Wrenches
By
Diane Shillington Parks

AUSTRAL SKIES

First edition. August 9, 2024.

Copyright © 2024 Diane Parks.

ISBN: 979-8227808332

Written by Diane Parks.

For my guys:
Jeff, Ryan, and Connor
Nerds, one and all.
Your love of history and aviation were an inspiration.
I love you.

Prologue

1931   Northern Territories

AGGIE GAZED SKYWARD, enthralled.

The small biplane swept across the sky at the neighboring ranch. Small and fragile, it flitted past her family who stood amazed at its aerobatics. The Ryan children had never seen an airplane; they had never had the opportunity. Living the wilds of Australian sheep and cattle country on a small cattle station, they went nowhere beyond their home, neighboring cattle stations, and the occasional trip to the general store in distant Birdum.

Their neighbors, the Sullivans, hired the plane to fly out and survey their property and take photographs of their home from the sky. They invited the nearby families to join them for a cookout and a chance to see the flying machine.

Aggie smiled as the lovely green plane bounced as it landed and rolled to a stop before them. Its double wings and long tail reminded her of a dragonfly. Mr. Sullivan clambered out of the plane with a wide grin on his sun-reddened face.

"What an adventure!" he enthused as he shook the pilot's hand. "What an amazing world we live in! Thanks for the ride."

The pilot smiled past his goggles and nodded his head. "Who's next?" he asked.

In their excitement, the children clamored forward with their hands waving in the air at the chance to experience the clear skies and open landscape.

"No, no," said Mum, addressing the Ryan children as they revealed their enthusiasm. "The Sullivan kids can fly if their parents let them. None of my babies are going inside that crate."

Aggie sighed. She would love to take a flight in that pretty green dragonfly, but even at ten years old, she understood. Mum pretended to worry about safety, but Aggie knew her mum didn't want to be beholden to Mr. Sullivan. Mum and Da couldn't afford to repay Mr. Sullivan for airplane rides for six children.

Da slid his arm over Aggie's shoulders, leaning down to whisper in her ear, "Look at that machine, Aggie."

"Oh, Da. It's magical."

Her Da smiled. "It is, isn't it?"

Da shared her imagination and he entertained her interest in all things mechanical. He allowed her to help fix both the tractor and the old jalopy they relied on for family travels.

"I wonder how it stays in the air."

"Sure, you said it yourself, Aggie. It's magic." Da winked at her.

She smiled and blushed. Her Da enjoyed teasing her with a twinkle in his bright blue eyes.

"Do you think someday I might fly in an airplane?" she asked.

"You might, dear Aggie. Anything is possible."

"Girls can't fly!" laughed her brother, Joe. He and their younger brother, Casey, were holding their sides, laughing at the ridiculous idea of a woman pilot.

Aggie shoved them both. "Girls can fly! Look at Amelia Earhart. We read about her in the paper. She's famous for it."

"Yeah, but she's an American. Americans do all kinds of crazy things, like letting girls fly." The boys were off in gales of laughter once again.

Aggie's face burned with frustration. She knew it wasn't likely that a girl from a tiny cattle station in the Northern Territories would fly an airplane, but why wouldn't they let her imagine it? Everyone should have a dream.

Da squeezed her shoulder. "Don't mind those silly boys," he said. "You dream your dreams, sweet Aggie. Don't let them go, no matter what."

Aggie smiled. Her Da always knew what to say. As she watched the little green plane take off into the cloudless blue sky, carrying one of the Sullivan kids, she let her imagination take wing as well. Someday, she vowed, she would fly herself.

Chapter One

June 1943
Sydney, Australia

SYDNEY BOUND!

Aggie felt thrilled to be on a train bound for her new position with the Women's Auxiliary Australian Air Force. All those years of greasy knuckles and broken nails keeping the cattle station machinery working would finally pay off.

Aggie stretched. Since leaving Birdum, she had been on the train for hours. Once in Sydney, she would meet her team for their training at Mascot Airfield.

Her eldest siblings, Chester and Mary, were both married now and running the family cattle station admirably. Joe and Casey were off in the Army. Eddie and Edith were now old enough to help around the homestead and with the animals. Finally, Aggie could set down her family's struggles and figure out who she wanted to be now that she was a grownup at twenty-one.

It seemed everyone in Australia was signing up to do their bit for the war effort. After Mass one Sunday, several of her friends talked excitedly about joining the Army. They had signed up for nursing training and encouraged Aggie to join them.

"Nursing?" Aggie questioned. "I'm not sure I'd be good at that."

"Why not?" asked her friend Laura.

"All that blood and nastiness? No, thank you. Besides, I can barely tolerate my own brothers and sisters when they're sick and grumpy. How could I take care of strangers?"

Aggie wanted to serve her country and hoped to do something with airplanes. The memory of the dragonfly biplane was ever-present. She read an article about the American WASP program where women pilots ferried aircraft from factories to airfields all around the United States. Many of those women already had flight training, though; something Aggie's family could never afford. Not after their struggles through the Depression.

While at the general store, she discovered an advertisement for the Women's Auxiliary Australian Air Force. With so many men joining up and being shipped abroad, The Royal Australian Air Force (RAAF) had an urgent need for skilled maintenance personnel to fill wartime positions in Australia and to assist the Aussies serving in the Pacific. They were looking for women to take over those roles. Aggie was sure she could use her knowledge and skills for the war effort – she'd helped her brother keep the farm equipment maintained and working for years. As a bonus, she would be working around airplanes. She might not get to fly them, but she sure could help fix them, proving herself to her brothers who teased her about her fascination with airplanes and her mechanical aptitude while relying on her to keep their family equipment working.

Aggie contacted the RAAF committee and sent away her application. She was delighted to receive a provisional acceptance to the program pending the completion of her basic training and aircraft maintenance training course. She packed her meager belongings, and the family drove her to the train station to bid her a tearful goodbye.

There she was, on the train, far from home on a grand adventure – just like her younger brothers Joe and Casey – ready to do her bit.

Stepping off the train, the crowd and the noise were overwhelming. As she stood, clasping her suitcase in one hand and her WAAAF paperwork in the other, a glamorous blonde with the most stylish suit and shoes she had ever seen approached her, grasping her arm.

"You look lost, ducky," she said. "A fellow WAAAF adrift in the crowd. At least we've found each other."

"How do you know I'm a WAAAF?" Aggie asked.

"From the letterhead on the paperwork you're clutching in that death grip. Come on! Let's go find our transport." She switched her grip from Aggie's arm to her hand, towing her through the crowd.

"I'm Betty Carter," the blonde said over her shoulder. "I thought of changing my name to Bette Cartier. Far more stylish, don't you think? Now is our time to reinvent ourselves. Setting off on this adventure amidst a war."

Aggie never considered reinventing herself or changing her name to something more fashionable. *Who thought like that?*

Apparently, Betty Carter, this force of nature pulling her through the servicemen and workers in the crowded Sydney train station. She guided Aggie through the crowd, popping out of the throng like a cork from a champagne bottle. The exit led to a small truck labeled 'WAAAF – Mascot Field.'

"How did you do that; know exactly where the truck would be?" Aggie asked, in awe of this blonde whirlwind who had taken control of her.

Betty offered a blinding smile and shrugged. "I'm ever so lucky that way. What's your name? I didn't catch it with the crush and the noise."

"I'm Agnes, Agnes Ryan. I'm from the Northern Territories, up near Birdum." She offered the name of the largest town near their tiny cattle station.

"Did you say Northern Territories?"

The women turned to see a petite auburn-haired woman lugging an enormous suitcase. She stepped forward to greet them.

"Hi! I'm Katie Larkin. I'm from near Alice Springs. Nowhere near your home, but still the Northern Territories. We should stick together!" She smiled and pushed her wire-rimmed spectacles up her nose.

"Oh, don't say you're going to abandon this Melbourne girl for someone from the NT," Betty pouted, with a twinkle in her eye. Aggie was pretty sure no one would abandon Betty. Ever. Still, she smiled and patted her hand.

"I wouldn't dream of abandoning a new friend, but I'm happy to meet another. Hi, I'm Agnes Ryan. This breathtaking creature is Bette Cartier, formerly of Melbourne." Aggie introduced Betty with her reinvented name in the fanciest manner she could imagine.

"Cartier?" Katie asked. "Like the diamonds?"

Betty burst out laughing. "Oh, Agnes! You're a doll!" She turned to shake Katie's hand. "A pleasure to meet you, Katie. Really, it's plain old Betty Carter. I was telling Agnes that this would be our chance to reinvent ourselves, complete with glamorous new names."

A gruff-looking sergeant leaned against the truck, smoking a cigarette, and watching this interaction with a look of boredom. He dropped the butt to the ground and crushed it out with his boot heel as he stood up straight, approaching the women.

"If you're done making up movie star names, perhaps Your Graces would get into the truck."

The girls exchanged sheepish smiles, embarrassed that this fellow overheard them. He picked up a clipboard from the driver's seat of the truck.

"We have Carter, not Cartier," he said pointedly, looking at Betty. "As well as Ryan and Larkin. We are still waiting on Doyle."

At that moment, a statuesque brunette ambled up wearing trousers and a tweed jacket, carrying a battered suitcase.

"G'day! Jackie Doyle, at your service." She snapped a jaunty salute at the sergeant. Unamused, he ticked a box on his clipboard, rose to his full height, and clasped the clipboard behind his back.

"I am Sergeant Maguire, part of the training team at Mascot Field. Be prepared to work hard. We need serious-minded young women to do serious work." He eyed Betty. "Please get into the truck so we can get to the airfield to start your training."

When they arrived at the airfield, the women were outfitted with their uniforms. The Class A uniform was a smart, dark blue skirt suit with a pale blue blouse and a dark blue necktie topped off with a soft peak cap in dark blue to be worn for dress occasions and in the office. The Class B uniform was less formal with a skirt or trousers, a blue waistcoat, and tie. They also received two sets of coveralls for when they worked on the planes and parts.

Betty frowned. "I don't think I'm going to need coveralls. I'm assigned to the signals and radio team."

Aggie and the others looked at each other, surprised. They had not been told their positions prior to arriving.

"Take the coveralls, Miss Diamonds," grumbled Sergeant Maguire. "We'll determine what you need and what you don't."

After receiving the rest of their kit, Sergeant Maguire took them to the WAAAF barrack at the edge of the airfield.

As they reached the basic looking building that would be their new home, a well-disciplined woman introduced herself as Mrs. Harrington. She would be the housemother and chaperone for all the enlisted women. Sergeant Maguire quickly parted ways with them at the barrack's door after the hurried introduction. Men could not enter the women's barracks, not even RAAF staff. Mrs. Harrington showed the four young women a room with two bunk beds, two large wardrobes, and a small washbasin in the corner.

"It's now 1500 hours...which is 3 p.m. for civilians," said Mrs. Harrington. "You have one hour to unpack and get your room squared away before meeting in front of the building at 1600. We will march to the dining hall for tea and introductions to the rest of the squadron. Please dress in your Class A uniform." She nodded curtly to the girls and left them crowded in the small space.

"Four of us in this tiny room?" Betty questioned. "We'll be on top of each other all the time."

Aggie glanced around. The room was larger than the one she shared with her sisters back home. With bunk beds, she would have a bed to herself. For years, she shared a bed with Mary, who was a terrible blanket hog. Having a bed to herself would be luxurious.

"I think we'll be fine. My sisters and I shared a room smaller than this. I think it will be cozy," Aggie said.

"Sure," said Jackie. "We won't be here in the room much, anyway. Just to change our clothes and sleep."

"It will be fine," agreed Katie with a teasing smile. "As long as nobody snores."

The girls set about unpacking their belongings from home and storing away their new uniforms and gear, chatting about where they were from and their families. Jackie, they learned, had traveled farther than any of them, coming clear across the continent from a town outside Perth.

When they changed into their uniforms for tea, they laughed as they bumped elbows and backsides as they tried dressing at the same time. Aggie helped Betty and Katie tie their neckties, as they'd never tied a tie before. She had plenty of practice from helping her little brothers get ready for church.

"We'll have to set up a rota with times to get dressed," Jackie joked. "Otherwise, we'll all be black and blue from bumping into each other."

At the front of the building, they met sixteen other young women. Mrs. Harrington organized them in two lines of ten as Sergeant Maguire made his way over to stand before the group.

"Cadets!" he barked in a booming voice. Several of the young women jumped. "We will march to the mess hall for tea and the beginning of your training. Stand tall and keep in step. Ready, march!"

There was stumbling and stepping on other people's feet as the women shuffled along. Aggie hopped and skipped to stay in step with Katie. At long last, they made it to the dining hall.

"We need to work on that," muttered Sergeant Maguire.

The women dined on a simple meal of tea and sandwiches with fruit as dessert, including juicy strawberries and ripe pears; fruits Aggie rarely saw at her dusty homestead. They were a delicious treat.

An RAAF officer stepped before them and began introductions. He was tall and confident with slicked back dark hair and an eye patch over his left eye. Aggie observed the subtle scarring on the officer's face before directing her attention to his remaining eye, which was a startling blue. She wondered how much of the war this man had seen.

"I am Captain Dempsey, the officer in charge of the WAAAF squadron here at Mascot Field. We will run this squadron like any other military unit. You will follow orders, be prompt, and be serious about your duties. Your work for the WAAAF is your primary focus and will be for the foreseeable future. You are not here to flirt with airmen or meet your husband. We are here to serve Australia and the Allied cause."

Some women frowned; clearly, they had been hoping to find a nice pilot to marry. Aggie sat up straight and proud. If she could help on the home front and allow a man to join the fight, she would do her best. No distractions.

"During the next week, there will be a series of aptitude tests to determine where you will best serve in the WAAAFs. For those already selected for special duties, you will still take part in the aptitude testing to determine if you can receive cross-training in another area."

The girls looked around at each other. Already selected for special duty? Aggie told her recruiter about her experience and skill in repairing farm equipment, but that wouldn't warrant special treatment. She glanced at Betty, who was looking down at her hands and appeared to be blushing.

Interesting, Aggie thought; *maybe Miss Bette Cartier had a special talent. Maybe she really was a movie star,* Aggie chuckled to herself.

"After tonight's meeting, you will retire to your barracks and lights out will be at 2200. We will reconvene at 0600 for calisthenics, followed by breakfast at 0700. At 0800, we will begin your aptitude assessments."

Katie leaned over and whispered in Aggie's ear, "We have to exercise at six o'clock in the morning? What have we gotten ourselves into?"

For the next few hours, the captain lectured them on the basics of military life. When the time came for dismissal to their bunks, the girls were showing signs of fatigue. Despite that, the excitement in the air among the new friends was palpable as they made their way back to their barracks.

They were settling into their room when Aggie turned to Betty, "What is your special skill?"

Betty flushed red. "No, darling. No special skills here," she denied.

"When we were getting our uniforms, you said you didn't need the coveralls. As if you knew you would work with radios and signals."

"You catch everything, don't you, ducky? Well, if you must know, I'm an amateur radio ham. I know Morse code. Back home, I built a radio that allows me to talk to people all the way in America and Europe. Don't tell anyone. It's all very embarrassing."

"Embarrassing?" Jackie cried, having eavesdropped on their conversation. "That's amazing! I'm studying engineering at university in Perth and have some interest in radios, though my area of focus is industrial engineering."

Aggie marveled at her new friends. In one day, Aggie Ryan, cattleman's daughter, and country girl, made two amazing new friends, one who could build radios, and another who was studying to be an engineer. What could she offer next to women like this?

Katie seemed to sense her uncertainty. "No worries, Agnes. I'm pretty good at fixing things, and you strike me as the handy type as well," she said with a wink. "You'll be fine."

Over the next week of training and testing, Katie's predictions proved true. While Betty could work wonders with the radios, she was inept with tools or fixing anything mechanical. Conversely, Aggie could disassemble and reassemble every machine placed in front of her. Katie was nearly as skilled as Aggie. Jackie's gifts seemed to lie in organization, outlining the most efficient method to complete a task. She was also a talented mechanic; she said her engineer's heart always made her wonder how things worked. Aggie smiled, thinking she might have an engineer's heart as well. If her Da saw her now, he would be amazed.

Aggie rarely allowed herself to think about Da after he abandoned their family. If she ever saw him again, she hoped he would be proud. He always encouraged her interest in fixing things, even if Mum thought it wasn't ladylike. Now look at her, surrounded by women with similar interests who didn't care if they were ladylike or not. Well, except Betty, she chuckled.

At the end of aptitude testing, Captain Dempsey gathered the women together to give them their assignments. Unsurprisingly, Captain Dempsey assigned Betty to the radio and signals team. Her ability to copy Morse was faster and more accurate than the radioman training the WAAAFs. Jackie went to the Supplies

Department, as well as being cross trained as a mechanic. Aggie was sure she'd have the department organized and running like a Swiss watch in a week. The trainers assigned both Katie and Aggie to the aircraft maintenance team, where they would work to repair broken airplanes and "Keep Them Flying," just like it said on the WAAAF recruiting poster.

The next weeks and months kept the women of the WAAAFs busy as they learned their new tasks. Aggie went from fixing her family's old car to learning how to rivet, patch holes in aluminum, and repair the radial engines on many war planes. She was always the first to understand a new topic and share what she learned with others, helping them do better as well.

Aggie was so pleased with her new life, with new friends and new challenges. She sometimes felt guilty that it had taken a war to find such happiness.

Chapter Two

November 1943
USS Enterprise

HENRY BOLANSKI WAS still amazed that this hard scrabble Polish kid from Chicago ended up on an aircraft carrier in the middle of the Pacific war.

When he arrived at the Bremerton Naval Station, he had his first sight of CV-6, the USS Enterprise. She was immense, with swarms of sailors working to prepare her to get underway. He climbed the gangway with his seabag over his shoulder. He saluted the ensign at the top of the ramp.

"Henry Bolanski, reporting, sir."

The ensign gave him a bored look and consulted his clipboard. "Bolanski...Bolanski...Oh, there you are. Pilot. Your bunkmate just arrived as well. Follow the signs to your berth and get unpacked."

Henry made his way through the cavernous hangar deck, filled with planes, equipment, boxes of fresh food, and other essentials being loaded onto the ship. After several wrong turns, he made his way to his berth. It was a small area lined with four sets of bunk beds. A line of eight upright lockers stood along the short wall.

A young man with short brown hair and hazel eyes greeted him.

"Hi! Welcome to the Dauntless squadron." He smiled and held out his hand. "Conor McLean, Chicago."

"No kidding! I'm from Chicago, too. Holy Trinity parish. Henry Bolanski."

"How about that? I grew up in the Montclare neighborhood. St.William's parish." The men laughed and shook hands.

"Sounds like we've got the Chicago mob here," said a low voice behind them. Henry and Conor turned, seeing a man reaching for a flight jacket in his locker. He shook his head and muttered, "Replacements."

Henry and Conor exchanged a glance. Henry introduced himself to the third man.

"I'm Joe Kowalski," he replied. "I'll be training you replacements. Do what I say, and nobody will get hurt."

Henry heard Conor snicker behind him. Kowalski gave him a disapproving glare. Conor flushed red.

"Sorry, sir," Conor said. "You sounded like a bank robber in the pictures."

Henry cringed. Laughing at your trainer wasn't a great start.

"So, can we grab any bunks? Or are they assigned?" Henry asked, trying to change the subject.

"These two bunks are available," Kowalski nodded to two beds next to each other. "You can use these lockers for your gear. Get your gear stowed and your bunks squared away. There's a briefing at 1600." With that, he left the berthing area.

"Oh, boy," said Conor. "That didn't go well." He shook his head as he sank down onto the bunk.

Two more men entered the berthing area. One was a tall, blond beanstalk of a man. The other was a shorter, red-haired fellow. The blond looked around, taking in the bunks.

"This reminds me of the bedroom I shared with my brothers on the farm," he said. "Sven Ahlstrom, Maple Grove, Minnesota. I'm supposed to be a back-seater for..." He consulted a handful of papers. "...for Henry Bolanski?"

Henry raised his hand. "Nice to meet you, Sven." He reached out to shake his hand.

"Does that make you McLean?" the redhead asked Conor. "Perry Mueller, Muskegon, Michigan."

Conor smiled and shook his hand. "Looks like we're more of a Midwest Mob, not just the Chicago Mob." He winked at Henry. "Now all we need is some guy from Wisconsin."

When they found their way to the briefing room, they learned they wouldn't need to look far for their guy from Wisconsin.

Kowalski stood before the new aviators and their back-seaters.

"I'm Lieutenant Joseph Kowalski, in charge of training aboard the Enterprise. I was studying at the Milwaukee School of Engineering with a Navy ROTC scholarship when the war broke out. They sent me for immediate flight training, and I joined the Enterprise just before Midway."

The men looked at each other, impressed. The Battle of Midway was the first big victory for the Americans in the Pacific, and the man before them had taken part.

"Many of the best pilots who flew at Midway now teach at the basic training programs you men have completed. Those of us left behind have been out at sea, fighting the Japanese and honing our skills. Listen to what the trainers and experienced pilots have to teach you, and you might just survive." He gave Conor a pointed look and Conor flushed. Henry sank lower in his seat.

"We depart Bremerton on November 1, heading to Pearl Harbor to meet up with the rest of the Task Force. On our way to Pearl, we'll be training. Practicing carrier takeoffs and landings, formation flying, everything we need to get you ready to face the Japs."

Once at sea, their carrier training began. Between leaving Bremerton and arriving at Pearl on November 6, Henry flew off the deck of the Enterprise more times than he cared to think about. Landing on the carrier in high seas took far more skill than the practice deck he used during his training in the placid Gulf of Mexico off Corpus Christi. He feared he wouldn't be good enough. His new friend and wingman, Conor, was a natural. His landings always looked smooth as silk, but privately, Conor shared that he was nervous every time.

They continued training once the ship arrived in Hawaii, focusing on formation flying and air combat tactics. The squadron was coming together with a good mix of old hands and new replacements. Henry and Sven worked well together as a team. They looked to Kowalski and his back-seater, Owen Kasprak, for advice and used them as their example. The group became close in the air and on the ship, with fellow pilots and others jokingly referring to them as the Midwest Mob.

When the Enterprise left Pearl Harbor in January 1944 as part of Task Force 58, they set a course for the Marshall Islands and were soon seeing action as the Big E raided Taroa.

Rumors aboard the Enterprise said they would launch their next attack against Japan's feared mid-Pacific fortress on Truk atoll. The fliers were excited and anxious to take on the equivalent of Japan's Pearl Harbor.

The Enterprise sent raid after raid over Truk. Henry and Sven flew so many sorties, Henry lost count. In the end, the Enterprise broke her own record for tonnage of bombs dropped in one day and launched the first night bombing attack in naval history.

From March through November, the Enterprise fought all around the South Pacific from covering the Marine landings at Emirau to the Marianas Turkey Shoot during the Battle of the Philippine Sea, the largest naval battle in history. Henry couldn't remember all the launches and landings and battles over the past year. Memories of some flights were so vivid; others were just a blur. He had lost friends, victims of bullets or crashes. It was hard to lose fellow pilots and see them replaced by fresh young kids right out of training. He now appreciated why Kowalski had been so hard on them that first day.

What a year it had been, Henry pondered as he stood on the flight deck as the Big E steamed into Sydney Harbor. Conor came up beside him as he looked out over the Sydney Harbor Bridge. Enterprise was making a brief stop in Sydney before returning to Pearl Harbor for a refit and training over the Christmas holiday. Henry and Conor were looking forward to shore leave. Neither were drinkers, so they weren't planning a booze-soaked expedition into Sydney's bars and pubs like most of the sailors lining the surrounding rails. They planned to find a pleasant restaurant with a good steak to celebrate surviving the past year.

As the Big E eased into her spot at the dock and her lines tied off, Conor clapped Henry on the shoulder.

"Let's go get some steaks, my friend! I can't wait for food not prepared in the Enterprise kitchen." Henry smiled and fell into step with his buddy.

Friday night. Time for a little adventure in Australia!

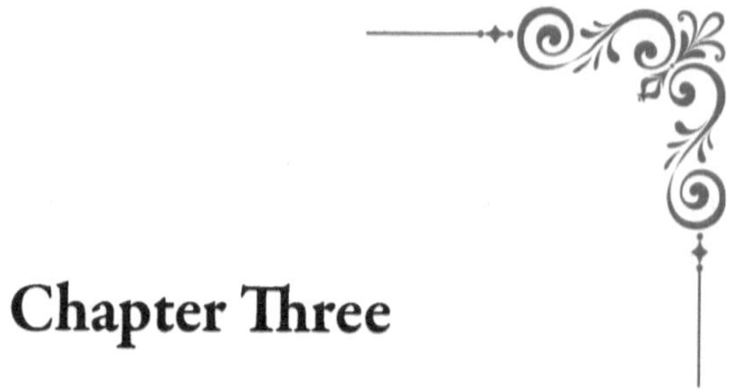

Chapter Three

N ovember 1944
Sydney, Australia

WHAT A YEAR IT HAD been! Aggie looked back on the past eighteen months in awe. She had learned so much. After completing basic training and her aviation maintenance training course, she had become one of the top aviation mechanics in her squadron, specializing in engine repair. Sure, other girls were more skilled with sheet metal work, patching bullet holes flawlessly, but if there was a difficult engine issue, Aggie was their go-to girl. Her mum always warned the Ryan children about pridefulness, but Aggie couldn't see any harm in pride in a job well done.

This Friday evening, Aggie and her friends were going out for dinner and a movie. They had saved up their pay to go somewhere special for a fancy meal. Katie and Jackie suggested going for steaks. Aggie felt guilty that she hadn't sent every penny of her pay home to her family, but her brother Chester assured her the cattle station was doing well. They didn't need her hard-earned pay to keep them afloat anymore.

Other women from the squadron mentioned an American aircraft carrier had pulled into port that morning. Several wanted to see if they could meet some American sailors. Aggie shook her head. There were plenty of Americans in Australia, as well as Brits and Canadians.

Betty was, of course, primping in front of the mirror.

"Rebecca was saying all the sailors from that carrier will be in town tonight. Maybe we'll run into some at the movie. What film are we seeing, anyway?"

"I hope the film's a romance," said Katie. In the past year, Aggie had learned that Katie was quite the romantic, though she was terribly shy when they would go to dances or activities at the RAAF Officer's Club.

"That's a great idea, Katie. We could use a little romance tonight," Aggie said with a wink. "Let's get going."

Betty had dressed to the nines in a lovely blue silk dress she kept at the back of her wardrobe for special occasions. It surprised Aggie that a night out with girlfriends counted as a special occasion for Betty, but she was a force unto herself.

Katie was wearing a floral cotton dress in a gentle green that highlighted her auburn hair. She allowed Betty to style her hair in victory rolls to frame her face and added a bit of pink lipstick.

Jackie dressed in tailored trousers and a tweed waistcoat over a cotton blouse.

"With that outfit, you look like Kathryn Hepburn," Betty teased Jackie.

"You say that like it's a bad thing, Betty. I'm completely satisfied with that comparison," Jackie said with a wide grin.

Aggie wouldn't mind being compared to the elegant actress, either. She was wearing a soft white cotton eyelet blouse and a khaki skirt.

"Oh, darling, that outfit is too dull. It looks like you could be in uniform," Betty said, surveying Aggie's ensemble. "What can we do to perk you up?" Betty pawed through a hatbox full of accessories on her bed, looking for the perfect finishing touch for Aggie's outfit.

"Here we go!" she said, brandishing a red silk scarf like a matador. She tied the jaunty scarf around Aggie's neck and pronounced her stylish.

When they got off the bus in downtown Sydney near the restaurant and theater, the place was a crush with soldiers and sailors. Betty's eyes lit up at so many targets of opportunity, as the pilots liked to say. This was a popular area for entertainment, and they found themselves pushed and jostled from all sides.

"Stick together, girls!" Jackie called over the noise of the crowd. "If we get separated, we'll never find each other."

"If we get separated, meet in front of the theater, to the right side of the marquee," Aggie suggested, remembering a technique her mum used when out in town with the whole brood of Ryan kids. Always have a rendezvous point.

"Good thinking," Jackie said. "Let's try to find the restaurant. McGillicuddy's Steakhouse, right? I think it's down the street a bit this way."

She elbowed her way through the crowd. Thank goodness Jackie was in the lead, she was a commanding presence and people often got out of her way. Betty waved and cooed to sailors as she followed in Jackie's wake, smiling, and apologizing for her friend, the human battering ram. Katie was clinging to the strap of Betty's handbag, towed along through the crowd. Aggie did her best to keep up but stumbled over her shoelace which had come undone.

What a place to stop and tie your shoe, she thought.

With the restaurant visible down the block, she stepped to the side out of the flow of the crowd and stooped down to tie her shoe. When she stood up, she could no longer see her friends ahead of her. She would need to find her way to the restaurant to catch up with them. She craned her neck to look for them.

At that moment, a large man stepped in front of her, blocking her path.

"Hey there, little lady. You looking for someone special?" he asked with an American accent, waggling his eyebrows at her.

Aggie nearly rolled her eyes.

"Um, yes. I'm looking for my friends. We're going for dinner at a restaurant up the street. Please excuse me." She attempted to step around him.

The man leaned over and braced his arm against the wall, blocking her path. He wore an American naval officer's uniform.

"Well, if you're looking to go out for dinner and have some fun, I can guarantee this Navy pilot will show you a better time than a bunch of girlfriends." He smiled wolfishly at her.

Aggie sighed. She had dealt with her share of unwanted advances when she was a slip of a girl working in the kitchen at Sullivan's cattle station, men pinching her bottom as she bent over to place platters of food on the table. Determined drovers cornering her, hoping for a bit of skirt. There was even a time...

She wouldn't think about that now. Now she had to deal with this ridiculous Yank.

"No, thank you," she said, straining to be polite. "I just need to get past you." She attempted to step around his other side, but he stepped in front of her, once again blocking her path.

"I think you should at least have a drink with me. We've been out battling on the high seas to save your little island here. Don't you owe me some gratitude?" he asked belligerently.

Aggie stared at him; she didn't know where to begin. Little island? Australia was an entire continent! As for having some obligation of gratitude to the US Navy? Was she supposed to have a drink with every one of them to say thank you? Or was he expecting even more to show her gratitude?

Aggie stood to her full height of five feet, three inches and squared her shoulders.

"I need to meet my friends. Now, please step out of my way," she said firmly.

The American laughed. He was over six feet tall and probably weighed twice her 120 pounds.

"What are you going to do if I don't get out of your way?" he smirked.

Well, this fellow had messed with the wrong Aussie, Aggie thought.

Growing up with four brothers, she knew how to throw a punch and the best spots to strike a man to slow him down. She had done it before at Sullivan's and she would do it again tonight if she had to. This was not the way she wanted to start her night out in town. She squared off the way her brother Chester taught her, preparing to get this bully out of her way.

HENRY HAD LOST CONOR in the crowd. They disembarked from the Enterprise with most of the crew and Sydney was now crawling with sailors off the carriers, as well as sailors from other ships and soldiers from all over. He had even spotted some of the famed Ghurkas in the crowd. It was like the League of Nations in this small entertainment area of Sydney.

The weather was remarkably warm, and Henry felt thirsty. He spotted a stand selling lemonade, which sounded refreshing. Tapping Conor's shoulder and shouting over the din, he said he was stopping for a drink.

After purchasing the bottle of lemonade, Conor was gone. Maybe he hadn't heard Henry telling him he was stopping. Henry glanced at the paper in his hand with the name of the steakhouse. A local dockworker had recommended the place when Henry and Conor asked where they could find a good meal: McGillicuddy's. It was supposed to be along this street somewhere. He'd find his way and meet up with his buddy.

As he maneuvered through the crowd, he sipped his drink, surprised to find it was fizzy, not like lemonade back home. He spotted a young woman stumble on something. He watched out the corner of his eye as she bent down to tie her shoe. When she stood, an American naval officer blocked her path.

Oh, no, thought Henry, recognizing the man.

Michael Richard, one of the Hellcat pilots from the Enterprise, who thought he was the greatest gift to aviation since Charles Lindbergh.

Michael came from money, growing up between a penthouse in Manhattan and his parents' swanky place in the Hamptons. He insisted on the French pronunciation of his last name: *Ree-shard*, and on being called Michael, not Mike or Mick or Mickey, like a normal guy. Michael had been studying business at Columbia, which he told everyone within five minutes of meeting them. He was an arrogant jerk, and a Yankees fan to boot. Henry and the rest of the Midwest Mob called him Jasper Theodore Worthington behind his back because it sounded like the name of a rich, snobby guy like Michael.

Henry tried to skirt around the pair when he heard Michael tell the girl she ought to have a drink with him to show her gratitude. For what, saving Australia? Henry felt his hand tighten around the neck of the bottle of lemonade. He didn't appreciate Michael talking to a lady like that.

He had seen enough men back home in Chicago try to take advantage of his ma that way; a widowed woman on her own. Like she should show some gratitude to the iceman for carrying blocks of ice up to their apartment when he was getting paid to haul ice.

Henry watched as she stood up as tall as she could and faced Michael. She was pretty, in a girl next-door way, with brown wavy hair and blue eyes. She looked neat in her skirt and blouse with a bright red scarf tied at her neck, but he could see her squaring off for a fight if needed. She asked Michael to step out of the way, more politely than Michael deserved, in Henry's opinion. When Michael asked what she was going to do if he didn't, Henry stepped in.

He walked up to the young lady and thrust his bottle of lemonade at her.

"Here's the lemonade you asked for," he blurted in a too loud voice. "Should we go meet your friends now?"

She glanced at him, confused, blinking her eyes. Then, with a shaking hand, she reached out and took the bottle of lemonade. She glanced quickly at his uniform, taking in his rank insignia.

"Why, thank you, Lieutenant..."

"Bolanski, ma'am."

"Of course, Lieutenant Bolanski. How could I forget?"

She was playing along; Henry could hardly believe it.

He nodded to Michael. "If you'll excuse us, we're meeting friends for dinner up the road at McGillicuddy's."

Michael looked between Henry and the young woman, incredulous with surprise.

"She's with you?" he asked in disbelief. "How'd a guy like you get a date with a dame like this less than three hours after we left the ship? You've never picked up a girl at any of our other ports of call.

Henry blushed as Michael mentioned his track record, or lack thereof, with the ladies in front of this lovely young Aussie.

"Maybe I could get a date because I didn't spend the last three hours drinking my way through every bar from here to the docks," Henry said, astounded that he came up with a pithy comeback on the spot. "Now, if you will excuse us, we're off to dinner."

He offered the young woman his arm. With slight hesitation, she took it, and he led them away from a slack-jawed Michael. Henry was pretty sure he was going to pay for this interaction back on the ship, but right now, he felt about ten feet tall for helping a lady out of a jam.

Once they had moved down the street, the young woman dropped his arm and breathed a deep sigh. He glanced at her and noticed she was trembling.

"Are you okay?" he asked. "I'm sorry, I didn't mean to be forward. It just seemed like old Jasper wasn't leaving you alone and you didn't look like you were interested. I only wanted to help." Henry knew he was blathering, but she was upset, and he worried he had contributed to her distress.

She shook her head and smiled.

"Oh, no, you don't need to apologize. I appreciate your help. I've had similar experiences when there wasn't someone to come to my aid. It just makes me shaky to think about it."

Henry frowned. What a world that a young lady minding her own business had to worry about fending off unwanted attention just for walking down the street. She said something that pulled him from his thoughts.

"I'm sorry. What did you say?"

"How did you know about McGillicuddy's? How did you know that's where my friends and I were going for dinner?"

"I didn't," he said. "That's where my buddy and I are planning to eat." They smiled at each other as they walked up to the front of the restaurant.

Conor jogged up.

"Hank! I thought I lost you in the crowd, glad you still found the place. Look who I got to join us, Kowalski..." Conor trailed off as he spotted the young lady next to Henry. "Oh, you found a date?" Conor looked crestfallen, worried they might leave him behind after he and Henry had planned this night out.

"No, no. I stopped to buy a lemonade when we got separated. I spotted Miss...?"

"Ryan," the young lady supplied.

"I spotted Miss Ryan here in the crowd. Jasper Theodore Worthington was bugging her and wouldn't take no for an answer. I stepped in to help her out."

"Is that really his name?" Miss Ryan asked. "What a posh name for such a lout."

"That's not really his name; it's what we call him behind his back. Pompous windbag," Henry said. He turned back to Conor. "Anyway, Miss Ryan is also having dinner here with her friends, so I walked her over."

"To keep the dragons at bay," she smiled at Henry, who promptly blushed to the tips of his ears.

Conor nudged Henry with his elbow. "Dragon slayer. Nice."

At that moment, a gaggle of young women rushed up.

"Oh, ducky! We lost you in the crowd!" exclaimed a glamorous blonde in a blue silk dress that clung to her figure.

"We were going to leave for the theater to meet you at our rendezvous spot," said a tiny redhead in a floral dress.

"A rally point. That's a smart idea," said Conor. When the women turned to look at him, it was his turn to blush and look at the ground.

Miss Ryan took a moment to introduce her friends. Henry returned the favor, introducing Conor and Kowalski.

"Thank you for your help, Mr. Bolanski," Miss Ryan said formally. "I hope you gentlemen enjoy your supper." She turned to take her leave.

"Are we going to let these lovely officers go their own way?" pouted Miss Carter. "We're all at the same restaurant about to have a meal. Why don't we push some tables together and make it a party?"

He and Conor exchanged helpless looks. Neither of them was very savvy with women and Kowalski was an 'all business all the time' kind of guy with them. Henry was amazed Conor had convinced him to join them for dinner. However, he noticed Kowalksi eyeing Miss Doyle in her trousers and vest.

Kowalski spoke up. "We'd be delighted to join you, ladies. One caveat: let's avoid war talk."

He then entered the restaurant with his usual take charge attitude, requested a table for seven, and promptly seized the seat next to Miss Doyle.

Henry sighed. So much for the quiet night he and Conor planned. Dinner with four lovely women was the opposite of a relaxing evening for the socially awkward pilot and his equally awkward wingman. What could go wrong?

Chapter Four

November 1944
Sydney, Australia

AGGIE WAS READY TO kill Betty.

Railroading these poor naval officers into joining them for dinner! Perhaps Betty was now learning a lesson. She had her eye on handsome Mr. Kowalski, but he only had eyes for Jackie. They chatted away, each leaning in with an elbow on the table to get closer.

While Betty tried to restrain her sulk on the other side of Mr. Kowalski, Aggie turned her attention to Katie. She was deep in conversation with Mr. McLean.

As Mr. Kowalski suggested, there was no discussion about the war. The dinner conversation started with discussion about their hometowns and pre-war occupations.

Upon learning that Mr. Bolanski and Mr. McLean were from Chicago, Betty cried out, "Like Al Capone!"

Both men winced. "Yes, like Al Capone," they agreed. Everyone associated Chicago with that one thing, they explained.

"We were in port in Majuro and the locals would say, 'Chicago! Bang bang!' when they heard where we were from," Mr. Bolanski said. Those gathered around the table laughed.

Mr. Kowalski told them he was from a city called Milwaukee. He had studied civil engineering prior to the war, which perked up

Jackie, who studied engineering in Perth. Soon they were off in their own little world, discussing bridge design and systems optimization.

Mr. McLean had been studying history at Loyola University in Chicago.

"What area of history is your focus?" asked Katie.

"Um, the Napoleonic era and the British response. Nelson at Trafalgar, Wellington at Waterloo," said Mr. McLean, blushing beet red at Katie's attention.

"I had an ancestor who fought at Waterloo."

"From Australia?" he asked, confused.

"Well, no," Katie said. "My family lived in Ireland. My great-great grandfather answered the drum, took the king's shilling. Before the family had to emigrate. The Famine, you know."

Mr. McLean's hazel eyes darkened. "Yes, the famine. My family emigrated to America." They locked eyes and nodded.

"I like history as well," Katie volunteered, to Aggie's amazement. Katie was usually so shy around men. "I planned to attend the teacher's college in Alice Springs and get my certificate to teach. I would enjoy teaching history." Then they were off, Katie and Mr. McLean sharing thoughts about long-ago events.

Aggie looked on. She wondered if Mr. Bolanski had been at university before the war. It made her feel rather inadequate; little Aggie Ryan, who left school at fourteen. What could she contribute to a conversation about history or engineering?

Mr. Bolanski looked across the table at her and smiled. Aggie thought he was rather handsome with his wavy dark hair and blue eyes fringed with black lashes. He had a slight cleft in his chin and a charming smile.

"What about you, Miss Ryan? Tell me about where you're from."

"Oh," she said. "Not much to tell. I was born and raised on a cattle station in the Northern Territories. What you would call a 'ranch' going by the Western pictures at the cinema."

"I like a good Western. Tell me about the place."

Aggie glanced away. "It's not very interesting."

Betty caught her eye and exaggerated mouthing the words, "Flirt with him."

Aggie turned back to Mr. Bolanski. "What would you like to know?"

"Tell me about your family and what you do on the ranch."

"Well, I'm the third of seven children."

"Wow, seven kids! Your mom must have her hands full."

Aggie wasn't sure she wanted to share this sad story.

"My mum died when I was thirteen," Aggie said.

"Oh, I'm sorry," Mr. Bolanski said. "That must have been hard. My father died when I was a kid."

Aggie nodded. "Then you can understand."

During the first years of the Depression, the Ryan family struggled. Her parents fretted over money, cattle, and putting food on the table. Mum never recovered from the birth of baby Edith, and when she passed away in 1933, it crushed Da. When the drought came in '34, he became undone. Aggie never imagined seeing Da in such a state. He would stand on the porch, staring out at the dusty ground, worrying his lower lip between his teeth, shaking his head.

One night, Da entered the bedroom shared by Mary, Aggie, and Baby Edith, gently kissing each of them on the head.

"Keep hold of your dreams, my girls..." he whispered. "...for I have lost all of mine." Then he rose to leave.

"Da?" Mary asked. He glanced back at her, shook his head, and slipped out of the room. In the morning, he was gone.

"Where's Da?" asked the younger boys.

"Perhaps he rode to the Austral Downs Station to look for work," said Chester, the oldest of the Ryan children. "I'm sure we'll get a letter in a few weeks full of Da's adventures on the grand cattle station."

Mary nodded in agreement. "I bet he will send some money back for us. Maybe then we can have a treat."

Joe and Casey, the inquisitive 12- and 10-year-olds, shared a skeptical look but didn't ask any questions.

"Oh! I hope Da sends us a treat!" chimed in six-year-old Eddie. Baby Edith, who wasn't really a baby anymore at three, had no opinion to offer on Da's whereabouts.

Aggie was worried. She hoped her Da would come home soon.

He never returned.

So began the odyssey of the next seven years. Chester, at 16 took over running the cattle station as if he were a grown man. Mary, 15, managed the homestead; cooking, cleaning, mending, washing, and caring for little Edith and Eddie. Joe and Casey helped Chester with the cattle and farm chores while keeping up their studies. Mum wanted her children to be educated and they would honor her by continuing their schoolwork.

As for Aggie, Aggie worked. Hard. She helped Mary around the house. The kitchen garden became her responsibility, growing what food they could. She put her clever mind and hands to work, helping Chester keep the tractor and farm machinery running. The big brother who always teased her about her interest in machines was now grateful to have someone who could diagnose a broken water pump and repair it with the parts on hand.

"Times were tough," Aggie said to Mr. Bolanski as she finished telling him about her family and life on the cattle station.

Mr. Bolanski looked at her with sympathetic and serious eyes. Aggie searched for a happy memory she could share with Mr. Bolanski and shake off the sadness that accompanied thoughts of her father's abandonment.

She grinned, thinking of her happiest childhood memory, and told him about that long ago day when she saw the green biplane at the Sullivan place and how she was so fascinated by the machine.

He seemed to brighten. "You like airplanes, huh? Have you ever flown in one?"

"Heavens, no! Why would a girl like me ever have reason to fly on a plane?"

"I don't know. Is it something you would like to do?"

"It would be like a dream come true."

Mr. Bolanski looked thoughtful. "Well, keep dreaming. You never know what might happen."

At that moment, Betty gave a start from her end of the table. "Oh, ladies! We must get going. The picture starts in thirty minutes, we need to get through the crowd to the theater."

The girls gathered up their things. There was a brief skirmish over the bill, with the men insisting they should pay and the ladies flatly denying them. In the end, they split the check with much grumbling from the gentlemen.

"Thank you so much for helping me tonight," Aggie said to Mr. Bolanski, stepping into the street. "And thank you for joining us for dinner. I had a wonderful time."

Mr. Bolanski looked down and scuffed his toe against the ground. "I had a really nice time, too. Glad I could be of service with old Jasper Worthington."

She smiled. "My slayer of dragons," she said as she briefly touched her fingers to the center of his chest. "Thanks again."

She and the other girls turned and made their way through the crowd to the theater. As she walked away, she looked back over her shoulder and raised her hand in a little wave to Mr. Bolanski. He was really a lovely fellow. Such a shame she'd never see him again.

HENRY, CONOR, AND KOWALSKI watched the women walk away. Henry absently rubbed the spot on his chest where Miss Ryan had touched him.

"Well, that was amazing," said Kowalski.

"What's that?" asked Henry.

"An evening out with women and you two actually talked."

"Says the guy who spent the entire night wooing a girl with engineering principles," Conor shot back.

"Hey, I'm just saying it was a good night for you two. Maybe when we get back to Pearl Harbor, you can try out your newfound skills on some navy nurses or local girls."

Conor gave him a shove. Henry was quiet, considering his conversation with Miss Ryan. It was easy talking to her, partly because he just enjoyed listening to her stories about life on the cattle ranch and her stories about her family. She clearly loved them very much. The story about the little green biplane stuck with him.

"She likes airplanes," he blurted to his friends.

"What?" asked Conor.

"She likes airplanes. She told me she saw an airplane once as a kid and taking a flight would be like a dream come true."

"She must have flipped when she found out you're a pilot."

"I didn't tell her I was a pilot," Henry admitted sheepishly.

"You didn't tell her you're a pilot?"

"No."

"You are a United States naval aviator trying to impress a girl who thinks flying would be a dream come true, and you didn't tell her you're a pilot?"

"No."

Kowalski shook his head. "You're hopeless. No wonder you don't have a girl."

"I know," sighed Henry, defeated. "Believe me, I know."

Chapter Five

November 1944
Sydney, Australia

IT WAS SUNDAY MORNING, and Aggie and Katie left the barracks for Mass. Aggie's family wasn't very religious, but her mum had insisted on Sunday Mass and evening prayers. With her brothers fighting in Europe, she often asked God to keep an eye on them.

Katie and Aggie took the bus to the cathedral in the city. It was beautiful and so different from the little chapel she attended back home with her family. The soaring pillars and stained glass were a treat to admire during Mass. She and Katie donned their headscarves and sat in their preferred pew halfway down the nave.

As the services began, Aggie listened to the readings and let the gentle Latin wash over her. She closed her eyes and sang along with the familiar songs and recited the prayers.

She prayed for her family back home and her brothers fighting abroad. Thinking about those fighting the war, her mind drifted to the American naval officers they had met on Friday night. She thought about Mr. Bolanski, who had helped her with the bully and listened to her stories. She said an extra prayer for him as well.

Returning to her seat after Communion and kneeling to pray, Katie elbowed her in the ribs. Aggie looked up from her folded hands and glanced at Katie.

"I think Mr. McLean is here!" she whispered. "I think I saw him on the other side of the aisle, waiting in line for Communion." Katie craned her neck as she searched the other side of the church.

"Stop that!" Aggie whispered back. "You look like an emu with your neck all stretched out. It's unseemly."

Katie continued glancing over her shoulder. Now Aggie wondered if Mr. Bolanski was also at church. Bolanski sounded like a Polish name, so he might be Catholic. It took every ounce of her self-control to keep from turning and scanning the crowd with Katie. If the men were at Mass, they might spot each other on the steps outside or as they walked to the bus.

Or not at all, most likely. Katie had been talking about Mr. McLean and his insights into history since they parted ways with the officers on Friday night. She may have conjured him as a figment of her imagination.

Aggie joined in singing the last hymn, though her singing was not very good. None of the Ryans could carry a tune. Katie gave her the side eye and shook her head. Aggie smiled and winked. She leaned over to whisper to Katie, "It's like the song says. How can I keep from singing?" Katie laughed.

Katie had been laughing a lot since Friday night, Aggie noticed. Even in the face of Betty's incessant teasing about "Mr. History."

"I've never seen someone use a history lesson as flirting," Betty declared. "I guess it worked for you two." Aggie laughed at Betty's observation.

"What are you laughing about?" Betty demanded. "At least she tried to flirt, even if it was the oddest way imaginable. You had that nice young man hanging on your every word and never even batted your eyelashes."

That surprised Aggie. Sure, she had found Mr. Bolanski to be a kind man, handsome too, but she couldn't imagine he would be interested in her. She was just little country girl Aggie Ryan; she wasn't fabulous like Betty. What could she offer a naval officer from the big city of Chicago who had traveled the world?

"I think you're mistaken, Betty. He was just being polite, asking me questions about where I grew up. It's very different from where he's from in Chicago."

"Darling, a man does not spend an entire meal asking you about Podunk Sheep Station in the Outback if he's not interested in you."

"It's a cattle station and it's in the Northern Territories."

"Whatever! The next time you find yourself with a man who shows a passing interest, and you're interested in return, FLIRT!"

Aggie shook her head, thinking back on Betty's insistence about Mr. Bolanski, but she would keep her advice in mind.

Aggie and Katie made their way out of the church and greeted the priest as he stood on the steps outside.

"Have a wonderful week, ladies. Keep 'em flying!" he said cheerfully.

As they strolled down the street to the bus stop, they noticed an American jeep at the side of the road with its bonnet up.

"They must be having car trouble," Katie said. "Maybe we can help them. I know you have experience fixing cars."

Aggie considered. She had worked on her family's car and the farm truck back home and knew the jeeps were simple machines, made to be serviced in the field. She could take a look if the men driving it would let a girl fix their car.

"Let's ask if we can help," she said to Katie, and they headed for the broken-down vehicle.

HENRY STARED AT THE engine of the jeep like he had any idea what he was looking at. He was a city kid from a poor neighborhood. If he wanted to get around, he took the bus or the streetcar or the good old Toe and Heel Express. Unless a sign saying "Fix Me"

with an arrow pointing to what was wrong suddenly popped into existence, Henry was at a loss. He looked at Conor, who stood next to him, scratching his head.

"What do you think?"

Conor shrugged. "No clue. We didn't own a car; I always walked or rode my bike everywhere back home"

Henry heaved a sigh. Why had he let himself be talked into going to the fancy cathedral for Mass? Conor said he was tired of Mass in the chapel on the Enterprise and listening to Father Palazolla's droning homilies and off-key singing. Henry had to admit that it was nice to be in a proper church with a proper choir. It was also nice to see the ladies dressed in their Sunday finery, rather than a bunch of sailors in their dungarees.

He just wished they had convinced Bill Lago, the crew chief for his Dauntless, to come with them. A fellow Chicagoan, Bill grew up in his family's three flat in the shadow of Wrigley Field. He had tales of skipping school to sneak into Cubs games that made Henry and Conor jealous. He also spent part of his youth under the hoods of his buddies' cars, souping them up to make them as fast as possible. Bill could fix anything, especially some broken down jeep.

"Do you gentlemen need some help?" a quiet female voice asked from behind them. A familiar female voice. Henry turned and found himself face to face with the lovely Miss Ryan from Friday night and her friend Miss Larkin.

"Oh, Miss Ryan! And Miss Larkin," he exclaimed.

Conor stood up so fast he cracked his head against the hood of the jeep, then whirled around.

"Miss Larkin," Conor said, rubbing the back of his head, then bowed slightly. Bowed? Henry tilted his head quizzically. Had he actually seen Conor bow?

"Good morning, Mr. McLean," replied Miss Larkin as she bobbed a small curtsey. Curtsey? *What was that about?* Henry thought.

Henry glanced at Miss Ryan. Was she seeing this as well? Miss Ryan was looking back and forth between her friend and Conor, a bewildered look on her face. Clearly, he wasn't the only one watching his buddy play out a Regency era greeting with the little Aussie redhead.

Miss Ryan appeared to shake herself to attention.

"Are you fellows having some trouble with your jeep?" she asked, nodding to the useless vehicle with its hood up.

"It won't start," Henry explained. "Neither of us ever owned a car. We don't know what's wrong with it."

"Then why were you looking under the bonnet?"

"Because when you have car trouble, you pop the hood and look underneath."

"Even if you don't know what you're looking at?"

"Apparently."

Miss Ryan chuckled. She had a warm laugh, Henry noted, like hot chocolate on a chilly day. He was glad he could make her smile even at the expense of him looking ridiculous.

"Would you mind if I take a look?" she asked.

Henry remembered her talking about helping her dad and brothers with the family car. He stepped aside. "Be my guest."

She rolled up the sleeves of her blouse, bent over the engine, and fiddled with the jeep's innards. Henry stood there watching, impressed by her competence.

Growing up with his ma, he knew women could be mechanically minded. She had taught herself to do basic plumbing and household repairs to keep their house running during the Depression. Miss Ryan seemed to have a similar "can do" spirit. He stood back and smiled and let her get to work.

AGGIE DELIGHTED AT running into Mr. Bolanski again. She never expected to see the American again, despite Katie's fanciful imaginings that they would all meet again. Yet here they were, two days later, and she was up to her wrists in grease from his jeep. It was a simple fix, a couple loose connections to the battery that were easily adjusted and reconnected.

"Mr. Bolanski, would you please try to start the jeep?" she called from under the bonnet.

"Just a sec!" he called back. She felt the vehicle dip as he climbed into the driver's seat. The ignition clicked and the engine roared to life. She stood up, dropped the bonnet of the jeep, and tried to rub the grease from her hands.

"Thank you so much!" said Mr. Bolanski, walking up to her. He offered his handkerchief so she could wipe her hands. "We would have been here forever without your help. Probably would have ended up AWOL and in trouble for losing a jeep."

"Aggie can fix anything," Katie piped up. She shared a grin between Mr. Bolanski and Mr. McLean. *Mostly for Mr. McLean,* Aggie thought.

Aggie glanced toward Mr. Bolanski, who looked back at her in admiration despite her greasy hands. Then she heard Betty in the back of her mind. Flirt. She smiled brightly at Mr. Bolanski.

"Happy to be of service. Wouldn't want you stranded and AWOL."

He smiled back. "Well, we appreciate it. Our captain can be a dragon when guys get out of line."

"So, it was my turn to slay your dragon," she said cheekily. *Where had that come from?* Aggie thought. Betty must be rubbing off on her.

"Yes, ma'am, I guess so," replied Mr. Bolanski with a devilish grin. *Oh, this man,* thought Aggie. *Too charming by half.*

His friend cleared his throat and cast a hopeful glance at Katie. "Um, would you ladies maybe like to join us for lunch? Just–just so we could thank you for your help!" He blushed to the roots of his hair as he stammered through his invitation.

Katie turned to Aggie with an equally hopeful look, eyes wide, as if pleading for Aggie to say yes. Aggie hid a smile; it was so fun to see shy Katie giddy over a boy.

"I think we could probably do something like that," Aggie agreed.

"Great!" Mr. McLean said. "Hank, you can drive. Miss Larkin and I will ride in the back because we're shorter." He helped Katie into the back of the jeep, holding her hand just a little longer than necessary.

Aggie and Mr. Bolanski shared a look and smiled.

"I think he's smitten," Mr. Bolanski said to her in a soft tone.

"He's not the only one."

With her direction, he drove them to Aggie's favorite inexpensive café, close to Mascot Field. They served simple food that reminded her of home, and she was happy to explain some of the Australian dishes to Mr. Bolanski, including cheese and bacon rolls and meat pies.

"Is this anything like your food back home?" she asked.

"Not exactly," he said. "My Ma is Polish, so we eat a lot of Polish food. Or whatever she brought home from work."

"Your mum brought home food from work?"

"Tons of food!" Mr. Bolanski said. "When my Tatus – my father – died, she had to go to work. Ma had a great job as a cook at the Allerton Hotel in downtown Chicago and she would bring home leftovers from the hotel kitchen. We were poor during the Depression, but we always had enough to eat. With my appetite, that was no small thing."

"I brought home food from my work as well," Aggie shared.

"I thought you worked on your family's ranch," Mr. Bolanski questioned.

"Oh, I did, but I also worked in the kitchen at a larger cattle station nearby to earn extra money for our family."

Aggie thought back to her work during the Depression. As hard as the Ryan children worked, it was not enough to pay the taxes and bills and keep food on the table. The oldest, Chester, Mary, and Aggie, sat on the front porch one night after their younger siblings were in bed trying to find a solution.

"I could go work on one of the bigger stations," Chester offered.

"Then who would take care of our livestock?" Mary asked. "We are barely keeping the herd fit and healthy now. How would we manage without you?"

"I don't know," he sighed. "But we need to do something."

Aggie looked at her siblings. Chester couldn't leave the station and Mary was working hard keeping everyone fed, clothed, washed, and the house clean, not to mention caring for little Edith.

"I'll do it," Aggie volunteered. "I'll find work."

At fourteen, Aggie made her biggest sacrifice, leaving school so she could go work to bring home extra money. She took a position at the Sullivan's cattle station as a cook for the drovers in the bunkhouse.

Every Sunday evening, after a simple family supper, Chester would escort her to the Sullivans. She prepared gallons of coffee, fried dozens of eggs, and rashers of bacon, made multitudes of sandwiches, and myriad stews, roasts, biscuits, and pies. On Thursday afternoon, her brother would bring her home to help with chores at the Ryan's place.

At the end of her first week, Mrs. Sullivan handed her a hamper along with an envelope with her pay.

"What's this?" Aggie asked, looking into the wicker basket.

"Oh, leftovers from this week. I thought your family could use them up. I'd hate for the food to go to waste, and I know you kids are in need," Mrs. Sullivan said, with a pitying look in her eyes.

While Aggie disliked taking charity and the way Mrs. Sullivan looked at her, she took the food gratefully for her family. With seven mouths to feed, anything extra was a boon.

"Wow, that's great that you did that for your family. I bet it was hard for you to be away from them," he said. "I didn't see my Ma much when she was working. She had to be at the hotel for the dinner service, so she would prepare a cast-iron skillet with the previous night's hotel dinner. She would start with a layer of leftover potatoes, then add whatever meat had been served, chicken, beef, pork. It didn't matter. She would top the meat with vegetables and smother the whole thing in gravy. The skillet would be on the stovetop for me to warm up when I got home from school."

"That sounds delicious."

"It was. My Ma is the best cook!"

Aggie did her best to follow Betty's advice and flirt, but she was not sure if it was working. Mr. Bolanski was attentive to what she said and asked questions like he had the other night, but who could tell? And did it really matter? He was an American sailor and would be leaving soon.

After their meal, the foursome clambered into the jeep as the men offered the women a ride home.

"Where to?" asked Mr. Bolanski as he settled behind the steering wheel.

"Just down the road to Mascot Field. That's where our barracks are located."

"Barracks? At the airfield?"

"Of course," said Aggie with a proud lift of her chin. "We're WAAAFs. Women's Auxiliary Australian Air Force."

He gaped at her. "So, you work on planes?"

"Yes, Katie and I are on the aviation maintenance team."

"No wonder you could fix this old jeep in two seconds flat," he said. "How about that? The little girl who fell in love with a green biplane grew up to fix planes. That's pretty amazing." He shook his head and smiled.

Aggie stared at him; he remembered. She had tossed out the story about her green dragonfly the other night as an anecdote and he had remembered it. Maybe Betty was right, maybe he was interested.

As the jeep drew to a stop at the gates to the airfield, the girls climbed out and the group said their thanks.

"Goodbye, Mr. Bolanski. It was so nice to see you again," Aggie said as they parted. She even remembered to do that thing Betty recommended, looking up at him through her eyelashes.

"It was a pleasure. Maybe we'll run into each other again. Seems like Australia isn't as big as some people make it out to be." He winked at her as he climbed back into the vehicle.

Wouldn't that be lovely? Aggie thought as the men drove away.

Chapter Six

November 1944
Sydney, Australia

"CAN YOU GIVE ME A HAND, Aggie?" Jackie called out as Aggie passed the storage area where Jackie ruled with an iron fist. "I need to get these parts pulled and loaded on the truck. It's a delivery for that aircraft carrier before they pull out. It seems they want to get a lot of work done during their trip back to Hawaii."

Aggie had just finished her most recent repair on a US Navy Hellcat. The engine was a mess. Aggie broke down most of the engine and pieced it back together. *A bit like Humpty Dumpty,* she thought. With no immediate assignment for Sergeant Maguire, she was available to lend Jackie a hand.

Jackie handed her a list of parts and Aggie sorted through the parts drawers, removing what was needed and signing the parts out, using the system Jackie had designed to maintain inventory and keep things organized.

In the afternoon, they loaded the parts onto the Army truck designated for their use. One girl with an artistic flair had painted a wrench wielding Valkyrie on the bonnet of the truck, like nose art on an airplane, and painted "WAAAF Mobile" on the doors in looping sky-blue script. Sergeant Maguire made a big show of being unimpressed, but Aggie suspected the artwork delighted him.

Jackie jumped in the driver's seat of the loaded truck and invited Aggie to ride with her to the naval base. Aggie climbed in; she was interested to see the big aircraft carrier up close. She knew the Hellcat she repaired was off the Enterprise.

They drove through the gates where one of the crew chiefs would inspect the parts and confirm the order was complete before having crew members unload the truck and move the gear onto the ship.

Aggie and Jackie stood outside the tailgate, looking up at the immense ship. A dark-haired man approached the truck and held out his hand to shake.

"Bill Lago," he introduced himself. "We sure appreciate your help with these parts. Our onboard stores are pretty low after Leyte Gulf."

"Happy to help," said Jackie, all business. "We had most of what you requested. Let's review your order and get the truck unloaded."

Jackie's in her element, Aggie thought. She was happiest when bossing around a bunch of underlings. Aggie worked in the back of the WAAAF Mobile, passing down airplane parts to the waiting sailors as Jackie and Bill consulted over their mutual clipboards. As she worked, she thought about Henry and wondered if he was aboard the Enterprise.

HENRY WALKED DOWN THE gangway of the Enterprise, heading for the Commissary at the post exchange. He heard a rumor that they had received a delivery of honest-to-God American Coca-Cola and he was on a mission to get his hands on a bottle. He hadn't had a proper Coke since they'd left Hawaii last January.

Sven was coming with him as well, hoping to buy some new socks. Sven and Conor's back-seater, Perry Mueller, were best friends, but were always pulling crazy pranks and practical jokes on each other. The most recent had been Perry hiding all of Sven's socks in the cockpits of the squadron's Dauntless airplanes. When the aircrews found them, they discovered the socks were perfect for small detail work and polishing.

Sven now had the pair of socks on his feet, and nothing more. Their berthing area smelled of his single pair of unwashed socks. Kowalski threatened to throw him overboard if he didn't get more before they departed for Pearl Harbor. Kowaski was in tow as well to make sure Sven bought the darn socks and to stock up on cigarettes before they hit the high seas heading for Hawaii.

As they reached the end of the gangway, they stepped aside for a line of sailors carrying boxes from a nearby truck, which had a stylized Viking woman holding a wrench painted on the hood and the words "WAAAF Mobile" written on the door. He perked up. Miss Ryan was a WAAAF. Could she be part of the delivery crew? He began planning to steer his group closer to the truck.

In the end, he didn't need an ingenious plan. Kowalski spotted Bill near the truck and strode over.

"Are these the replacement parts we ordered from that Australian outfit?" Kowalski asked Bill.

Bill snapped a quick salute. "Yes, sir. Miss Doyle and her colleague are helping us unload. Everything seems ship-shape, all very organized and ready to be added to our parts department."

"Miss Doyle?" Kowalski asked as Jackie turned to him, clipboard in hand.

"Yes, Mr. Kowalski. So nice to see you again."

Then, Miss Ryan popped her head out of the back of the truck.

"Oh! Hello, Mr. Kowalski. And Mr. Bolanski, a pleasure." Her cheeks flushed a faint pink. Henry was thrilled to see her.

"We must stop meeting like this," she said and blinked at him a few times.

Wait, Henry thought, *is she batting her eyelashes at me?*

Sven looked around the group, wide eyed. "Hold on," he asked. "You guys all know each other?"

Kowalski cleared his throat. "Well, yes, we met in town on Friday evening. I believe Hank assisted Miss Ryan, and we all had dinner together afterward."

Sven's guileless Minnesotan face broke into a smile.

"Oh! So, you're the girl Hank's been talking about. Nice to meet you! I'm Sven Ahlstrom, Henry's back-seater." He reached out, grabbed Aggie's hand, and started pumping it up and down.

Oh, geez, thought Henry. Sven and his big mouth. Really, he was the nicest guy on the planet, but he never knew when to keep quiet. Thank goodness he wasn't in military intelligence.

Miss Ryan looked at Henry with wide eyes before turning her attention to Sven.

"So very nice to meet you, Mr. Ahlstrom." She extricated her hand from Sven's mad pumping.

"Nah, call me Sven. Everyone does. Or Swede, that's my nickname, which is odd because it's not any shorter than Sven." Sven kept babbling, which was fine with Henry because it took the attention off him.

"You know, you all should join us at the beach tomorrow," Sven said, turning to Henry and Kowalski while including the women. "We went on Saturday. It was amazing. Perry decided he wanted to learn how to surf. He thinks if he masters it, he could surf in Lake Michigan back home if there's a big storm and the waves get big enough. Mostly, I think he's trying to impress that girl at the surf shop. Anyway, we're gonna go tomorrow and have a bonfire on the beach. Becky, the surf shop girl, said we could grill shrimp over the fire and make an evening of it. Wanna come?"

Henry wasn't sure if Sven had paused for breath during this invitation. He really was the nicest guy, with the energy and enthusiasm of a Labrador puppy.

The women looked like they were still processing the sheer number of words Sven had spewed at them.

Kowalski took over. "I believe Sven is inviting us to a grilled shrimp dinner on the beach while Perry tries to woo fair Becky from the surf shop with his middling surfing skills."

Jackie snorted. "Sounds like fun. Which beach?"

Sven broke into an even wider smile and provided the details. He invited Bill along as well, but he declined, stating he needed to get the parts unpacked and put away.

Miss Ryan looked at Henry and smiled. She did that thing where she looked up at him through her eyelashes making his stomach flutter.

"I look forward to seeing you again, Mr. Bolanski. Do you think your friend Mr. McLean might come?"

Henry's heart sank. Why was she asking about Conor? She was fluttering her eyelashes and looking up from under her lashes for him, wasn't she? Or was she interested in Conor? Henry was so confused.

"Perhaps if Mr. McLean were to come, I could persuade Katie to join us as well?"

Oh, right, Henry got it now. She was trying to set up her little redheaded friend with his buddy. That made more sense.

Sven nodded approvingly. "Sure! Conor will probably come. Bring whoever you want, the more the merrier! Though I suppose we'll need more food if there's a crowd..."

Jackie patted him on the back. "Never fear, Sven, we'll get the food sorted."

The group parted ways as the truck was unloaded, and the ladies needed to return to the airfield. As they waved goodbye, Henry was tickled to think the irrepressible Sven had wrangled him a date on the beach with the lovely Aggie Ryan.

"C'mon, Sven. Let's get to the Commissary. I owe you a Coke!"

Chapter Seven

November 1944
Sydney, Australia

AGGIE DIDN'T KNOW WHAT to wear for a beach party.

She never went to the beach before she moved to Sydney. Since she never learned to swim, she didn't have a bathing suit. Luckily, Betty grew up swimming at the beaches near Melbourne and outfitted her. She dressed Aggie in khaki shorts and a short sleeve white blouse which she knotted at Aggie's waist. Aggie wasn't sure about baring her midriff, but Betty thought she should show off her flat stomach.

Aggie was excited to see Henry Bolanski again, especially after learning he was a pilot. Sven told her he was Henry's back-seater, so he must fly one of the Dauntless dive bombers, a plane with a back seat machine gun. How exciting it would be to hear about his flight experiences! She wondered why he hadn't mentioned he was a pilot when she told him about her interest in airplanes.

The friends drove to the beach in high spirits. Piling out of the borrowed jeep with beach bags, blankets, and bottles of lemonade, they followed the path to the surf shop run by the mysteriously enchanting Becky and spotted their party near the water's edge. There were a few beach umbrellas and surf boards planted in the sand.

"The WAAAFs have arrived!" announced Betty to one and all.

Sven turned to them with a big smile. "We're so glad you could come."

Conor rushed over to relieve Katie of the bags she carried.

"It's very nice to see you again, Miss Catherine," he said. Aggie hid a grin. Miss Catherine, he sounded like Rhett Butler.

Henry came splashing out of the water with a wide smile.

"Greetings!" he called with a wave of his hand.

Aggie looked down, embarrassed. Mr. Bolanski was quite...fit, with broad shoulders and toned stomach muscles. She hadn't thought about what he might look like without a shirt and in swim trunks. He caught up a white undershirt from a blanket spread on the sand and pulled it over his head.

"I just went for a quick dip. I couldn't resist taking a swim. Plus, I thought I might need to rescue Perry."

The figure with the surfboard caught everyone's gaze as he flailed in the waves. A pretty girl with long blonde braids stood ankle deep in the water, shouting encouragement. That must be Becky.

"He's determined. I'll give him that," said Henry.

"Faint heart never won fair lady," Aggie observed.

Is that so?" Henry asked, turning to her with a charming smile.

Maybe Betty was right about flirting, thought Aggie. Since she'd tried it a few times, Mr. Bolanski seemed more interested in her.

The friends began to relax and enjoy their time at the beach. They cheered when Perry finally stayed upright on the surfboard and rode it onto the beach. Becky squealed and threw herself into his arms. Perry looked bedraggled but triumphant. Becky's friends arrived with a sack of fresh shrimp and a grill. It was time to build a fire and get cooking.

"I can build the fire," volunteered Conor. "I'm an Eagle Scout."

"Of course you are..." muttered Kowalski. He stood up and dusted the sand from his trousers. He held out a hand to Jackie to pull her to standing.

"Let's go gather some driftwood. Tell me about the system you developed for your maintenance inventory. I think something like that would help our maintenance crew."

They wandered off down the beach, heads close together in conversation.

"Love amongst the engineers," sighed Betty. Then she turned bright eyes to Sven. "So, tell me about yourself, you handsome Viking." She batted her eyelashes.

"Oh, wow. Well, uh..." Sven stuttered.

"You're overwhelming him, Betty," Aggie said, laughing. "Dial down the charm."

Betty gave a pretty pout. "You can't blame me. I'm feeling left out with all the love and romance in the air."

Sven blushed bright red. "Oh gosh, I'm sorry, Betty. I didn't mean to mislead you. I've got my Anneliese back home. We're gonna get married once I get back, and the war is over."

He pulled out his wallet and showed her a photo of his girl and began extolling the virtues of Anneliese and life in Minnesota to Betty.

"Poor Betty," said Aggie. "She's not used to being a third wheel. She's always the belle of the ball."

"I only see one belle here tonight," Mr. Bolanski said, looking into her eyes. She glanced down shyly.

As Conor got the fire going, Aggie and Henry settled onto one of the blankets to enjoy some small talk about the weather and their activities that day. Aggie spotted Betty discreetly holding up three fingers out of the corner of her eye as a reminder of Betty's tips about flirting.

"If you ever meet a pilot, remember that pilots like to talk about three things: themselves, flying, and themselves flying," Betty had told her with a wink. *It was worth trying,* Aggie thought to herself.

"You never told me you were a pilot. Sven revealed your secret, that you fly a Dauntless," Aggie said.

"Oh, I didn't want to sound like I was bragging, talking about being a pilot."

"No! It's fascinating. I know you said your family was quite poor. How did you learn to fly?"

ENJOYING HIS TIME ON the beach with Miss Ryan, Henry couldn't believe it was going so well. He was happy to tell her about his life in Chicago.

"We were very poor. Times were tough, especially growing up without a dad. I never realized how poor we were, though. Everyone around us was just as poor."

Miss Ryan nodded.

"I know my life could have turned out a lot different. I never even thought about being a pilot when I was a kid. I spent most of my time hanging out with guys from my gang."

"Gang?" Miss Ryan asked.

"Well, that's what we called ourselves. We were just kids getting into mischief. Since my Ma worked at the hotel in the afternoons and evenings, I had plenty of time on my own without supervision. That meant plenty of time for fun with Porky, Skinny, and Curly, my best friends. We'd chase each other along the rooftops of the garages lining the alleys, sneak into the rail yard to throw rocks at rats and passing train cars. In the winter, we'd skitch behind cars and buses."

"Skitch?"

Henry laughed. "On a snowy day, we'd grab the back bumper of a car or a city bus and have it pull us down the snowy street."

"That doesn't sound dangerous at all," she deadpanned. "My younger brothers would probably love doing something like that."

"It was mostly harmless fun when we were kids. As we got older, though, Porky and Skinny started to push things a little farther. There was drinking and smoking and gambling. They got us into a lot of fights. It was starting to feel dangerous, and not just fun shenanigans anymore."

Henry reflected back toward the end of their senior year in high school when Porky proposed the idea of selling car parts to raise a little extra money.

"Where are we gonna get car parts?" Skinny asked.

"From cars, ya knucklehead," Porky said.

"Um, from what cars?" Henry asked nervously, not sure he liked the sound of this plan.

"I dunno. Any cars. We're gonna liberate 'em," replied Porky. "Curly's good with taking things apart and putting them back together. We can pull apart whatever we need from cars parked along the street. Or we could steal the whole car and take it apart somewhere else."

Henry was anxious about the idea. He loved his buddies; they'd been friends forever. He didn't want to be a wet blanket but stealing car parts was a bad idea. Stealing a whole car was even worse. He knew his mom would punch him in the head if he got arrested. Waleria Bolanski would not tolerate a thief in her home.

When the weekend rolled around, he told Porky he had to help his ma paint the dining room and couldn't hang out with them. None of the guys really believed him, but no one was going to question Mrs. Bolanski about this alleged dining room painting project. Henry might not have a dad, but Mrs. B made up for it. All the boys in the gang were terrified of her.

It was a good thing Henry spent that Saturday night at home doing chores for his ma while she was working. The police arrested both Porky and Skinny while trying to steal a car on Saturday night. When his ma heard the news after Mass on Sunday, she was incandescent.

"How can you be friends with these characters?" she demanded. "Haven't I raised you better than to associate with thieves?"

Henry didn't know what to say. He never thought the gang's activities would ever advance to outright law breaking.

On Monday afternoon, when he returned from school, his ma was not at work, but at the house waiting for him with a look of thunder.

"Those boys! They're trouble!" she cried, still angry and upset about the events of the weekend and the gossip around the neighborhood. "Everyone is talking about those boys trying to steal cars. And they know you are a part of their group, so they are talking about you as well." She looked him straight in the eye. "We are going to talk to Father Parkolewicz."

Father Parkolewicz, Henry thought. Boy, he must be in some real trouble if his ma was dragging him to see the parish priest. She led him down the block, past chattering women on their doorsteps, who lowered their voices and pointed at him surreptitiously as they walked by. *People really are talking,* Henry observed. Ma hauled him up the steps of the rectory to Father Parkolewicz's office.

"Henry," said the priest. "Your mother tells me you're involved with some troubled fellows. She came to me and asked me to set you on the straight and narrow."

Oh, no, Henry thought, panicked. His ma was going to sign him up for the seminary. *Please don't let it be the seminary.* Henry might be nervous about talking to girls, but he did like talking to them. He'd like to kiss one someday. Being a priest would prevent that activity altogether.

Father Parkolewicz sensed his panic and hid a smile. "I have a friend who serves with the Christian Brothers. They've started a small technical school near Lockport called the Lewis School of Aeronautics. They teach young men about aviation, flying, fixing planes, that sort of thing. Airplanes are an up-and-coming technology, young man. Knowing how to work with them or even fly them would be a chance to build a productive life."

Henry breathed a sigh of relief. No priesthood. Phew! But Lockport? Where was Lockport? Somewhere in the hinterlands, out in the country, no doubt. Far away from the city...and his friends.

"I don't know that I could go to a school so far away," he prevaricated. "My Ma needs me."

"Your Ma needs you away from those troublemakers before you go to prison!" Ma huffed.

Well, that was dramatic. Henry rolled his eyes.

"Besides, I don't know how we would pay for some school a million miles away," Henry said, stalling for time.

"The Christian Brothers provide scholarships and there's a generous scholarship available from the Polish American Association," said Father.

"I doubt my grades are good enough for a scholarship."

Father Parkolewicz sighed. "The Christian Brothers created this school to help get young men off the streets and teach them a trade which will earn them a good living. They are interested in helping ... er ...wayward youth find a different path."

Ma gave him the hairy eyeball, her patented look of withering disappointment. Henry shuddered. Clearly, Ma didn't appreciate him being described as a "wayward youth."

Henry paused for thought. The gang had been getting out of hand of late. Their antics were no longer just fun, they were taking on a more dangerous edge. An edge that scared him, if he was honest. Father Parkolewicz was offering him a lifeline. All he had to do was grab it.

He looked at his ma. She was gripping the arms of her chair and had tears in her eyes. '

"I'd be so far away from you, Ma. I'd worry about you alone in the city," he said, looking into her eyes.

"I worry about you staying in the city. This is a chance to build a life, Heniu. Away from those boys who are leading you into trouble. I know you are a good boy. Prove it to yourself."

Airplanes, huh? He had always been interested in airplanes. They were elegant and took people to places and adventures far away. He'd never considered flying in a plane, much less piloting one himself. That wasn't something people from his neighborhood would ever dream of. Still, it was an intriguing prospect, and a chance to break from the gang, whose increasingly reckless activities were making him more and more anxious.

He glanced back at his mother. She was smiling and nodding through her tears. "Go, Heniu. Go, fly."

That was how Henry Bolanski found himself at the Lewis School of Aeronautics in the fall of 1941. While an indifferent student in high school, he discovered he enjoyed his classes at Lewis. He was challenged and interested in learning subjects important to his training as a pilot. Mostly, he loved flying.

When Father Parkolewicz told him about the program, Henry thought he would learn about aircraft maintenance, but Brother Joe and the other flight instructors saw a spark in Henry and selected him for flight training. The Christian Brothers at Lewis had an eye to events in Europe and sensed there would be a need for more pilots soon.

As his skills developed, Henry felt proud of his accomplishments, something he'd never experienced before. He began to see a life beyond the old neighborhood and the troublemakers in his gang.

On the afternoon of Sunday, December 7, the students and faculty at the aeronautics school heard the news of the Japanese attack at Pearl Harbor and realized their country was now at war. In the dining hall, many of the students were ready to leave school to enlist immediately. Brother Joe, Henry's flight instructor, admonished the young men to stay calm and finish their training.

"There will be a great need for your skills now. Be patient and finish what you are learning to use your flying to the best effect. You don't need to enlist; the military will come looking for you."

While some boys did not heed Brother Joe's advice and dropped out to enlist, Henry remained to finish his training. The Christian Brothers and the Polish American Association had put faith in him by giving him those scholarships, and he wasn't about to throw that away. He had made his way out of the old neighborhood, he wanted to make his ma proud.

In the end, Brother Joe was right. The military came looking for pilots, specifically the Navy came looking. In fact, the Navy took over the school to train more pilots. After completing his flight training and course work at Lewis, Henry commissioned as an ensign and would begin his type rating for his new plane soon after graduation.

At his graduation from Lewis, his ma was there in a new dress and tears in her eyes.

"You're gonna pop the buttons off that new dress, Ma," Henry teased.

"Oh, but I'm so proud of you, Heniu. Of course, I am popping my buttons," she said, dabbing at her tears with a hankie. "I am so proud of you, but I am worried about you, too. Off to fight in a war." She shook her head. "At least you joined the Navy. Your Tatuś was in the Army. It was terrible, living in trenches, poisonous gas. Awful! At least you will be safe from all that in the Navy."

Henry rubbed the back of his neck. The Navy wasn't exactly safe, he reflected. Following the war news, he knew about the naval battles in the Pacific and places like Iron Bottom Sound, where a thousand American sailors perished in one encounter with the Japanese. Plus, he was flying for the Navy. While his Ma was right, he wouldn't have to deal with trench foot and poison gas attacks in the Navy, he wasn't sure if his mother understood that his job in the Navy would involve flying his plane off the deck of a ship and then returning to land on that same ship. While it was moving. On a rolling ocean. He wasn't about to share that with her now if she didn't already know.

"Do you know when they are going to ship you out?" Ma asked.

"I have two weeks of leave and then I need to catch a train to Corpus Christi, Texas, where I will get my plane assignment and training on that type of plane."

"But you already know how to fly a plane. What more can they teach you?"

"Yes, Ma, I know how to fly, but all planes are different. You need to learn how to fly each one, where the controls are, and so forth. You can't just hop into any old plane and take off."

"I hadn't thought of that. I guess it would be like knowing how to drive a car and expecting to know how to drive a bus. That makes sense. Anyway, I will be glad to have you home for a few weeks to cook for you and fatten you up before you leave."

Boy, she wasn't kidding about fattening him up. After two weeks of his ma's cooking, Henry was lucky his uniform trousers still fit!

He took the train to Corpus Christi and learned the Navy assigned him to fly the SBD Dauntless dive bomber. While a little disappointed not to be assigned to fly fighters, he knew the Dauntless was a good plane and that he would see plenty of action. Once he earned his type-rating on the Dauntless, he waited to hear from which aircraft carrier he would be flying.

Late in the summer of 1943, he received the news that they had assigned him to the USS Enterprise. Enterprise! The Big E! Henry was beside himself with excitement. The Enterprise had been part of several major battles, including Coral Sea and the Battle of Midway. Pilots from the Enterprise were legends in the Navy aviation community, and Henry was proud to join their ranks.

Henry shared his stories with Miss Ryan as she asked about his flying experiences. Thrilled at how the evening was progressing, Henry thought he might get a kiss by the end of the night if he played his cards right.

AGGIE ENJOYED LISTENING to Mr. Bolanski's stories about his life in Chicago and his flight experiences.

The sun was setting, and the stars were coming out. Mr. Bolanski was scooting closer to her on the sandy blanket. *Maybe he'll hold my hand or give me a kiss before the evening ends,* she thought. She secretly delighted at the idea of a kiss.

"I was thinking," he said. "We've gotten to know each other. We can probably dispense with the Miss and Mister stuff, don't you think? Would you mind if I called you by your first name? The girls call you Aggie, right?"

"Well, yes. My name is Agnes, but my friends and family call me Aggie. When I came to Sydney, I tried using Agnes because it seemed more grown up, but everyone still calls me Aggie." She smiled at him. "I've heard your friends call you Henry and Hank. Which do you prefer?"

"The guys usually call me Hank. Most of the guys have nicknames. We're kind of informal amongst each other aboard ship. My Ma always calls me Henry. Or Heniu."

He paused and tilted his head in thought.

"I'd like you to call me Henry. You remind me of my Ma."

Aggie froze. She reminded him of his mum? Well, so much for thinking the flirting was working. She wasn't experienced with beguiling men, but she had been trying. She must be terrible at it.

Here she was in the firelight on a golden beach, with stars flickering to life overhead, and the young man she thought about so often in the past week told her she made him think of his mum. She scooted a little farther away from him on the blanket.

She forced a smile. "Henry it is then."

He looked at her quizzically.

"Is everything alright, Aggie?" he asked.

"Oh, fine. Just fine. It looks like the coals are burning down and they're ready to throw the shrimp on the barbie. I'll see if Becky needs any help with the cooking. I have plenty of experience cooking for a crowd."

Aggie was babbling but couldn't seem to stop. How embarrassing. She felt like she had been throwing herself at Henry and it turned out he wasn't interested at all.

Aggie jumped to her feet and brushed the sand off her shorts. She flashed Henry a strained smile.

"I'll go help with the food."

She strode off to help unload the picnic hampers and set up the grill over the fire. As she kept her hands busy, her mind was spinning, going over her interactions with Henry over the past week.

She thought he returned her interest. He seemed attentive to her stories, but that was foolish, she realized. He was probably being polite. Why would a man from a big city like Chicago be interested in a country girl like her? He had been to that aviation school and she left school at fourteen to work as a cook. What was she thinking?

Aggie helped with serving the food, a task she found familiar and mindless. She did her best to smile with her friends and the men from the Enterprise, laughing as the group teased Perry, as he bragged about his surfing skills and his plans to continue surfing on Lake Michigan when he returned home.

She didn't want to sulk and have her disappointment spoil the evening for everyone else. She was quiet, though, so embarrassed that she read the situation with Henry so poorly.

HENRY WAS CONFUSED. He and Aggie had been getting along swimmingly, sharing a blanket on the beach, and talking about his flight experiences. He felt like he was getting to know her, and he really liked what he saw. Henry had been slowly scooting closer to her on the blanket, hoping to build up the nerve to hold her hand. They even agreed to call each other by their first names.

Asking her if he could use her first name seemed old-fashioned to him, but Australia was more traditional and formal than back home, so he figured he should ask and show her he was a polite guy.

After that, things changed. She jumped up to help with the food and appeared to be avoiding him since then. Not rudely, but subtly. He would try to stand near her, and she would slip away, saying she needed to get something from one of the picnic baskets. When he tried to engage her in a private conversation, she would turn and include one of their friends in the chat. It baffled him.

He reviewed their conversation in his mind. Had he said something that had offended her or scared her off?

He told her about growing up in Chicago and his gang of friends and their shenanigans. When she heard he was in a gang, did she think he was a mobster? He didn't think so. She seemed amused by his descriptions of his gang's mischief.

Her attitude changed after they agreed to use first names. She asked which name he preferred her to use, Hank or Henry. He told her to use Henry, which was more formal and seemed to suit her. Plus, his ma always called him Henry, which made it special, and Aggie was special. He told her to call him Henry because she reminded him of his ma.

Henry froze. He told her she reminded him of his mother. *Good gravy!* What a thing to say to a girl he was falling for. That must be where he went wrong.

Don't misunderstand. In Henry's mind, his ma was the woman he admired most in the world. Ma traveled from Poland to America not knowing a word of English and was seasick the entire voyage. She married her beloved and when he returned home an invalid from the First World War, she cared for him and their family and created a loving, happy home.

After being widowed, his ma worked to support herself and Henry, keeping them fed and a roof over their heads throughout the Great Depression. She was loving, the best kind of mother, but she didn't take guff from anyone, including Henry.

He remembered coming home one Saturday night, drunk after a night out with his friends, trying to sneak into the house. He was bumping into things in the dark, making a terrible racket as he groped for the string hanging from the ceiling light fixture in the front room. As soon as he caught the string in his outstretched hand, he pulled it to turn on the light and found himself face to face with his irate mother, all five feet nothing of her. She promptly punched him in the nose.

The next morning, she dragged his pathetic, hungover self to Mass, where he had to explain to Father Parkolewicz the source of his two black eyes was his own mother. Henry quit drinking after that episode. Maybe the occasional beer at a ball game, never to excess. Getting slugged by your ma went a long way toward showing a fellow the error of his ways. Ma loved him like no one else and did all she could to keep him happy, healthy, and on the straight and narrow.

He could see the similarities between the two women. How Aggie helped to care for her younger brothers and sisters on the ranch. How she left school to work on the bigger ranch to help support her family once her father abandoned them. Both women cared deeply about their families and worked hard to serve them and others. Saying that Aggie reminded him of his ma was the biggest compliment he could give her. Ma was extraordinary, so was Aggie. He just needed to explain to her what he had meant, and how he felt about her.

The fire on the beach was burning low as he tried to approach her again. She was talking to Betty, who was grumbling about leaving and heading back to base. He knew he needed to act quickly to set the record straight.

"Good evening, ladies," he began, wondering how he could get rid of Betty.

"Hello, Henry," Aggie said with a smile that did not reach her eyes. "We were getting ready to pack up and head back. Sergeant Maguire will make us do press ups if we don't return on time."

Betty snorted. "I can handle Sergeant Maguire. I don't want to deal with Mrs. Harrington haranguing us about behaving like ladies and displaying fine moral character."

Aggie chuckled at her friend as she scooped up a blanket and shook the sand out. Henry stepped forward to help her fold the blanket, but she waved him off, stating she could manage it herself. Henry sighed.

People from their group were clearing up their belongings and making their way toward their vehicles. Perry was helping Becky stow the surfboards, umbrellas, and barbecue grill in the back of her surf shop. Jackie and Kowalski were in the lead, carrying blankets and bags back to the men's truck and the ladies' jeep.

Aggie finished folding the blanket and reached for the beach bag at her feet. Henry snatched it up before she could take it.

"I'll carry this," he volunteered as he dropped into step beside her. Conor and Katie were bringing up the rear, holding hands and whispering to one another.

"Listen, Aggie," he began, but she interrupted him.

"I hope you enjoyed your time at the beach. This was my first Australian beach party as well; it was a lot of fun. I hope all you boys leave with wonderful memories of your time in Australia," she said too brightly and with a forced smile.

They reached the jeep. He placed the beach bag in the back, then took her blanket and placed it on top. He turned to face her.

"Aggie, about what I said before? About my Ma. And you reminding me..."

"It's okay," she interrupted again, looking down and not meeting his eyes. "You don't have to explain anything or be polite. I understand."

She held out her hand. "It was a pleasure to know you, Henry. I hope you have an uneventful trip back to Hawaii."

He took her hand and shook it, holding it longer than he should. "It's been wonderful meeting you, Aggie."

At that moment, Betty walked up and started chivvying the girls into the vehicle, warning about the wrath of Sergeant Maguire and Mrs. Harrington as she clambered into the passenger seat. They looked away as Conor gave Katie a kiss on the cheek and offered his hand to help her into the back.

Aggie extricated her hand from his grasp. "Take care of yourself, Henry. Fly safe."

With that, she climbed into the back of the jeep across from Katie. She raised a hand in farewell as Jackie fired up the vehicle. He waved back and watched as the jeep drove away. He saw her reach up and touch her cheek, as if she were wiping away a tear.

Henry was disappointed he hadn't been able to explain himself. What did she think she understood? Certainly not that he thought she was the best girl he'd ever met, that he hoped he could see her again if the Enterprise returned to Sydney, that he'd be thinking about her all the way back to Pearl.

Chapter Eight

December 1944
Oahu, Hawaii

HENRY AND CONOR WERE at the beach, trying to enjoy a day off before the Big E returned to action.

Their time in Hawaii was challenging. The captain and admirals wanted the Enterprise to run nighttime flight operations. The fliers worked hard, mastering night takeoffs and landings on the carrier deck. It had been exhausting.

With an afternoon off, Perry wanted to practice his surfing. He'd wrangled Sven into trying it as well. The back seaters invited Henry and Conor to join them. The Chicago boys passed on the surfing lessons but sat side by side at a small tiki bar on the beach watching as their fellow Midwesterners fell into the azure waves of the Pacific Ocean.

Henry sipped on an icy cold Coca-Cola and sighed as he looked out over the ocean. It was beautiful here, but so strange to be celebrating a second Christmas season amidst the palm trees, sandy beaches, and gentle ocean breezes. The tiki bar had a small potted palm in the corner festooned with colored lights and Christmas ornaments.

He never thought he would miss slushy Chicago streets and the cold whipping down State Street when he and Ma would go to look at the Christmas decorations in the windows at Marshall Field's and Carson, Pirie, Scott, but there it was. Homesick for a proper Midwest winter. Henry had a stack of postcards in front of him on the bar. He brought them, planning to send them to Ma and some friends back home in place of Christmas cards. Who wouldn't like a Christmas postcard from Hawaii?

Conor was next to him, pen in hand, bent over a pile of papers. Writing to Katie back in Australia, no doubt. He knew the pair exchanged addresses at the beach party in Sydney. Conor had already written a letter to her every day since they set sail back to Hawaii.

"Are you writing your girl or are you writing the Great American Novel?"

Conor looked up and smiled.

"Writing my girl. I'm telling her about how the beach here in Hawaii compares to Australia. Also sharing my observations of Perry's atrocious surfing skills."

"So, you met some girl in Australia, huh, McLean?"

They turned to see Michael Richard take a seat down the bar from them. The Hellcat pilot had been looking for a chance to mix it up with Henry since their encounter in Sydney.

Conor ignored him; he didn't want Jasper Theodore Worthington to spoil his day. He returned to his letter.

"Did you ever score with that Aussie dame, Bolanski?" Michael asked Henry.

Henry felt his teeth clench. He didn't appreciate Michael talking about his Aggie that way. *His Aggie.* Didn't he wish?

"Don't talk about women like that, Michael," Henry ground out. "You sound like a jerk."

"Guess that means you didn't score," grunted Michael. He threw back a shot of something brown and ordered another. "No surprise you screwed that up."

I'll say, Henry thought. He met a lovely girl who had appeared to return his affection, and he had messed it up for sure. Henry sighed.

As Michael ambled off to pester Kowalski, who was chatting up the barmaid farther down the bar, Conor looked up from his letter.

"How did you screw it up?" he asked Henry. "You and Aggie were getting along like a house on fire. Katie told me Aggie was so excited when they ran into us at church and when Sven invited them to the beach thing. It looked like you both really liked each other. Did something happen that evening?"

Henry sighed again. "We were sharing a blanket, getting cozy, talking about planes and my flight experience. I was trying to work up the nerve to hold her hand, but first I asked her if we could drop the Mister and Miss thing and use first names."

"That sounds good," Conor said.

"Sure, until she asked if I preferred to be called Henry or Hank and I said she should call me Henry because she reminded me of my mother."

Conor looked at Henry, slack jawed.

"I'm such a knucklehead! I realized how she probably took that, like I wasn't interested, and I tried to fix it, but I never got to explain. She kept avoiding me."

"Yeah, you are a knucklehead. I mean, wow, I don't know a lot about women, but I'm pretty sure no girl wants to remind a guy of an immediate family member. It would be bad enough if you compared her to a sister, but your mom? That's not good."

Henry dropped his head to the edge of the bar.

"I know that now! But my Ma is the person I admire most in the world. So, when I said that, it meant I admired Aggie too. But she jumped up like someone had lit her on fire and stayed away from me for the rest of the night. She left before I could fix it."

"Maybe you could still fix it," Conor said.

"How am I supposed to do that? I'm in Hawaii, she's in Australia."

Conor tapped Henry's stack of postcards with his pen.

"Write to her. Send her one of those cards and explain."

"I can't write to her; I don't have her address."

Conor shot him an incredulous look and tipped his head toward the stack of papers in front of himself.

"You might not have her address, but I have the address of her best friend, who stays in the same barracks. I'm pretty sure a couple of smart guys like us can figure out how to get a postcard to her."

Henry perked up. "Do you think that would work? You don't think she'd be mad or think I was being too pushy?"

"You'll only know if you try. Get it off your chest, clear the air, and stop being such a sad sack. The worst that can happen is you never hear from her again. If that happens, you're no worse off than you are now. And who knows? Maybe she'll be happy to hear from you. Maybe she'll write back."

Conor was right. He could write to her, he could explain, and let her know he was still thinking about her, weeks later.

Henry thumbed through the postcards in front of him. He selected one with a colorful sunset beach scene and the words "Greetings from Oahu" splashed across the upper left corner. It reminded him of their evening on the beach in Sydney.

He plucked the pen out of Conor's hand and started writing.

Chapter Nine

January 1945
Sydney, Australia

AGGIE SAT AT THE SMALL table in the common room of the WAAAF barracks writing a letter home. She was updating her family about the holidays.

The girls had gone to Christmas Eve Mass at the cathedral in Sydney. For New Year's Eve, they attended a tea dance hosted by the Royal Australian Air Force squadron at the Officers Club. They had worn their best dresses and Betty had helped everyone with their hair and make-up, so they looked their best as they rang in the New Year.

At the dance, the girls sat at a table together, enjoying the music and nice Australian wines.

"I don't know about you girls," Betty said. "But I plan to dance the night away!"

Katie sat beside her, tapping her toes to the music.

"I'm just going to enjoy the music. I wouldn't feel right dancing with someone besides Conor."

"That's more men to dance with me, then," Betty laughed. "What about you, Aggie? Will you dance, or are you going to keep moping about Henry?"

"I'm not moping!" Aggie defended herself. Sure, she'd been thinking about Henry a lot and what happened at the beach and how embarrassed she was, but she wouldn't call it moping.

"Then get up and dance!" Betty said.

A pair of RAAF officers stopped by the table and asked Jackie and Betty to dance. Betty accepted with alacrity, taking the man's hand as he led her to the dance floor. Jackie assented more slowly. She asked the gentleman if he would get her a drink before dancing. He wandered off toward the bar.

"Why did you put him off like that? Are you worried about Mr. Kowalski?" Aggie asked.

"No," Jackie said, smiling. "Not everyone is as obsessed with those Americans as you two are. I doubt Mr. Kowalski is worried about me. He strikes me as a fellow who has a girl in every port. I enjoyed chatting about engineering with him but he's not really my type."

"Then why the hesitation to dance with this fellow?"

"Look at Katie, so wrapped up in her romance with her pilot. I'm not sure I want to get attached like that while everything is so unsettled, and people keep dying. I'll just have a dance, have some fun. No strings."

The officer returned with Jackie's drink, and she joined him on the dance floor.

"I don't want to speak out of turn, Aggie, but Betty's right. You've been awfully mopey since our night at the beach," Katie said.

"Not you too!"

"Yes, me too. I keep telling you, you blew the whole thing out of proportion."

"He told me he thinks of me like his mother! Obviously, he wasn't interested in me like that."

"I think you're wrong. Maybe what he was trying to say came out the wrong way. You said he tried to explain himself, but you stopped him before you heard what he had to say."

"Maybe. I don't know, I was just so embarrassed."

Katie reached over and hugged her friend.

"Let's leave that behind us for now. You should dance tonight. Let's have fun! It's the start of the New Year, let's look on the bright side."

Aggie squeezed Katie's hand in thanks. She would do her best to stay positive. She prayed 1945 would bring the end of war and see her brothers and all the other servicemen safely home.

As the night progressed, she danced with several servicemen, and everyone sang Auld Lang Syne at the stroke of midnight. She wished Henry had been there.

Aggie was finishing her letter home when Katie bounded into the room with a handful of mail. She received a steady stream of letters from Conor McLean over the past few weeks. He must have written to her every day since leaving Australia. *Lucky girl,* Aggie thought.

Katie rushed up to her with a huge smile on her face.

"You got something in the post today!" Katie said.

She was practically bouncing up and down on the balls of her feet. She seemed awfully excited about a letter from Aggie's siblings back home. Maybe it was a letter from one of her brothers serving in Europe.

She received a letter from Joe early in December, but nothing from Casey for a while. She would enjoy a letter from him. He always had such funny stories about the men in his unit and their adventures, as he called them. As if calling them adventures hid the fact that he was sharing his war stories with his older sister. She held out her hand.

"Thanks, Katie."

Katie did not give her the envelope she was expecting. She handed her a postcard. On the front was a sunset beach with gentle blue waves lapping the stand and the words "Greetings from Oahu."

Aggie looked up at Katie, stunned. Katie hopped back and forth from one foot to the other. Aggie turned over the card and read.

My dearest Aggie,

Conor and I are here at the beach, watching Perry and Sven try to surf.

I'm thinking of the last time I was at the beach. I was with you, and I messed everything up. I'm sorry if I made you angry or sad because I said things the wrong way.

I want you to know that I think you are special and extraordinary. You have been on my mind since the first time we met.

I hope you will allow me to write to you. If we stop in Australia on our way back out, I hope you will let me take you out again.

Know that I am thinking of you.

Yours,

Henry

Aggie looked up at Katie. She felt giddy with relief and could feel an enormous smile spread across her face. Katie looked at her expectantly.

"Well?"

"He apologized for messing things up at the beach party. He says he thinks I'm special and that he's thinking about me." She glanced down at the card. "He would like to write to me and see me again if the Enterprise returns to Australia."

"Yay!" Katie whooped. "I knew it! He likes you! I knew you were blowing what he said about his mum out of proportion. Of course, he thinks you are special. You *are* special and amazing!"

Aggie laughed as she clutched the postcard to her heart.

"You're going to write back, aren't you?" Katie asked.

"Well, I can't write back. He sent me a postcard, not a letter. I don't have his address."

Katie shot her a dubious look. "Did he have your address?"

"Well, no. I never gave it to him."

"And yet, he managed to get a card to you. I wonder how that happened?" She tapped her finger against her lips. "How convenient that your best friend has the address for his best friend, and they share the same berthing compartment. I imagine a couple of bright gals like us can figure out how to get a letter to your Henry."

Her Henry. Aggie sighed. She liked the sound of that. Aggie rose from her seat and scampered into their bedroom to grab more paper and an envelope. She had a letter to write!

DEAR HENRY,

Thank you for your postcard. It was so lovely to hear from you.

I appreciate your apology, but it's not necessary. Katie keeps telling me I blew things out of proportion and should have given you a chance to explain what you meant. So, I apologize for not listening to you.

I would be honored if you would write to me. I would enjoy hearing about your flight experiences and getting to know you better. If you should ever return to Sydney, I would be delighted to see you again.

Yours,

Aggie

DEAR AGGIE,

It was wonderful to receive your letter and forgiveness. I've never been very smooth with girls, so hopefully I won't make a hash of things again.

Our time here in H was very productive, with lots of training and flying at all times of day and night. We went to the beach a few times. Perry is still terrible at surfing.

I apologize in advance if my letters are cryptic. We must be careful not to share information that might aid the enemy if our mail goes astray.

But I can say we are heading out soon and will be in your part of the world in not too long.

Thinking of you,
Your Henry

Chapter Ten

L ate January 1945
    Sydney, Australia

THE ENTERPRISE LEFT Pearl Harbor on Christmas Eve and was steaming into Sydney Harbor. It was a brief stop to load up with fuel and fresh food before heading out to meet the Japanese.

The sailors lined the deck as they came into port. Henry was excited to return to Sydney. He received one letter from Aggie after sending his postcard and he was relieved that she had forgiven his bumbling. She agreed to write and said she would be happy to see him again if he found himself in Australia. Well, she was in for a surprise!

He and Conor had a plan; they would get to see their girls before other sailors ever got off the ship.

A Stearman Kaydet trainer was on board the Enterprise to be delivered to the Aussies as a training plane. All Navy pilots trained on the Stearman. It was a simple biplane, but responsive and fun to fly. Conor and Henry convinced the flight officer to allow them to deliver the plane to the RAAF at none other than Mascot Field, home of the Women's Auxiliary Australian Air Force.

Imagine the look on Aggie's face when he showed up flying the bright yellow plane.

The plane rested at the end of the flight deck. Henry and Conor donned their caps and goggles and they walked toward it. The Stearman was an open cockpit biplane with one seat behind the other. They would need the leather caps and goggles to protect themselves from the wind.

Henry climbed into the back seat, letting Conor take the front. The launch crew gave them the thumbs up, and they sped down the flight deck. Rumbling down the deck, the plane took off like a kite. They buzzed past the carrier's island and waggled their wings at the sailors manning the rails. Then they turned inland, heading to Mascot Field and the chance to surprise their girls.

AGGIE WAS UP TO HER elbows in the guts of a RAAF Kittyhawk fighter. The pilots had abused the poor thing on flights fending off Japanese attacks. She needed to rebuild the engine to get it back into action.

Betty scurried into the hangar, which was unusual. She enjoyed her work with the radio team, helping receive and relay radio traffic, as she was a wiz with Morse code. What she did not enjoy was getting grease on her uniform whenever she had to relay messages out to the hangar. However, today she was making a beeline for Katie, who was working on the Wirraway trainer next to Aggie's Kittyhawk.

Betty skidded to a halt in front of the plane. "Katie! The Enterprise is coming into the harbor today! I just heard the news on the radio report."

Katie dropped the wrench she was holding and reached up to fix her hair, as if her beau was going to materialize out of thin air, this instant in the hangar.

"Betty!" Aggie admonished. "Loose lips sink ships! You can't come in here bellowing about a ship coming in."

"Oh, please! Her boyfriend's on that ship. It's not like she's going to snitch to the enemy. And that carrier is so big, it's hardly a secret she's pulling into port."

Betty makes a fair point, Aggie thought. Everyone was so cautious, keeping quiet about the things they heard in the last few years. You never wanted to say anything that could give aid to the enemy.

"I need to get back. You might get to see those officers of yours soon if the Enterprise gets shore leave." With a wink, Betty turned on her heel and sashayed back to the radio area in her neat uniform.

Aggie looked down at her stained coveralls and the grease on her forearms. Katie had a smear of dirt on her cheek and her red hair was coming out of the scarf she had wrapped around her head to hold her hair out of her face while she worked. Both would need some time to tidy up if Henry and Conor came to find them. She reached for a nearby rag and began rubbing the grease from her hands.

"Do you think they'll get leave?" Katie asked excitedly. "I hope they do. Do you think Conor will want to see me if he has time off the ship?"

"I'm pretty sure the man who has been writing to you daily will want to see you if he gets leave."

She secretly hoped that Henry was of the same mind and eager to see her now that they had the chance.

Aggie looked up as Sergeant Maguire strode into the hangar bay.

"Look sharp, ladies! We have a US Navy Stearman coming in shortly. When it lands, we'll bring it in for a maintenance inspection. It's been sitting on the carrier in the salt air for a while now. We want to be sure it's in tiptop shape for our lads."

"Yes, Sergeant. Shall we stop work on these planes for now and focus on the American?"

"Yes, you can take a break from these for the moment. The Stearman should be in decent shape. They're flying it off the carrier to bring it here, but I want you to give it a good going over. The RAAF boys will need it in a few days."

"Yes, Sergeant."

They heard the call from the radio stating the Navy plane was on approach and walked to the front of the hangar to watch it land. Aggie was interested because Henry had told her he'd flown a Stearman when learning to make carrier landings during his training in Texas.

After receiving his postcard, she tried to learn what she could about the planes Henry had flown. She even found manuals for the Dauntless dive bomber he flew. Betty teased her as she studied the information about the planes, saying it was a strange way to show her romantic interest in a man. Aggie simply shrugged. It made her feel closer to Henry, and that's what mattered to her.

As they reached the front of the hangar, she raised her hand to shade her eyes. It was a beautiful blue-sky day in Sydney with not a cloud in sight. The sky was a rich blue with the color growing to a darker indigo farthest from the horizon. It was easy to spot the brilliant yellow biplane against the blue of the sky as it neared the field.

The plane flew over them in a low pass and dipped its wings in greeting before turning to land. It floated to the ground, touching down as smooth as silk. It reminded Aggie of the long-ago day at Sullivan's cattle station when she first saw that green biplane. This one was just as charming, with sunshine yellow paint and blue US Navy roundels.

Taxiing to a stop before them, the pilots climbed out in US Navy khaki uniforms, flight jackets, leather helmets, and goggles. As the pilots turned toward them, they began removing their protective gear. The women were astonished to see it was Henry and Conor. Katie shrieked and threw herself into Conor's arms. He laughed as he lifted the tiny redhead off the ground and spun her around.

Henry smiled shyly at Aggie.

"Surprise!"

She burst out laughing and stepped forward to give him a quick embrace. All thoughts about the grease on her hands and the fact that she was wearing her work coveralls went out of her mind. Henry was here and giving her a warm hug. She felt on top of the world.

"This is a surprise. We were told a Stearman was flying in from the Enterprise, but never expected to know the pilots!"

She was delighted to see Henry, but the plane also intrigued her. Even after spending so much time around airplanes in the past couple of years, she still found them magical. This biplane represented a bygone era, with its painted fabric skin and wooden struts and structure. It was such a beautiful machine, a bright yellow dragonfly this time.

Henry showed her around the plane, and she briefly inspected the engine. She tested the tether lines between the two sets of wings and admired their construction. As Henry showed her how the control surfaces worked, Conor walked over with his goggles and leather helmet and handed them to her with a wink.

"What are these for?"

Henry smiled at her. "Put them on. We're going for a flight."

She stared at him in shock. Going for a flight in this beautiful little machine?

Henry laughed. "Come on. I know the helmet is going to crush your curls, but isn't it worth it to take your first airplane ride?"

He helped pull the leather flying helmet over her head and settled the goggles on top of her head.

"Ready to climb in?"

Aggie was more than ready. She listened carefully as he instructed her where to place her feet as she stepped up on the wing to climb into the front seat. She had to be careful to step in the correct places so she would not damage the fragile fabric skin of the plane.

Once she settled in the seat, Henry leaned over to show her how to secure the seatbelt and instructed her on how to use the speaking tube. There was no radio headset to communicate with the other occupant of the plane, like a modern aircraft. They would need to rely on an old-fashioned speaking tube and hand signals if they needed to communicate while in the air. Once buckled in, Henry flashed her a blinding smile and climbed into the backseat of the cockpit.

"Ready to roll?"

She heard his voice through the speaking tube. She looked over her shoulder at him and smiled, then flashed the thumbs up so he knew she was ready. He reached forward and patted her shoulder, then turned the ignitor.

The engine roared to life and Henry radioed the tower for clearance to taxi. Once granted permission, he began taxiing to the end of the runway. He received approval for take-off, and she felt the plane gain speed as it rolled down the runway. She could feel every bump and crevice in the pavement as they rolled along toward take off.

Suddenly, she could no longer feel the bumps and jolts of the wheels on the tarmac, and she looked to the side and realized that the plane was rising into the sky. She turned sideways in her seat and gripped the edge of the cockpit as they gained altitude. Henry made a looping turn and flew past their friends standing at the edge of the runway. Aggie spotted Katie waving wildly and waved back.

She could hear Henry's laughter through the speaking tube. He turned the plane, flying north toward the Harbor. They passed over the Enterprise, docked at the piers, and swept low along the water beneath the Sydney Harbor Bridge. Flying out over the ocean, they followed the peninsula south, past the beaches, and back toward the airfield. Aggie thought it was magnificent. The view of the city and ocean and beaches from this height was breathtaking. How lucky Henry was to do this for his job!

"Do you feel up to doing something exciting?"

She heard his question through the tube. As if flying alone was not exciting enough! She nodded and gave him a thumbs up. He took her through some basic aerobatics, including an aileron roll and an Immelman turn. She shrieked and laughed as they briefly inverted. She loved the way her stomach seemed to rise and fall with the maneuvers and was giggling like crazy as he returned to level flight.

"Are you okay up there?"

She looked over her shoulder at him and nodded vigorously.

"Do you want to fly it?"

She looked at the control stick between her legs and contemplated it, then shook her head no.

"Let's try this. Put your hand on the stick. You'll feel what I'm doing to hold the plane level."

She gently placed her hand on the stick. She could feel the engine and the tiny movements Henry was making to keep the plane straight.

"All you need to do is keep the wings level with the horizon. Easy peasy."

She looked out ahead of her and saw how he was keeping the wings level as they glided over the ocean.

"Alright, your turn. You have control."

She could feel the stick change in her hand and could tell that Henry was no longer holding the controls in his compartment of the plane. Looking ahead, she used the stick to keep the plane as level as she could.

While she only had control for a few minutes and could feel the moment Henry took hold of his stick again, it exhilarated her. She couldn't wait to tell her little brothers that she had helped to fly an airplane. She could feel her cheeks beginning to hurt from so much smiling.

"Great job, but I think I'll take it for the landing, okay?"

He radioed the tower, letting them know the Stearman was on approach. He guided the plane gently to the ground, where they touched down with nary a bounce. They taxied back to the hangar, where Katie was jumping up and down and clapping.

Henry climbed out of the cockpit first, then moved to help Aggie get down. As soon as he was on the ground and reached up to help her balance as she stepped off the wing, Aggie launched herself into Henry's arms. He staggered backward.

"Oh Henry, thank you so much! This was a dream come true! Flying an airplane! It was amazing! Thank you!" she exclaimed as she clung to his neck. What a magical experience it had been.

Henry hugged her back.

"I remembered you talking about seeing that biplane when you were a kid and that you dreamed about flying. As soon as I saw this plane on the Big E, I knew I would figure out a way to give you a ride. Sorry that it's yellow and not green."

"No, it's perfect. Thank you for a perfect day and a perfect flight, Henry."

HENRY FELT LIKE HE was ten feet tall as he held Aggie in his arms. He was so proud that she had the chance to take a flight and that she had been willing to fly the plane herself. Sure, he'd had his hand hovering over his stick while she had control, but she had done a fine job holding the plane level and steady.

Conor and Katie came running up. Aggie turned away from him to hug her friend. Conor strode over and clapped him on the back.

"Well, if she wasn't in love with you before, I bet she is now," Conor grinned. Henry wasn't sure about love, but at least now he knew she liked him. He smiled at his friend.

"You want me to give Katie a ride?"

"No way," Conor laughed.

Katie turned to them.

"No, thank you. I know too much about what can go wrong with planes. I'm not interested in flying."

She reached out and took Conor's hand.

"I'm happy on the ground with this one." Conor planted a kiss on her cheek.

Henry consulted his watch. Time was ticking by, and they needed to get back to the Enterprise. They were only in port overnight, enough time to drop off the Stearman, load up on some fresh vegetables, and then hit the open seas. Conor saw the gesture.

"I'm afraid we're going to have to go, ladies. They're sending a jeep to pick us up. We only had permission to deliver the plan and need to head back to the ship now. Hank and Aggie's little joy ride was an add-on."

Katie tried to convince Conor to stay a little longer, maybe go to the mess hall and grab a bite to eat so they could spend more time together. Henry took Aggie's hand and led her back to the shadow of the biplane to give their friends, and themselves, some privacy.

"Did you really enjoy the flight?"

"You know I did. It was absolutely spectacular."

"Spectacular enough to forgive me for saying the wrong thing the last time we were together?" he asked shyly. He wanted to be sure she knew he didn't think of her as a close family relative.

"There's nothing to forgive, Henry. I explained that in my letter."

"I know, but it's different hearing it face to face."

He reached out and brushed a strand of hair away from her cheek and tucked it behind her ear.

"I want you to know I think you're about the best girl that I ever met. I don't know what is going to happen with the war, but I'm glad I have a girl to write, and who will write me back."

"And if you're ever back in Australia..." she began.

"This will be my first stop. Just like this time."

As she smiled up at him, Henry decided to ask for a kiss. He didn't want to swoop in without warning.

"May I give you a kiss before I go, Aggie?"

"Yes, please."

Henry bent down and kissed her gently. Her lips were soft and warm, and she reached up to touch his face. He pulled back and looked down into her happy blue eyes as they fluttered open. Aggie pulled her hand back to lightly touch her lips in astonishment.

"That was lovely," she whispered.

The moment ended with Conor and Sergeant Maguire coming around the side of the plane. Sergeant Maguire was glaring at Aggie with a disapproving look that Henry did not appreciate. He raised his eyebrows and gave Maguire his ma's patented hairy eyeball and watched as the sergeant glanced away. He wasn't about to let the sergeant make his girl feel bad about sharing a moment with him.

"We gotta go," said Conor. "Not that I want to leave any more than you do. Maguire said our ride is here to take us back to the ship."

The ladies walked with them to the front of the hangar where a Shore Patrol Marine was sitting in a jeep, waiting. Both men stepped apart from each other, each with their respective girl.

"It was a great day," Henry told Aggie. "I'm so glad I got to take you on your first flight."

"Me too. Please be careful, Henry. Fly safe."

He reached out and touched her cheek, then he dropped a chaste kiss on her lips.

"I'll keep you posted about my safe flying. Be sure to write."

He and Conor climbed into the jeep. As it drove away, they watched the girls wave goodbye.

"Was it worth it?" Conor asked.

"Very much worth it."

"So, you're out of the doghouse now?"

"So far out of the doghouse," Henry laughed. "Now we need to figure out how we are going to see these girls again."

DARLING HENRY,

I wanted to write and thank you again for the wonderful flight in the Stearman. What a magical day!

How lucky you are to fly all the time! It was amazing to see Sydney from the air; it was such a different perspective. I still can't believe you let me fly the plane. I wrote my brothers and let them know I got to fly a plane. When we were kids, they laughed at the idea of women pilots. I showed them!

Thanks again for making my dream come true. Take care of yourself, Henry. Fly safe.

Yours,

Aggie

Chapter Eleven

J anuary 1945
    Pacific Ocean

DEAREST AGGIE,

I'm so glad you enjoyed your flight. I love flying that Stearman and I'm glad you enjoyed flying it as well.

The Big E is busy making waves all along the Philippines. I can't share where we are, but Admiral Halsey is in the mood for carrier hunting. Seems sinking four carriers and a battleship at Leyte Gulf wasn't enough for him. We've been starting some nighttime flight ops, something we practiced in Hawaii. But so far, no luck finding any carriers or capital ships. We had some success against some coastal convoys, though.

The weather is awful as we've hit the edge of a typhoon, so no flight ops today. Poor Sven is seasick. He's in his bunk, clutching a bucket, and retching, moaning about how he's from the Midwest and used to being landlocked. Poor guy.

When I got my commission in the Navy, my Ma was so happy that I didn't join the Army, thinking I'd be safer in the Navy. It's a good thing she can't see me now!

I hope this letter finds you well, in sunshine and without a seasick roommate.

You are always in my thoughts,

Your Henry

DEAR HENRY,

I hope you are well. I am writing to let you know our squadron is on the move.

Captain Dempsey called us together for a meeting to tell us. With the fighting moving north and closer to the home islands of Japan, the RAAF has decided that Sydney is too far south and will be moving us to the Northern Territories. We are packing up our gear and tools to be transported to Darwin, which is on the northern coast. Jackie is in her element; organizing, packing, and labeling everything to be loaded on the lorries and trains.

Katie and I are excited to return to the NT. I'm hoping to take a few days' leave to visit my family once we reach Darwin. I haven't been home since I left for Sydney two years ago.

I will write with my new address as soon as I know it.

Yours affectionately,

Aggie

DEAREST AGGIE,

Boy, have we been busy!

The Task Force has been along the coast of China. I can't be more specific than that due to operational security. Though I'm pretty sure the Japanese know where we have been! It's hard to believe this kid from the old neighborhood is flying in such distant lands.

The weather has improved now, but we were still battling typhoon winds for a while. One of our Hellcats disappeared on a night mission, just flew off into the wind driven rain never to be seen again.

Conor and I are currently cooling our heels in the briefing room, waiting for our flights. There were two aborted launches this morning that needed replacement planes sent up to the flight deck. Then another plane returned to the ship with engine trouble. So, we are off to a slow start today.

I wrote to my Ma about you yesterday. She always used to badger me to find a nice Polish girl and settle down. I can only imagine her reaction when she hears I met a great girl, and she lives on the other side of the globe.

Sven is telling me it's time to go. I'll write more later.

Yours,

Henry

PS: Back aboard. This was a rough one. We lost many planes today. Michael Richard, the pilot that bothered you the night we met, was shot down today. His buddies are packing up his personal effects next door. While we didn't get along, I feel terrible for his parents back in NYC.

That makes me think about my Ma. I'm all she has in the world. If something were to happen to me...There are so many losses. I worry I might not see the end of the war.

I'm sorry. I don't want to scare you , my darling, but I can't talk about this with Conor or the guys. Everyone is trying to be brave. I hope you don't mind me telling you.

❧

DARLING HENRY,

Greetings from the Ryan homestead in the NT! I could take a few days' leave as we waited for the rest of our gear to be transported from Sydney to Darwin.

It is wonderful to see everyone. My home looks just as I remembered, but with a fresh coat of paint and a newer truck for Chester. With the need for beef and leather for the war effort, the family is finally doing well. The cattle look fat and healthy and so does my family. Chester and Mary's husband Louis are doing a fine job running the place.

Chester and Lily married the year before I left, and Mary and Louis married just before I went to Sydney. Now the Ryan family has expanded! I have met my new niece Natalie (Mary's daughter) and nephew David (Chester's son) for the first time. They are just darling!

I'm so proud of how well everyone is doing. Eddie is learning so much from Chester and Louis about running the station and Edith is top of her class at school. They are so grown up now. I'm grateful I've had a chance to visit.

I hope my letter finds you well. Fly safe, Henry.
I am thinking of you, and I am always,
Your Aggie

DEAREST HENRY,

I have returned to Darwin and I'm helping unpack the gear at the new hangar.

What a wonderful visit back home. Still, it was strange to be back after being gone for so long.

The homestead seems frozen in time. While things are so much better than during the Depression, life there is very much the same.

I enjoyed being with my family, but I felt restless and like I didn't quite fit in anymore. I feel like my life has gotten bigger than that small place. Maybe I'm not such a country girl anymore. Perhaps my life after the war could be something different from returning to a cattle station in the Northern Territories. It's given me much to think about.

I hope you are well. Fly safe, darling.
With love,
Aggie

MY DEAREST HENRY,
You won't believe it, but we are on the move again!

You must be making progress against the enemy because we need to move farther north. We'd barely set up our new HQ in Darwin. Now the RAAF's sending half of the squadron to New Guinea to better service the Allied planes as the fighting moves north. Jackie is back to packing and bossing everyone around as we prepare for the move.

This will be my first time on a ship and my first time leaving Australia. I imagine that seems like nothing to you, having traveled all the way from America to Australia and beyond. I can tell you, it will be a big step for this Aussie girl!

Once we arrive, I will write you with my newest new address. Ha ha.

Fly safe, my Henry.
Love, Aggie

DEAR HENRY,

Arrived safely in Aitape, New Guinea. Please see my address below. I wonder how many of your letters will find me after traveling from Sydney to Darwin to Aitape. In my imagination, I picture your letters trying to jump on trains and planes and ships to reach me. A fanciful thought, I know.

The planes we are seeing here at Aitape are far more damaged than those we worked on in Sydney. The bullet holes and flak damage are terrible. It makes me worry about you, seeing what can happen to these fragile airplanes that hold you aloft. Katie won't talk to me about it. She is as worried about Conor as I am about you.

Please be careful, darling. Fly safe.
All my love, Aggie

DEAREST HENRY,

We are following the exploits of the "Big E" through the war news, both in the papers and from what Betty overhears in the radio shack. Jackie found a large map of the Pacific Ocean, and Katie and I have been using it to plot the movements of the Enterprise. The South China Sea, Hong Kong, and Formosa. You fellows are certainly getting around!

I'm sending a photograph I had taken with a Dauntless dive bomber. I thought you might enjoy a photo of me alongside a plane like yours. Hopefully, that's not silly.

I pray you are well. With all the moving around, I haven't had a letter from you in weeks. I know there were some terrible storms in your area this month. I hope you are safe.

Know that I am thinking of you. Fly safe.

My love, Aggie

Chapter Twelve

February 1945
USS Enterprise

IT WAS FREEZING OUTSIDE.

Henry thought back to December in Hawaii when he was missing Chicago winters. Well, he could forget that now.

As they moved north towards the home islands of Japan, the weather got colder and grayer, with drizzle and choppy seas. The Enterprise had pulled out of Ulithi atoll, a tiny island in the Pacific now the largest US Naval Base in the area. North of the equator, but at a similar latitude as the Philippines, it was a tropical paradise compared to the chilling cold they were now experiencing.

The bomber pilots were reclining in the briefing room, waiting for their latest targeting plan. They sat up straighter as Kowalski walked into the room with his briefing clipboard in hand.

"Gentlemen, I think you might like this next mission. Our target: Tokyo."

There was a murmur throughout the room. Tokyo! Taking it to the enemy's capital city was something many of the fliers had imagined since they heard about the attack on Pearl Harbor.

"The Marines are landing on another island, and our attacks will be a diversion. We'll keep the Japanese distracted by attacking their capital while the Marines prepare for landings at..." Kowalski looked down to consult his notes. "Landings at Iwo Jima. Be aware, gentlemen, that when some Hellcats went up earlier today, they experienced icing issues above 3000 feet. Keep below that ceiling, boys."

Icing, Henry thought. He hadn't had to worry about icing since he was doing his training at Lewis outside Chicago. Flying in tropical climates for so long, part of him had forgotten icing existed. He shared a look with Conor, who was shaking his head, no doubt having similar thoughts.

"Okay, fellas, let's go get 'em," Kowalski dismissed the pilots.

The men scrambled to their feet and went to prepare for their flights. Henry tapped Conor's shoulder.

"I'm going to run down to the bunks. I think I have some long underwear buried at the bottom of my footlocker. Sounds like it's gonna be cold up there today."

"Already wearing mine. Be prepared!" He winked at Henry, and they parted ways. Conor really was a Boy Scout.

When Henry reached the berthing area, he knelt before his locker and rummaged for his long underwear. He carefully set aside the stack of letters he had received from Aggie when the Enterprise stopped at Ulithi.

He was reading them slowly, savoring them. She had sent him a photograph in one letter, a picture of her in her WAAAF uniform sitting on the wing of a SBD Dauntless, his plane. He had carefully tacked the picture to the wall of his bunk. He wondered if she was getting any of the letters, he had sent to her after her squadron had moved from Sydney.

Henry tried to keep things light in his letters, not wanting to scare or worry her, but he couldn't help but open his heart to her. He had written about the losses near Formosa and that Jasper Theodore Worthington had crashed, as well as his fear that he wouldn't survive to the end of the war.

Her letters were a balm. He enjoyed hearing about her visit to her family. Her descriptions of the ranch brought the place to life. While she delighted in the visit and meeting her new nephew and niece, he thought she realized that maybe life on the ranch wasn't what she would want after the war. Would she want to stay in Sydney? Or would she consider traveling farther to make her way in the world? Maybe come to the US?

Henry shook his head as he grabbed his long johns and pulled them on. Talk about getting ahead of himself. He'd kissed her once and now he was wondering if she would consider moving to the States. Wow. Perhaps he'd better focus on the task at hand, namely getting his bomber over the skies of Tokyo.

Over the next two days, February 16 and 17, the fliers from Enterprise conducted bombing raids around the Japanese capital. The resistance from the Japanese land-based air forces was minimal, and the Enterprise lost just one Avenger crew.

Jubilant from their success over Tokyo, Kowalski informed the pilots they were heading to Iwo Jima. Alongside sister carrier USS Saratoga, Enterprise would fly combat air patrols to protect the Marines amphibious landings on the island.

During their briefing on February 21st, Kowalski confirmed a rumor that had been spreading throughout the Pacific fleet, a terrifying new twist on aerial combat: the kamikaze.

These pilots would stop at nothing to damage or destroy an American ship. If they couldn't drop a bomb or a torpedo to do the job, they would use their planes as a weapon and crash into a ship. Suicide by airplane. Horror filled the American fliers. While they were dreaming of returning home to their loved ones, they couldn't imagine purposely killing themselves by crashing their planes to win the war. How could you fight against something like that?

Henry, Sven, Conor, and Perry discussed the situation on their way up to the flight deck.

"We'll have to make every shot count," said Sven with grim determination. "We can't let anything get through our air defenses at this point. Now it's not just the fear that they'll get a bomb off before we can stop them, but that they'll crash into the flight deck or something."

The men looked around the flight deck, with its milling sailors, ordinance racks, fuel supplies, and airplanes fueled and loaded with ammunition. If something got through, it would be a conflagration.

By the end of the day, they would see that very thing.

While Henry and his friends were aloft, battling to protect the Marines on the landing beaches, bombers and kamikazes flocked southward from Japan to defend the island. Saratoga took five bomb hits which turned its flight deck into an inferno of burning planes. Sara was out of the fight.

Five pilots from the Saratoga landed on Enterprise and joined the battle from the Big E. Enterprise now stood alone as the source of air power for the invasion and protection of surface ships.

Everyone was on edge and anxious after the kamikaze attacks that were coming in waves from Japan. The anti-aircraft teams from the various ships in the Task Force were on high alert for anything coming at them.

That evening, Kowalski descended out of the overcast sky to line up for the approach to Enterprise. Nervous American anti-aircraft crews from one destroyer, anticipating a kamikaze attack, started firing on him and other ships joined in. Kowalski's plane was in tatters. Forced to ditch in the ocean, he signaled a nearby patrol boat for rescue. When the boat arrived, the sailors were unsure if he was an American until they heard the unmistakably American profanity he and Owen, his back seat gunner, hurled at them during the rescue.

Henry and the rest of the Midwest Mob rushed to meet Kowalski as he came back on board.

"I can't believe they shot up my plane! Don't they study their aircraft recognition cards?" Kowalski grumbled. Henry and the guys were just happy that they had their grumpy leader back on the ship safely.

The next day, they met in the briefing room for an update and the day's briefing. Pilots from various squadrons, as well as the five crews they had adopted from the Saratoga, crowded into the space.

"I'm not gonna sugar coat this," Kowalski announced. "The landings on Iwo Jima are slowing down. Our Marines are having a hell of a time moving off the beaches, the Japs have them pinned down. They're going to need all our support and then some to crack this nut. And we're gonna give them our best. We're going to have planes in the air day and night as long as we can to help get them off those beaches and inland."

Henry and Conor exchanged a glance. Kowalski painted a stark picture in this briefing.

"If you're not in the air, I want you sleeping or preparing for your next flight. No gambling, no horsing around. We're gonna be all business and we're gonna get this job done."

He continued outlining the plan for flight operations for the next 24 hours. The ambitious plan presented amazed Henry. Kowalski and the air bosses weren't messing around.

So began Enterprise's heroic effort. At 1630 on February 23, the night fighters launched for the first round of combat air patrols. In a steady rotation, fighters and bombers launched off the deck of the Enterprise, the beginning of a string of seven days of continuous flying. Enterprise never ceased flight operations for 174 hours straight.

Henry was exhausted. He'd flown daytime flights, nighttime flights. Flights at dawn, flights at sunset. They had just landed and were riding the elevator down to the hangar deck. He didn't know what day it was or even the time of day. He only knew it was still light outside. As he picked his way across the hangar deck, heading to his rack, he saw sailors and air crew members sleeping in corners and on the floor. One ordinance man was curled up under a bomb rack. Despite the non-stop noise from flight deck operations, men were so exhausted they would doze off as soon as they stopped moving.

When he reached his bunk, he took a moment to shake Conor and Perry awake. During the endless cycle of launching and recovering planes, their flight times had gotten out of sequence, so Conor hadn't been his wingman as he usually was. Henry thought there may have been a mechanical issue with one of their planes at some point that forced them out of the same rotation, but the past week was a blur and he could not remember.

"Your turn. You guys are up in the next wave. Time to rise and shine."

Conor rubbed his eyes and emitted a jaw cracking yawn. "Thanks. How are things going?"

"The hangar deck looks like your kid brother had a gigantic sleepover. Guys are asleep on their feet. Poor Bill Lago is exhausted. You know how he can't sleep when he's trying to figure out a problem? Well, he's got about a billion problems to solve to keep these planes flying. He's barely slept in the past six days."

"Any word about progress on the island?"

"Some guys raised the American flag on top of the mountain the other day, so that's good, I guess. The Marines are getting inland and winning? I'm not sure. I'm so tired, I can't remember what they told us in the last report. Sorry."

"Don't worry about it," Conor said as he climbed out of his bunk and started pulling on his clothes. "I'll get the update when I go for my briefing. You guys get some rest."

Sven shambled in with his toothbrush still hanging out of his mouth. "I'll see you in the morning. Or evening. Whatever." Then he flopped into his bunk, already asleep when his head hit the pillow.

"How long can we go on like this?" Henry asked.

"I guess as long as it takes," Conor responded. He patted his friend on the shoulder, grabbed his flight jacket out of his locker, and left.

Henry crawled into his bunk. He curled on his side and looked at Aggie's picture. With her soft smile looking down on him, he fell asleep.

Chapter Thirteen

February 1945
Ulithi Atoll, Caroline Islands

AGGIE WAS TAKING HER second flight in an airplane, and it was nowhere near as dizzyingly romantic as her first.

She was aboard a transport flight with a group of WAAAF and RAAF aviation mechanics flying toward a tiny Pacific atoll called Ulithi. It was the home of the biggest US Naval installation in the Pacific theater, and they desperately needed mechanics to repair damaged aircraft. The US Navy lads did not have enough skilled hands to manage all the work themselves, so they had called the Aussies to ask for help. They had such a shortage of mechanics they seconded several WAAAFs, including Katie, Jackie, and herself to the mission.

She and Katie sat squashed together in the uncomfortable webbed seats that lined the sides of the fuselage. Aggie and Katie had been following the news and knew about the battle that was raging at Iwo Jima. They knew about the damage to the US carrier, Saratoga, with its planes burning on the flight deck. She wondered if they would repair any of those planes. Or planes from the Enterprise.

Henry was never far from her mind these days. As reports came in about the struggles of the Marines landing on the beaches at Iwo Jima, she was grateful he was not part of the landing parties. The new kamikaze threat was terrifying, though. Brave pilots like Henry and Conor were in the skies fighting two battles: to complete their bombing runs to aid the Marines on the island while protecting their carrier and task force ships from the suicide pilots in the air.

When the flight landed at Ulithi, the Navy delivered the WAAAF mechanics to a small metal shed near the airstrip, a short walk from the hangars where they had dropped off their tool bags. As they stood in the doorway, Aggie took in the oil-stained dirt floor, bunk beds, and the lack of windows. The space smelled stuffy with a faint tinge of engine oil.

"What swanky digs," Jackie said with a snort.

"I'm sorry, ladies, it's the best we could do for you," apologized the young Navy mechanic who was showing them to their quarters. He was worrying his white sailor hat in circles between his hands. "The only women's housing on the island is for the nurses at the hospital and that's a pretty far hike from the airfield. They wanted y'all close to the strip and the hangar to do your work, so we cleared out this old storage shed and dragged a few bunks over from our barracks." He was chewing his lip nervously.

"I don't mean to complain..." drawled Jackie. "But there are no windows or ventilation. We're in the tropics, can we at least have a fan to move the air around?"

'Well, ma'am, I don't think a fan would do y'all much good since there's no electricity out here to plug one in."

The girls looked around at each other, nonplussed. They were all imagining baking in this airless hut at night. Aggie spoke up.

"Is there a corner of the hangar we could use, perhaps? We could squeeze the beds together and hang up some sheets or tarps for privacy? We won't need much space, just room to sleep and change clothes. What we do need is proper ventilation and a working fan if we are going to do the work required of us. Now, please ask whoever is in charge. We're going to store our bags here, for now, and get to work."

The young man scurried off to find his superior, and Aggie turned to her fellow WAAAFs.

"Let's get out of our dress uniforms, into our coveralls, and start working."

The ladies changed quickly, trying to get out of the stifling hut as quickly as possible. As they left the hut, red and sweating from the heat, a Petty Officer met them, trailed by the young sailor from earlier.

"I've been told you ladies are unhappy with your accommodations. You need to understand that I am running a naval air station here, not some fancy hotel. We know the Aussies thought sending you would be helpful, but you will be no help if you kick up a fuss the moment you arrive on the base just because your quarters don't have a window with a view," he blustered.

Aggie raised an eyebrow. *So, this is how it's going to be,* she thought. Some man explaining to the womenfolk how they were making things difficult. Well, she had seen enough of that in her time; men on the cattle station, mechanics from the RAAF. It was rather exhausting. Still, she plastered on a sweet smile and addressed the man.

"Thank you for your kind welcome," she said. "We appreciate the Navy's attempt at providing accommodations so close to the hangar. However, the issue isn't that we don't have a window with a view, but no window at all, or ventilation of any kind. We propose partitioning a small area of the hangar for our quarters, so we're not sleeping in a baking tin can."

"I don't think it's necessary to exaggerate, ma'am."

"I'm not exaggerating, sir. We just spent five minutes in that hut changing into our coveralls and, as you can see, we're already hot and perspiring. May I ask you a favor, sir? Please go into the hut and lie on a bunk for five minutes and tell me if you think that would be acceptable accommodation for your sailors."

The man grunted and stomped into the hut. Five minutes later, he was directing a group of sailors to move the bunks to the back corner of the hangar and instructing them to hang tarps to provide privacy for the WAAAFs. He left briefly and returned with a table fan.

"From my office," he said as he thrust the fan into Aggie's hands.

"Why, thank you," she smiled. "Now, shall we let our team get to work?"

Initially, the Navy mechanics assigned the women basic maintenance tasks such as oil changes and changing tires. Then Aggie offered some tips to one mechanic struggling to repair the engine on a Hellcat next to the P51 Mustang on which she was performing an oil change.

"You need to tune the cylinders in sequence," she called over the roar of the misfiring radial engine.

The mechanic looked at her blankly and cupped his hand to his ear. "What was that?"

Aggie jumped down from the Mustang and strolled over.

"I rebuilt a couple of Hellcat engines back in Sydney."

She leaned in to shout in his ear to be heard over the struggling engine. "You need to tune the cylinders in sequence so they fire smoothly to turn the prop. You keep hopping from one to another across the engine. That's why you're getting the misfires."

"You're kidding me. How long have you been doing this?"

"Two years."

"No joke? I just finished training two months ago and then they stuck me on a ship here. Back home, I work on cars, not planes."

"Would you like me to show you how it's done?"

The man smiled and handed her his wrench.

By the end of the second day, the Navy mechanics were so impressed by not only the women's work ethic, but the quality of the work they were doing, that the Navy men started assigning them more complex and complicated repairs. The Hellcat mechanic Aggie had helped kept sending over other new mechanics to ask her questions and get tips with their repairs. The petty officer who had given them such a hard time about their lodgings approached the women at the end of the third day to apologize for doubting their skills and to thank them for their work.

Katie, Aggie, and their fellow WAAAFs were working long hours to keep 'em flying. They woke early, around 0500 when mechanics began arriving at the hangar. While this was a downside of their makeshift accommodations in the hangar, it was better than sweltering in a dirt floored shack. They would work on planes from dawn to late in the evening. There were so many to be repaired, some so terribly damaged that Aggie could not imagine how the pilots flew them. When she touched the battle-scarred machines, she thought of Henry and whispered a prayer for his safety.

Everyone on the base was following the reports of the battle at Iwo Jima. The maintenance teams had unloaded what undamaged planes they could off the Saratoga when she stopped at Ulithi on her way back to the US for repairs. They listened breathlessly as word spread in the mess hall about the heroic effort of the Enterprise, keeping aircraft continuously aloft for 174 hours. *The men must be exhausted,* Aggie thought about both the fliers and the aircrews who kept the planes maintained and flying.

Rumors began that Enterprise was returning to Ulithi around March 9. After their work at Iwo Jima, the sailors and fliers needed rest and relaxation.

Aggie and Katie arranged a few hours away from the maintenance hangar on the day Enterprise was pulling in. Jackie discovered them in the parts storage area, using large pieces of paper that had wrapped engine parts and leftover paint to create large signs reading, "Hello, Conor!" and "Welcome, Henry."

"What's the plan here?" Jackie asked.

"We're going to meet the Enterprise and surprise the boys when they get off the ship," Aggie said.

"Well, they'll be in for a shock, seeing the two of you her in Ulithi."

"It's going to be fantastic!" Katie said. "Do you want to come along, Jackie? You could see that handsome Mr. Kowalski."

"I told you not to worry about me and Mr. Kowalski. If we run into each other, we'll see what happens. Like I said, I enjoyed talking to him about engineering, but he's not my type and I'm not looking for anything serious."

With that, Aggie and Katie prepared to see their fellas. Scrubbing the grease from under their fingernails, they fixed their hair and donned their dress uniforms. They carefully rolled up their signs and walked to the harbor in time to see the gangway being extended from the Enterprise. Standing near the gangway on the dock, they held up their sign as men began streaming off the ship. The women looked at each other in anticipation. Wouldn't the guys be surprised to see them?

Chapter Fourteen

March 1945
Ulithi Atoll, Caroline Islands

HENRY FELT LIKE HE had done nothing but sleep since they left Iwo Jima. Most of the crew had been sleeping as well. The captain, knowing how hard everyone had worked during their epic seven days of non-stop flight operations, was being lax about crew members grabbing shut eye whenever they could. He was still feeling groggy as he pulled on a fresh set of khakis and tied his tie. Conor was bent over, shining his shoes.

Kowalski strolled in and grabbed his garrison cap.

"You guys gonna join us at the O Club?" he asked. "They're saying it's going to be unlimited beer and shots all around for the men of the Enterprise to celebrate our record-breaking achievement."

"Yep, we'll swing by," Henry said. "Not much beer for me, but we'll come over."

"They're talking about a dance as well. Navy nurses, you know." Kowalski waggled his eyebrows.

"You can have all the nurses to yourself, Kowalski," Conor said. "I wouldn't mind a little music, though. We'll be there."

"Good to hear. See you there." Kowalski tipped his hat and left.

"I'm still so tired," Henry yawned. "I'm still trying to get into some kind of normal sleep schedule. For a while, I didn't know if it was day or night."

"I hear you," Conor said. "I'm just looking forward to getting off the ship. It's so big, but after a while it gets small."

Henry chuckled, then nodded.

The men crossed the hangar deck and joined the line to walk down the gangway to the shore. Just about everyone was going ashore. Heavens knew they had all earned it. As they were halfway down the gangway, Conor shook his shoulder and pointed down to the pier.

"Are you seeing what I'm seeing?"

Henry sighted down Conor's arm to see what he was pointing at on the dock. There were two women holding large signs, on with each of their names.

"What in the world?" asked Henry.

As they continued down the gangway, he realized the women were not wearing US Navy nurse's uniforms but Australian WAAAF uniforms. As he got closer, he recognized Aggie's sweet face. Conor was already pushing his way through the crowd of sailors to reach Katie. As soon as he reached her, he caught her up in a massive hug.

When Henry reached Aggie, he looked at her in disbelief. He took her face in his hands and brought his lips to hers. As she wrapped her arms around him, he pulled back and touched his forehead to hers.

"What are you doing here?" he whispered. "Or am I still sleeping?"

She smiled up at him. "The Navy needed more hands for repairing planes. The RAAF sent over a group of mechanics, including a few of us WAAAFs. We've been here for a couple weeks and following your exploits at Iwo Jima."

He pulled her into a tight embrace.

"I'm so glad to see you, Aggie. I can't even tell you how glad." He kissed her again. Having her with him, he felt a wave of relief and contentment wash over him.

Conor and Katie waked over; Conor's arm wrapped tightly around Katie's shoulder.

"Let's get these ladies to the O Club for some dinner and dancing."

Henry was so delighted to have Aggie by his side. He had spent the last weeks of flying and battle dreaming of being able to see her again and here she was, like magic. They walked hand in hand to the Officer's Club and requested a table in the dining room.

Over dinner, Aggie and Katie told the men how they had been on their own island-hopping campaign over the past month, moving from Darwin to New Guinea, and now Ulithi. It sounded like quite the adventure for two girls from the Northern Territories.

Henry and Conor told them about some of the flying they had done since they had seen them in Sydney. They talked about experiencing the typhoon and embellished the story about poor Sven clutching his bucket to his chest in the horrible waves. The women shared their stories about refusing to sleep in the airless hut and the different aircraft they'd been working on.

As the meal ended, Henry found he was censoring himself, only telling amusing or exciting stories, keeping the worst of what he had seen from Aggie. He didn't know how many of his letters she had received since she had been moving around. He longed to talk to her alone, more seriously, about what he'd seen and experienced and what was in his heart when he thought of her.

As they were leaving the dining room, Kowalski caught sight of the foursome. He waved them over.

"How did you fellas get your gals here?" he asked.

He currently had an arm around a pretty navy nurse, who he introduced as Dolores. They briefly explained the WAAAF's presence on the island.

"Jackie Doyle is here as well," Katie said, hopefully. Kowalski raised an eyebrow and glanced at Dolores who smiled up at him. Henry knew Jackie and Kowalski had a spark back in Sydney, but it seemed like Kowalski had a spark with some girl in every port.

"Well, how about that?" Kowalski said, glancing at his date, then changing the subject. "Now you guys don't have any excuse for not coming to the dance. One of the ship's bands is gonna play."

Henry wasn't a great dancer, but if Aggie was up for it, he'd give it a go. Hopefully, her toes would survive. They followed Kowalski and Dolores into the ballroom of the O Club as the band was striking up "Moonlight Serenade." Conor took Katie's hand and led her out onto the floor.

Henry looked sheepishly at Aggie.

"I'm not much of a dancer," he said.

"That's okay," she said. "It will just be nice to have you hold me in your arms."

He held out his hand to take her to the floor. Aggie placed her hand in his and he pulled her close, his free arm wrapping around her back. She rested her temple against the side of his chin, and he led her into the dance.

"This is so lovely," she murmured. "I've been so worried about you. It's nice to have you here so close, safe in my arms."

Henry felt a warm pleasure wash through him at her words. He thought of the crazy hours of flying and fear, and always coming back to his bunk and her picture.

"Thank you for sending the photo, I put it up by my bunk. It's the first thing I see when I wake up and the last thing I look at before I close my eyes."

She kissed his cheek.

"I'm glad you like it. That pilot thought I was crazy asking to pose in front of that Dauntless."

"Oh, yeah? What did you tell him?"

"I told him my fella is a Dauntless pilot and that he'd like a picture of his girl next to his plane.

"His girl, huh?"

"Well, yes, I hope that's okay. I like to think of myself as your girl," she said, looking down and biting her lip.

He tipped up her chin to look her in the eyes. "I think of you that way myself."

Henry held Aggie close and swayed to the music. The tempo of the song changed, but he kept swaying, enjoying the feeling of her in his arms. It felt so good to have a moment that was peaceful and normal.

He thanked his lucky stars that he could share this moment with her. What an amazing surprise to find her here on Ulithi. Really, what a surprise to have met at all, an American and an Aussie in the middle of a world war. *What are the odds?* he pondered, and then was just grateful the odds were in his favor.

Katie and Connor came over, and Katie tapped on Aggie's shoulder.

"It's getting late. We need to get back. We were only supposed to be gone for a few hours."

Aggie looked up at Henry with her bright blue eyes. "I'm so sorry, Henry, but we need to go, we have to be up early for work tomorrow. We don't want to get back too late; we'll wake up the other girls in the hangar."

"Would it be okay if we walked you ladies back?" Henry was not ready for the night to be over.

"Of course," she replied and took his hand.

They ambled back to the airfield and the WAAAF's makeshift accommodations in the hangar, hand in hand. They trailed a distance behind their friends, wanting some privacy and to allow Conor and Katie some time alone as well.

"I still can't believe you're here. It really is like a dream coming true. I think about you all the time, Aggie. I feel guilty because I write to you more often than I write to my Ma."

"I write to you more than the rest of my family combined," she admitted.

He laughed.

"Oh, it feels good to laugh. We joke around and razz each other on the ship, but it's different. Gallows humor, you might say."

"Is it hard?" she asked in a serious tone. "Are you losing a lot of pilots? I see these planes come in, all torn to pieces... I think about you, up there, where somebody could shoot up your plane, too. Then I realize, even if the plane is damaged, the pilot must be okay, because he landed this busted up plane, and I think to myself, I bet Henry could land any plane he's in."

"Thanks for the vote of confidence, sweetheart. So far, I have landed everything."

"I pray for you every morning and every night, Henry, and sometimes in between."

"Well, I'll take all the prayers you've got for me. Between you and Ma, I should be covered."

He squeezed her hand.

"Listen, I'm not sure how long we'll be here at Ulithi, and I know you have important work to do, and you're busy, but I'd like to see you again before we hoist anchor."

"I'd like that too, Henry."

"I'll probably have more free time since we aren't doing any flying while we're here. Rest and relaxation and all that. I can stop by from time to time, maybe at mealtime and we can hit the chow hall together."

"Oh, the chow hall," she teased. "You're such a wild romantic, sir."

"Anywhere with you is romantic," he teased back. "Even the chow hall." He tipped her a wink.

They reached the side entry to the hangar. Conor and Katie had slipped off into the shadows for a private kiss goodbye. Henry took Aggie in his arms and held her tight. She felt so soft and warm in his arms, he could hold her forever. She raised up on her toes to bring her lips to his and they melted into the kiss.

"I'll try to stop by tomorrow," he whispered as they broke apart.

"I look forward to seeing you." Then she slipped through the doorway and was gone.

ALTHOUGH SHE BARELY slept, Aggie felt like she was floating off the ground the next morning. It had been such a lovely evening. Spending time with Henry was so special – the dinner, the dancing, walking home, holding hands. How has she found such a nice guy during a war? They laughed and teased each other, but also started talking about more serious topics. She wanted to know everything he was thinking, how he felt when he was flying.

For the moment, she needed to get to work. She donned her shapeless coverall and tied her hair up with a navy scarf with stars speckling the fabric. It made her think of the stars on the Australian flag or the American flag, which made her grin. She ducked out between the tarps that separated their sleeping area from the rest of the hangar.

Working with one of the US Navy mechanics, Aggie was doing her best to bring the abused, poorly maintained Pratt and Whitney engine of an F4U Corsair back to life. Marty was a Navy mechanic, and they had been working on this plane for the past couple of days.

This morning, they were at it again, doing battle with the battered machine.

She had her head and shoulders practically inside the engine cowling as she worked. Marty was on the other side of the plane, asking her about the next step in the repair when he suddenly snapped to attention and saluted.

"Don't worry about saluting, sailor. I'm just here to see my girl," she heard a familiar voice say.

She popped her head out of the cowling, surprised and pleased to see Henry.

"Hey there, lady," he grinned. "Don't they let you take a break for lunch around here? I've been watching you work for the past forty-five minutes."

She glanced at the clock on the hangar wall. It was already 1330, an hour past when she was supposed to have had lunch.

"I'm so sorry, Marty! Why didn't you say anything? You must be starving."

"Oh, I'm fine, ma'am," Marty said, rubbing his belly. "I won't waste away if I'm late for a meal. We were making good headway and you were so focused, I didn't want to disturb you."

"Well, you should have. Go, get something to eat." She shooed him away.

"All right, *Mom,*" he said, chuckling. "We'll get back to it after lunch." He waved and sauntered off in search of a meal.

Aggie turned to Henry.

"And what's a pilot like yourself doing in a place like this?" she flirted.

"I came with Bill. He needed to check on a few of the planes from the Saratoga that were brought here for tune ups. We're going to fly them onto the Big E to fill in some gaps for planes we've lost."

His eyes darkened and his mood turned serious as he looked over the planes that lined the hangar and along the airfield beyond.

"We've lost so many."

She reached up to touch his shoulder but noticed the grease on her hands. It wouldn't do to spoil his clean khaki uniform. He seemed to shake himself out of his reverie and turned to her with a smile.

"Can you grab some lunch with me?"

She pulled a rag out of her pocket and began cleaning her hands.

"Let me go wash up. I won't have time to change and go to the mess hall. There's a small canteen here at the airstrip where we can have a sandwich and a soft drink if that's okay."

"Sounds perfect."

She hurried to the sink at the back of the hangar and washed her hands. There was a mirror over the sink, so she checked her hair and then rushed to meet Henry.

They each chose a ham and cheese sandwich from the canteen truck. She had a lemonade while he had the ubiquitous Coca-Cola that the American sailors loved so much. They found a spot under a palm tree, looking out toward the ocean and unwrapped the waxed paper that protected the sandwiches.

"It's rather beautiful here," she said. "It's hard to believe there's a war on."

"Other than the Navy ships at anchor, hundreds of people in uniform, and a hangar load of broken-down warplanes for you to work on."

"I know but sitting under this palm tree with the errant tropical breezes blowing, the sound of waves in the distance, and the smell of the salt air, it's nice to forget, at least for a minute."

She looked at Henry.

"Or maybe you can't forget when you've been in combat so much."

"It's impossible to forget," he said as he looked out at the sea and the cruisers and destroyers in the harbor. "I don't know how we will all go back to normal when this is over. Will we even know what normal is after all this? When we've seen so much and lost so many?"

She watched him as he spoke. He looked so bleak.

"I got a letter from Ma this morning. They heard that Porky, my buddy from my gang back home, died in Belgium this winter during the Battle of the Bulge. I can't imagine what the old neighborhood will be like without a guy like Porky. He was one of my best friends." Henry released a shuddering breath and wiped away a tear.

"I'm so sorry, Henry," Aggie said. She reached out to take his hand. "It must be hard to hear about an old friend dying like that."

"It's not just the old neighborhood friends, either. Guys I went to school with at Lewis, flying for the Army Air Force in England, have been killed. A couple of guys were bomber pilots, flying B-17s over France and Germany. Another is now a POW, they hope. Imagine that? Hoping he's a POW."

He sighed. The words were spilling from his mouth, faster and faster.

"I think about the friends I've made here as well, guys on the Enterprise. When we first arrived, Kowalski was really hard on us. He didn't want to be friends with the replacement pilots because he didn't know how long we'd be around. Now we're the old hands and I feel the same way about the new guys. We thought we lost Kowalski when he had to ditch. What if I lose Conor or Sven? Conor's my best friend here. I rely on Sven as my radioman and gunner. There are a few pilots who survived crashes and enemy fire and their back seaters haven't. I don't know what I'd do with myself if something happened to Sven."

Aggie was at a loss. She wasn't sure what she could say to ease Henry's mind. Compared to him, her wartime experience had mostly been a grand adventure. Leaving home, going to the big city. Learning to work on the different airplanes and discovering how good she was at her job. Even traveling here to Ulithi, despite the discomfort and inconvenience, was an amazing experience.

While Henry was getting to fly, and that too was an adventure, she could see it came at a significant cost. Every time his squadron left the flight deck of the Enterprise, there was no guarantee that they would all return. Aggie held tight to Henry's hand. She didn't want to offer platitudes.

"I don't know what to say, Henry. Is there anything I could do to help?"

"No, sweetheart. I just appreciate you listening. I don't want to scare you, but I don't want to hide things from you either. It would be nice to tell you what's going on in my mind and in my heart. I hope that's okay."

"Of course, that's okay. I won't always know what you're going through, but I can't understand if you don't tell me. I'll always be happy to listen."

"Thanks, sweetheart."

He leaned over and kissed her cheek. "I'm sorry I spoiled your admiration of the beautiful day."

"Not at all."

"Good, now eat your lunch. I need to get you back to work or that Marty will give me the hairy eyeball for making you late."

"The hairy eyeball?"

"Yep. That's what I called it when my Ma would give someone a dirty look. I was usually on the receiving end of that look."

She laughed. "I think I'd like to meet your mother."

Henry cast her a thoughtful look.

"I think I'd like that, too. For you to meet my Ma."

Aggie felt flustered. Meet his mother? She had been teasing him about meeting his mum, but he seemed to take the thought seriously. Henry's mum sounded amazing. Look at the son she'd raised all on her own, through the Great Depression, working at that big hotel in Chicago. She must be a formidable woman.

What would she think of Aggie? A girl from Australia who met her son in the middle of a war. Would Mrs. Bolanski like her? Would she accept her as...? Aggie stopped herself before her imagination could run away with her. There was no way Aggie Ryan from the Northern Territories, Australia was going to meet Mrs. Bolanski from Chicago, USA.

"Hey," Henry nudged her with an elbow. "You okay over there? You got awfully quiet. Did I scare you off talking about my friends?"

"No, not at all," Aggie assured him. "I'm happy to listen, anytime."

She smiled. "Now, I need to get going before my sergeant gives me a hairy eyeball."

Henry smiled and pulled her to her feet.

"Well, let's not let that happen."

AFTER RETURNING AGGIE to work on the Corsair, Henry tracked down Bill for a ride back to the ship. He had been arranging for the Saratoga planes to be finished and ready to fly out to the Enterprise the next day, March 14.

"Looks like we're going to be heading back out," Bill said.

"Bound to happen," Henry agreed. "Not like they're gonna let us hang out here in paradise for too long."

"Speaking of paradise, that's a fine young lady you've got over there." Bill nodded to where Aggie once again had her head in the engine of the Corsair.

"Yeah, she's pretty great, huh?"

"She's smart as a whip, too," Bill said. "I was watching her earlier while you were mooning over her, waiting to take her to lunch. She's running rings around that kid over there on that Corsair. I was talking to a few of the other mechanics. She's been teaching all of them the past few weeks they've been here. She knows her stuff. I could use her on the Enterprise if she were a guy."

Henry puffed up with pride. He respected Bill, the guy who kept Henry's plane in the air. He was happy that Bill recognized Aggie's talents and brains. Henry, however, was grateful that Aggie wasn't a guy.

As they drove the jeep back to the ship, Henry could see the signs that they were getting ready to be underway again. Food and fuel were being loaded onto the Enterprise, as well as ammunition and ordnance.

"Wonder where the war will take us next?"

"No clue," Bill responded. "But it probably won't include a pretty WAAAF on a tropical island."

Bill tipped a wink at Henry and hopped out of the jeep to report the status of the Saratoga planes to the air boss.

Henry caught up with Conor on the hangar deck. Conor was off to see Katie but took a moment to give Henry the latest scuttlebutt.

"Looks like Admiral Spruance wants to go kamikaze hunting," Conor said.

"How's that? Seems like they find us just fine on their own."

"Spruance wants us to attack the kamikaze hatcheries on some island called Kyushu. The Japanese are training these guys up there. The Admiral wants to catch them in their nests."

"Any word on when we're pulling out? Bill said something about flying the Saratoga planes aboard tomorrow."

"Yep, the word is one more night of shore leave here on Ulithi and then heading to sea tomorrow. I was going ashore to see Miss Catherine before we weigh anchor."

"Miss Catherine? Since when do you talk like a proper British gentleman?"

"Since she likes it," Conor said with a wink. Then he sobered. "I really like her, Henry. Maybe more than like her. I'm pretty sure I'm in love with her. What am I gonna do?"

Henry didn't have any answers for his friend. He was pretty sure he was in the same boat with Aggie, and that boat wasn't the USS Enterprise.

He was falling for Aggie, probably since he saw her square off to fight old Jasper Theodore Worthington, rest his soul. How had he fallen in love in the middle of a war? On the other side of the globe?

Earlier, she had joked about meeting his mother and it had gotten him thinking. He was even thinking out loud when he said he, too, would like Aggie to meet his Ma. How would that work? He'd only known Aggie a short time, but it seemed longer. Time moved so differently, so much more quickly, during the war. He'd only know Conor for two years and he felt more like a brother than a friend.

He and Aggie had only known each other for five months. He was already sharing deeper and more meaningful thoughts with her than any other girl he'd ever dated before, admittedly a small sample. Other girls wanted him to be funny or smooth; they didn't really wonder about who he was underneath. He opened up to Aggie about his fears of losing his friends and she had offered her quiet support.

Bill was right; she was a bright girl. Henry also thought she was the right girl for him. He'd be a fool to let her get away, but how did you hang on to the right girl when she lived halfway around the world?

SOMETHING'S GOING ON, Aggie thought.

Earlier that day, there was a big push to wrap up the work on the airplanes from the USS Saratoga. Planes that needed basic maintenance, like oil changes and changing tires, were suddenly a priority. There were rumblings amongst the Navy mechanics that the plane would fly out soon, hence the rush.

Henry and Conor arrived at the hangar as she and Katie were packing up their tools for the night. They invited the girls to join them for dinner at the mess hall. Both were quiet, without their usual teasing and joking with each other.

After dinner, Conor and Katie split away from them. There was music being played at the Officers' Club and they planned to do a little dancing if they could.

Aggie and Henry went to the beach, where they slipped off their shoes and socks and held hands as they walked along the shoreline with the sand between their toes. Henry was not his usual chatty self – he seemed pensive to Aggie.

She wondered if Henry regretted his show of emotion the other day. Men could be funny if they thought they showed signs of weakness. Aggie always noticed that her brothers tried to be unemotional and stoic when they were hurt or sick.

When her brother Casey's appendix needed to be removed, he downplayed his symptoms and denied there was a problem, even when the doctor drove all the way to the homestead to check on him. They had barely gotten him to the hospital for surgery when his pain had become so unbearable, he couldn't hide it any longer. As he was wheeled into the operating room, he looked up at his family and said, "I guess I really was sick." *Ugh, that boy was the worst.*

Perhaps Henry thought telling her about his concerns and worries would make her think less of him. Nothing could have been further from the truth. Aggie was so honored that he shared his thoughts and fears with her. She hoped she could give him the love and support he seemed to need.

Aggie stopped short. She had finally said it out loud. Well, out loud in her own head, anyway. *The L word.*

In her mind, she had been tiptoeing around that word for a while now, but there it was. She had been falling for Henry since the moment he intervened with that fellow in Sydney back in November. Five months, a handful of encounters, a stack of letters, and she found herself in love with this charming pilot from Chicago.

Chicago, a big city halfway around the world from her tiny home in the Northern Territories.

Henry had said something that she missed, as her mind had wandered to their geographic differences. She felt guilty.

"I'm sorry. What did you say?"

He pulled her into an embrace.

"I'm just so glad to be here with you. To have time to talk and to hold you," he whispered into her hair.

He bent down to kiss her as she rose up on her tiptoes to meet his lips. She slid her fingers int the short hair at the nape of his neck as he trailed kisses across her cheek to nibble at her earlobe and she sighed. As he began kissing his way down her neck, she started to giggle and pulled away.

"Do you want me to stop?" he asked, looking stricken.

"No, it just tickles," she giggled as she rubbed at her neck.

He looked at her wryly. "That's not the way ladies react to someone kissing their neck in the movies. Maybe I'm doing something wrong."

"I don't think so. I'm just very ticklish."

"Maybe if I stick to regular kissing, it would be okay?"

"I think we could certainly experiment," she said cheekily.

They stood, wrapped in each other's arms, kissing and caressing until Henry pulled back and took her face in his hands. He gazed into her eyes.

"What am I going to do with you, Aggie?"

"Do you have to do something with me?"

"I'm falling in love with you, Aggie," he said. "And I don't know what's going to happen next."

Her breath caught. *Wow!* He just admitted he was falling for her, too. At least she wasn't alone in her feelings. She looked into his eyes and smiled.

"I don't know what's going to happen next, either, but I'm falling in love with you, too."

"Really?"

"Yes." She reached up to touch his face. "You're so dear to me."

He pulled her down to sit next to him in the sand.

"I'm not sure where this war is going to take me next. We might not see each other again for a long time. I don't know what our next steps should be."

She held his hand.

"I don't know that we need a plan, do we? We can continue to write to each other like we've been doing. That we've been able to see each other here on Ulithi these past few days was a miracle. I'm just happy for any time we have together."

He lifted her hand to his mouth and kissed her knuckles, one at a time. It sent shivers up her spine. He leaned close and captured her mouth.

"This is so much better than our trip to the beach in Sydney. I'm so happy I got a do-over. You make me happy, Aggie."

She felt a warm rush in her heart. He made her happy as well.

"I'm so glad I found you. In this whole world, I found the best girl. How is that possible?" He looked at her wonderingly.

"Well, I found the best guy," she said in return, kissing him. "How could I resist the man who taught me to fly?"

He ran a hand down the side of her face and cupped her cheek, looking at her with serious eyes.

"Speaking of flying, we're going to be getting underway soon. I can't give you any details, but you probably won't see me after tonight."

"I understand." She made a gesture like turning a key over her lips and then throwing the key away. "I'll write and pray for you every day."

"I would appreciate that, though mail delivery is spotty when we are underway. I'll write to you as well."

"You can write anything you like, Henry. Even if it's saying you're bored or scared or angry. I want to hear your thoughts, even if they aren't pleasant. You don't need to hold anything back or censor yourself for me."

"You really are extraordinary. I don't know what will happen next, but I'm so glad you're mine."

He stood and pulled her to her feet.

"I need to get back to the ship before the Shore Patrol comes hunting for me. Let me walk you back to the hangar."

They crossed the beach, donned their socks and shoes, and slowly made their way back to the airfield, hand in hand. Aggie felt soft and dreamy as she rested her head against Henry's shoulder as they walked. They had admitted they loved each other, which she found nothing short of amazing. For tonight, she would be content that he loved her. The rest would have to wait.

He kissed her one last time and whispered, "I love you, Aggie Ryan."

"I love you, too," she replied with a kiss of her own. "Be safe."

Chapter Fifteen

March 1945
Pacific Ocean, off the Japanese Home Islands

CONOR HAD BEEN RIGHT.

Admiral Spruance wanted to attack the kamikaze hatcheries on Kyushu to stop the kamikaze attacks before they could get started. He was also hoping to distract the Japanese prior to the Okinawa invasion. The Enterprise departed Ulithi on March 14 and headed to sea.

Henry had one last chance to see Aggie before he left. He was part of the team flying the Saratoga planes out to the Big E.

They didn't have time alone, as she was busy with her work. She took a moment to give him a hug and kiss before he entered the plane. He slipped a letter into the pocket of her coveralls as he hugged her back.

He hadn't slept the night before, so he poured out his heart into a letter to her.

My darling Aggie,

We're heading back out, as you will know when you read this letter. I'm not able to sleep, thinking about our time together here at Ulithi and our discussion on the beach this evening. Know that I'll be thinking of you while we are apart and how much I love you.

I hope someday you would consider coming to Chicago. I know you and my Ma would be thick as thieves in about five minutes after you meet. The two of you would probably gang up on me! I'm sure Ma will love you just as much as I do.

When you come to Chicago, I'll be over the moon to show you around the old neighborhood. I might even show you off to Father Parkolewicz so he can see how far I've come from that troublemaker in a would-be gang to a military pilot who found the loveliest young lady. I also want to show you the city; take you shopping on State Street and wander through Grant Park. We could go to the Field Museum and the Planetarium. Maybe even go to the Art Institute if you feel like doing something more cultured. We can walk through the city and see the skyscrapers. Did you know Chicago is the birthplace of the skyscraper? I want to show you my city and hope you will like it as much as I do.

Mostly, I just want to spend time with you, somewhere peaceful. Some place where we can be together without being pulled apart by the war.

I keep hearing you whispering I Love You in my ear and it makes me the happiest guy in the world. I love you, too, my Aggie.

Please keep writing, you know I look forward to your letters. I hope we will see each other again soon. Know that I love you.

Yours, with all my love,

Henry

He hoped he didn't scare her off, sharing all these thoughts with her. But his heart had been so full after they had said good night and she'd said she loved him.

Perhaps he shouldn't have written. Maybe it wasn't fair to tell her his thoughts and feelings when they were heading out to sea. There were so many dangers when he left the deck of the Enterprise: enemy fighters, flak, training accidents. He had handed her his heart. What if he never returned?

Following the captain's orders, the pilots and aircrews did their best to rest as the Enterprise ate up the ocean on the way toward Japan. They remembered the non-stop cycles of flying over Iwo Jima and would take the rest when they could get it.

On March 18, the Enterprise and her task force were in striking distance of the kamikaze training areas on Kyushu. The Enterprise dive bombers and fighters took to the skies to begin their attacks on the airfields. The night fighters used the hours of darkness to harry enemy bases and attack known radar sites.

There were airborne targets aplenty for all: the fighters, the anti-aircraft gunners aboard the Enterprise, and her escort task force. Sven splashed a Zero, blasting away at the enemy aircraft during one of their bombing runs. Several pilots from the Enterprise took down enemy planes, some pursuing their quarry through the clouds and rain squalls all around the fleet.

Operating in a confined area off the coast of Japan, the carriers were easy to find. An enemy dive bomber broke through, mistaken for a friendly by the radar operators. The plane roared over the Enterprise from bow to stern, dropping a bomb that struck the forward elevator. The fuse broke off the bomb and it lay there in the middle of the flight deck, unexploded, until a few brave souls rolled it to the stern and shoved it overboard.

For four days, the Enterprise and her fellow carriers from the task force attempted to damage the kamikaze sites on the island. Enemy aircraft streamed out from shore to attack the carriers and their task force.

The carrier Wasp took hits that killed 100 men but could steam away under her own power. Enemy dive bombers hammered the Benjamin Franklin. Men on the Enterprise watched as a sickening plume of greasy black smoke rose from the Franklin with flashes and flames of exploding ordinance. Big Ben had to be towed out of the area, with the loss of eight hundred crew.

The Japanese kept coming. The captain kept the Enterprise at general quarters day and night, Henry was glad he had taken what rest he could on the cruise from Ulithi.

On the morning of March 20, he and Conor headed to the hangar deck in their flight suits, ready to take to the skies for another day of midair battle.

"Bad news," Bill Lago said, looking at Conor. "The fuel line that got hit yesterday is still leaking. Your bird isn't going anywhere. They're working on bringing up one of the Saratoga planes for you to use today."

Conor's shoulders slumped, whether in disappointment or relief, Henry couldn't tell.

Bill turned to Henry. "You're good to go. She's gassed up and ready to fly. The guys just loaded her onto the elevator. If you and Sven hurry, you can ride up to the flight deck with her."

"Thanks, Bill," Henry replied, then he turned to Conor. "I'll see you up there, right?"

"As soon as they get me a ride," Conor said, clapping Henry on the shoulder. "Be safe up there. They're getting desperate. Don't do anything stupid."

"Nope, nothing stupid. See you soon."

He sprinted over to the elevator to ride up to the flight deck with Sven and the plane.

The crew rolled the plane into place at the end of the flight deck. Henry and Sven climbed in and clipped into their safety belts. Sven checked the radios and made sure the ammo cans for his machine guns were in place. He gave Henry a thumbs up. Henry repeated the gesture to the deck crew, letting them know the Dauntless was ready to fly. Seconds later, the plane was hurtling down the flight deck and into the air.

Henry pulled up and joined his flight group at their rally point. The squadron would bomb an airstrip used by the kamikaze for take-off. As they headed toward the island, Japanese aircraft swarmed them. Henry did his best to keep them off his tail while Sven pounded away with the big machine guns.

"You gonna splash another one today, Sven?" Henry called over the radio as he twisted and dove to avoid enemy fire.

"I'm gonna try! Four more and I'm an ace."

Henry located the airstrip they were aiming for. He dropped to a precipitous angle, ready to release his bombs.

Henry loved the dive on the bombing run. It was such a rush to plummet at an impossibly steep angle to drop the payload. He could hear Sven whooping behind him and smiled. Sven loved roller coasters, but nothing would ever compare to the 70-80 degree drop they would experience when diving with the Dauntless. Henry dropped his bombs and pulled up, avoiding the triple A from the ground, and joined the fray with the fighters above.

Sven continued firing his twin machine guns, swiveling side to side to fend off attackers. Henry was doing his best to let the Hellcats handle the Japanese fighters. Besides Sven's guns, which faced rearward in a defensive position to protect from attack from behind, Henry had a machine gun to engage the enemy. Firing and flying, he noticed his ammo was running low. His best option was to get back to the Enterprise as quickly as possible to reload with additional munitions before another bombing run.

"Hey, Hank! They're all over us!" called Sven.

Henry was doing his best to jink and dodge as he flew toward the Big E. Then he heard the bullets raking the side of the plane and Sven cry out.

"Sven! What's happening back there, man?"

"They got me in the shoulder! Oh my God, that hurts!" Sven screamed.

Henry had a moment of panic. They hit Sven. There were a few guys in the group who had lost their back seater, and the thought of that happening to Sven haunted Henry.

"I've got you, Sven. I'll get you on the deck as soon as I can and we'll get the docs to patch you up."

"He's coming around again," Sven said weakly. "I can only fire with my left arm; I can't lift the right one to hold the gun."

Henry heard another rattle of gunfire hit the tail of the Dauntless and another cry from Sven.

"Sven! Talk to me!"

"I think... I got hit again... I think maybe in the chest... It's hard...to breathe..."

Henry had the Enterprise in sight He just needed to get lined up for approach and put it on the deck.

"Sven, can you radio us in? Ask for priority landing?"

"I don't...I think the...radio...got hit...too."

"Never mind. They'll see me," Henry reassured him, at least he hoped he sounded reassuring. Henry tried to call with his radio. No dice. They were without communications.

As Henry prepared to line up for his approach and landing, a Judy dive bomber dropped out of the overcast over the bow of the Enterprise and dropped a bomb close to the hull. The assailant sped for home followed by a hail of gunfire. Misdirected fire from escorting ships caused projectiles to detonate above the Enterprise's forward anti-aircraft guns. Henry watched in horror as the explosion caused six fueled and fully armed Hellcats on the deck to burst into flames. There was no way Henry could land in that inferno.

He looked around for one of the other carriers. Perhaps he could land on one of their flight decks, the way the guys from the Saratoga had landed on the Enterprise. He couldn't see anything nearby and he could hear Sven struggling to breathe over the intercom.

He glanced at the map on his knee board. No good. The only nearby airfields were the ones they had just bombed. They wouldn't have a very good reception if they tried landing there. He'd heard stories about how the Japanese treated POWs, and he wouldn't put himself and wounded Sven through that.

Henry thought fast. He checked his gauges. He was low on fuel. The bullets had likely damaged his fuel lines.

He needed to decide quickly. He looked down at the ocean. There were several cruisers and destroyers within reasonable distance. The Navy was good about picking up downed fliers; their search and rescue was amongst the best. He could ditch the plane near one of the friendly ships and hope they could pluck them out of the water in time to get medical attention for Sven.

Suddenly, on the horizon, he spotted another flat top. He thought it might be the San Jacinto. He changed course and directed his wounded bird toward the carrier. If he couldn't land on her deck, he'd get as close as possible so they could send out a rescue crew.

"Hang in there, Sven. I spotted another carrier. We're gonna land and get you some help."

There was no response from Sven. Henry said a brief prayer that his buddy would be okay, then an Act of Contrition, just in case. He thought about his Ma. What would happen to her if he didn't make it? She'd lost her husband to wounds from the last war, now she could lose her son in this one. Henry shook his head. He couldn't think about that now.

He tried to line up for a landing on the carrier. Enemy fighters swarmed her, and there was a hail of anti-aircraft flak in the air surrounding her. He was losing altitude, and he checked his fuel status. He was at Bingo, out of gas. His dive bomber just became a glider.

Henry prepared to ditch the plane as close to the carrier as he could. He ran through the ditching checklist and tried to plan how he would get Sven out of the back and into the life raft. As he guided the plane down, closer and closer to the waves, he thought of Aggie. He was glad he'd told her he loved her. He hoped he'd live through this to see her again.

Henry flared the nose of the plane before he hit the water. When he touched down, it was like hitting a wall. There was no gliding along the tops of the waves or skipping like a stone on a pond, just a sudden lurching stop. The plane appeared to be floating for the moment. He unbuckled his harness and slid the canopy back, climbing out quickly. He extracted the small life raft and pulled the cord to inflate the raft as he climbed along the wing to get to Sven.

As he reached the back seat and looked in at Sven, Henry had never seen so much blood. He reached in and shook Sven, who roused briefly.

"Let's get you out of here, buddy," Henry said, as he worked to unbuckle Sven's seatbelt. He grabbed Sven under the arms and pulled. Sven's eyes shot open wide, and he screamed.

"I'm sorry, buddy, but we gotta get you out of there. The plane is sinking."

"Planes don't sink... They fly..." Sven muttered.

"Yep, that's usually true, but this one's sinking. Let's get you in the life raft."

Henry wrangled Sven's lanky frame out of the plane and into the raft. He unzipped his flight suit, tearing off his undershirt to make a compress to hold Sven's wounds. He wished Conor were here. Surely the Eagle Scout would know more about first aid than Henry.

"Hang in there, Sven. Help should be on the way soon."

Henry looked around, hoping to see a skiff headed their way from the carrier. He hoped they would get Sven to the doctors in time to treat his wounds.

As they bobbed in the life raft, he held onto Sven, cradling him in his arms. He thought about the fire he'd seen engulf the flight deck of Enterprise and thought of Conor and their other crew mates. Henry was an altar boy growing up but had never been very religious. Now, he bowed his head and prayed. For Sven. For his friends on the Big E. For rescue. Prayed that he would see his Ma and Aggie again.

Chapter Sixteen

March 1945
Ulithi Atoll, Caroline Islands

RUMORS WERE FLYING thick and fast around the Navy base on Ulithi. The Wasp struggled into port for repairs, followed by the Franklin, under tow and likely out of the war. Damage on the Franklin was breathtaking, and reports said over eight hundred sailors had lost their lives.

Aggie and her fellow mechanics were busy with the planes ferried from the Franklin to the airfield for inspection and maintenance. The planes would transfer to other carriers to replace aircraft lost in battle. Meanwhile, their former home - Big Ben, as the Navy men called it - underwent emergency repairs to return to Pearl Harbor.

Aggie was most concerned about reports of a fire on the flight deck of the Enterprise. Details were scant, but there was an explosion and several planes on the deck had caught fire. Both she and Katie waited for word about Conor and Henry's safety.

On March 24, word swept through the base that Enterprise was coming into port for repairs. Katie and Aggie borrowed a jeep and drove to the pier to see the arrival. From their vantage point, they could not see any damage, because the flight deck was high above them. They watched as stretchers bearing wounded sailors came down from the hangar deck for transport to the base hospital. One sailor told them ten men had died in the attack.

The Shore Patrol waved them away from the dock, stating that all crew members were being held aboard the Enterprise until completion of a final damage assessment.

The women returned to the hangar more anxious than when they left. Aggie tried to lose herself in her work as they waited for more news. She kept repeating tasks because she was having difficulty focusing. She was so worried about Henry.

Late in the day, Conor strode into the hangar, looking for Katie. When she spotted him, she shrieked and ran into his arms. Aggie looked behind him for Henry. It seemed the friends were always together, like tea and jam.

When she didn't see Henry, her stomach dropped and her heart started beating hard and fast in her chest. After assuring Katie he was unscathed, Conor turned to Aggie, removed his garrison cap, and started worrying it in his hands.

Aggie was finding it difficult to breathe and felt her vision narrowing.

"What happened?"

Conor led the girls over to a group of chairs near their makeshift bedroom. As they sat down, Jackie also rushed over to hear the news. She and Katie each held one of Aggie's hands as Conor told them what had happened aboard the Enterprise.

"I was below, on the hangar deck. Bill was trying to get an alternate plane ready for me. Henry's plane was on the elevator, so he and Sven took off on their sortie as planned," Conor said.

He explained about the Japanese dive bomber who had overflown the flight deck and how the shells exploded, resulting in several planes catching fire. The fire had quickly spread across the deck and ignited thousands of rounds of anti-aircraft and machine gun ammunition.

"There was a Dauntless lining up for landing when the deck caught fire," Conor told them in a hushed voice. "It may have been Henry. He couldn't land on the flaming deck, so he peeled away. The landing crew on the flight deck thought they saw the Dauntless trailing smoke as he turned away."

Conor looked at Aggie, stricken.

"We aren't sure what happened to the plane or the crew. But Henry and Sven didn't make it back to the ship once the fires were out."

Aggie was stunned.

"When will we know?" she asked shakily.

Conor simply shrugged. "We just don't know. There was a report that the San Jacinto may have pulled a few of our guys out of the water, but there was no confirmation about Henry and Sven."

He reached out and rested a hand on her shoulder. "I will let you know if I hear anything."

Aggie thanked him and left Conor and Katie to have a private moment. She stepped between the tarps blocking their sleeping quarters as the first tears began falling. Aggie sat on her bunk and wept quietly. She reached under her pillow for her rosary and prayed for Henry and Sven that they were safe and whole. She prayed for Henry's mum. From Henry's stories, he was the center of his mum's world and Aggie was worried about this woman she'd never met if she should lose her boy.

When she finished the rosary, she put her beads back under her pillow and dried her eyes. She stood from her bunk and squared her shoulders. There was work to be done. Crying would not help Henry, nor bring him back safely. She would keep praying while she did her work and got through each day. Like she had done when Mum died, and when Da left them. She would do what needed to be done and move forward.

THE HOSPITAL SHIP ARRIVED at Ulithi two days later.

Henry had barely left Sven's side since they were in the life raft. They had drifted on the ocean for half an hour before the carrier had sent a skiff to pick them up. He was right; it had been the San Jacinto.

When the rescue party arrived, a young lieutenant helped Henry get Sven settled in the rescue craft and kept them company while the small boat raced back to the carriers.

"Sorry it took so long to get out here," he apologized. "The kamikazes were swarming us and we weren't able to lower the skiff until the firing let up."

"I'm just glad you got to us," Henry said. Sven had been in and out of consciousness while they were in the raft, but now appeared to be unconscious.

"I saw you ditch," the lieutenant said. "My plane's damaged and they're trying to repair it. I spotted you guys trying to get to us, but you were really losing altitude. Once you were in the drink, I grabbed a pair of binoculars and watched you, so I'd know where to direct them."

"You're a pilot? Do you usually do search and rescue missions?"

"No, this is my first. I had to bail out a while ago and wait to be picked up. So, I know how it feels to be floating out here. At least you'll have space on the carrier when we get back. I got picked up by a submarine," he winced. "Not recommended."

"Thanks for keeping track of us. I just want to get medical attention for Sven." He looked down at his buddy, worried. "He's so still."

The young man patted Henry on the shoulder.

"He's gonna be fine."

"How can you know that?"

"Read my lips: he'll be just fine. We've got the best docs in the Navy on our ship."

When they reached the carrier, they bundled the men on board and the ship's doctor was waiting to examine Sven. One bullet had passed through Sven's upper right arm but missed any bone or major vessels. The other had indeed hit his lung, which had collapsed. The doctor inserted a tube between Sven's ribs to re-inflate the lung. As soon as the lung was functioning again, Sven came around. They brought him to the medical area, and Henry opted to stay with him.

The lieutenant, who introduced himself as George, brought Henry a cup of coffee and peeked in on Sven.

"I told you he was going to be alright," George said with a wink. "They'll transfer him to the hospital ship, and then he'll go to the Navy hospital on Ulithi. We can't take you boys back; still battling it out with the Japs."

"Do you think I can catch a ride back to Ulithi on the hospital ship? It would give me a chance to catch up with the Enterprise."

And Aggie, he thought. She would be worried sick if the Enterprise arrived for repairs, and he wasn't on the ship.

"I'm sure we can arrange something," George replied. "Unless you want to stay aboard and fly with us."

"Thanks for the offer, but I need to get back to my squadron."

George nodded his understanding. Henry thanked him and shook his hand.

"I appreciate your help with Sven. It means a lot."

"I'm happy to help," George said soberly. "When my Avenger went down, I was the only one who got out. The rest of my crew died. I think about them every day. Helping you guys was part of my way of making amends for losing them."

The men shook hands again, wished each other well, and parted ways as they moved Sven to the hospital ship.

Two days later, they carried Sven down the gangway to a waiting ambulance. Sven looked much better. He still had the chest tube in place and would need a brief surgery to remove the bullet that was rattling around in his rib cage, but he was awake and talking a mile a minute like normal. Henry was so happy to hear him talking non-stop.

Once Sven was settled at the Navy hospital, Henry went to the Enterprise to let the captain know he had arrived.

Now that I'm done with that chore, thought Henry, *I'm going to find my girl and let her know I'm alive and well.*

AGGIE HAD JUST FINISHED her day and was heading to the back of the hangar to grab her shower gear. She wanted to wash up after a hard day, which had been physically challenging and emotionally grueling. She planned to walk over to the Officers Club with Katie and Conor to see if there was any news, but she needed to clean up first.

As she reached their partitioned area, she thought she spotted a familiar figure. She had been working on a plane out on the hangar apron, in the bright sunshine and her eyes had not yet adjusted to the gloom inside the hangar. As she squinted to make out the figure, the man turned to face her.

"Aggie, sweetheart..."

That was all she heard as her heart started pounding, her knees buckled, and she burst into tears. Henry rushed to her and caught her in his arms. He held her close and stroked her hair.

"It's okay, sweetie. I'm here. I'm okay," he soothed. He kissed her cheeks and looked in her eyes. "I'm good, it's all good. Please stop crying. I'm okay."

Aggie tried to pull herself together. She led him to the same group of chairs where Conor told her Henry was missing. She drank in the sight of him and held tight to his hands as he told her about Sven and having to ditch the plane. He told her about the rescue and their time on the hospital ship. She listened, rapt, as he told his tale.

She was so very grateful to see him again and said a brief prayer of thanksgiving to God for watching over this man.

He pulled a handkerchief out of his pocket and handed it to her to dry her eyes.

"I was so worried about you, Henry, but I tried to stay strong. This is only the second time I've cried, and this is sheer relief."

"I don't want to see you cry, but is it wrong of me to be pleased that you're crying tears of relief to see me?"

She smiled through her tears and shoved his shoulder. "You're terrible. It's a good thing I love you so much."

"That is a good thing. I love you very much, too." He leaned forward and kissed her gently. "Now, why don't we head over to the O Club for a proper meal?"

She looked down at her grease-stained coveralls and dirty hands.

"I was heading to my bunk to get my things to take a shower. I'm filthy from working on that Avenger. Can you give me a bit to wash up?"

"After the past few days I've had, I'm more than willing to wait for you to get dolled up so I can take you to dinner.

"Then wait right here, I'll be back in a flash!"

Aggie gathered up her bathing supplies and her clean uniform and rushed to the shower. She washed quickly, scrubbing hard to get the grease and dirt from under her fingernails. Dressing carefully, she did her best to arrange her hair into a fashionable style. She added a swipe of lipstick and hurried back to Henry – only to find him sound asleep with his feet propped up on a chair.

She looked down at him as he slept. He looked so peaceful and handsome, with a firm jawline and a slight cleft in his chin. He had a strong nose and dark eyebrows that framed his closed eyes. His hair was a little longer than usual and a lock of dark hair fell forward over his forehead. She sat and studied him as he slept, memorizing the lines of his dear face.

He must have heard her shift in her chair because his eyes slowly opened. It took a moment for him to pull her into focus. He rubbed a hand up and down his face.

"I'm sorry, I dozed off."

"Understandable. You've had a few very stressful days."

"I have, but it's all better now, just seeing you. You look pretty, Aggie."

She blushed and thanked him for the compliment.

"Shall we head for dinner?"

"Yes, please."

After the meal, she asked the waiter if there might be a bunch of grapes in the kitchen that she could have. He took his leave to see what he could find.

"Grapes?" Henry asked quizzically. "Why do you want a bunch of grapes?"

"For Sven, of course. Obviously."

Henry looked baffled. "What's obvious about Sven and grapes?"

"To bring to him in hospital," she said, not understanding why Henry was confused.

"You're going to bring Sven grapes? Because he's in the hospital?"

"Yes, that's what I said. You know, grapes for the ill, a gift to wish him well. It's traditional."

"Are you telling me it's a tradition to bring someone grapes when they're ill and in the hospital?"

"Well, yes. Don't you do that in America?"

"Uh, no," he said flatly.

"Then what would you bring someone in hospital?"

"Usually flowers, I think. I can't say I've visited many friends in the hospital."

"Well, it's what's done in the UK and Australia. Let's go visit Sven," she said as the waiter returned with a small bunch of grapes wrapped in paper.

After a visit to Sven, who thanked Aggie for the grapes, then sang Henry's praises for saving him from the ditched plane and helping him into the life raft, Henry and Aggie strolled down to the beach near the harbor. They held hands and talked and kissed in the moonlight.

This began a weeklong idyll for the two of them. Henry had no duties while the Enterprise was undergoing repairs, and Aggie's supervisor allowed her two afternoons off as the Navy had brought in more mechanics to service the myriad planes at the airfield.

They lounged in the sun on the beach, drinking Coca-Cola and splashing in the surf. Conor and Katie joined them for the occasional picnic lunch. They took long walks along the beach with their toes in the water. On the days she had to work, Henry met her for lunch at the mess hall or they would grab sandwiches at the canteen.

In the evenings, they would share meals together and go dancing at the Officer's Club. The days felt like being on holiday at the beach, the nights like they were carefree and dating – something Aggie wouldn't have thought possible since signs of war surrounded them.

They talked constantly about their lives before the war and then, tentatively, about what their lives might look like after the war. They could tell the Japanese were on their back foot. From the European news, the German defeat was coming. It was time to think about, and discuss, what came next.

Henry wanted to continue flying, maybe for an airline that shuttled people from one city to another. Aggie didn't have any plans and told him so.

"I hadn't really thought beyond going into the WAAAFs and serving in the war. A chance to move away from home and have some adventure. Look at me now!" She gestured around herself at the moonlit ocean lapping the shore, the palm tree overhead, and Henry himself.

Henry looked at her speculatively.

"Have you enjoyed traveling? Moving to the city? Working at different air bases?"

"Oh, yes. There's such a wide world beyond that cattle station in the Northern Territories. I feel like I've only had a little taste of it."

"Would you consider further travel?" he asked tentatively.

"I don't know," she said, a fluttery feeling starting in her tummy. "I guess it would depend on where I was traveling and why."

He looked at her seriously.

"Would you consider coming to Chicago?"

Aggie gasped softly. She had thought Henry was working his way toward this conversation. He had mentioned showing her around Chicago in the letter he'd slipped into her pocket. Over the past week, he had told her about his neighborhood in Chicago and about his mum. What their house was like, the food his mum liked to cook. He appeared to be gauging her interest in the life he had back home, trying to decide if he should ask her to come home with him.

"I don't know. It's so far, literally the other side of the world." She paused, then asked, "How would it work?"

He released a deep breath, breathing out the anticipation that had clearly built up on him before she responded. "A friend of mine from Lewis is flying with the Army Air Force in Europe. He's a bomber pilot. He met an English girl who lives near his airfield. They started dating and now they're engaged. After the war, he's going to bring her back home and get married. Maybe we could do something like that. What do you think?"

Engaged? Married? Moving to America?

My goodness, she thought, *this is moving fast.* Realistically though, this was the only option if she and Henry hoped to be together in the future. Either she would move to America or Henry would stay in Australia and she didn't think that would be possible. She knew he would want to be close to his mum.

What would happen if their relationship didn't work out? She would be in a strange country all alone. Although, that wasn't dissimilar to her leaving home to go to Sydney. She didn't know anyone in the WAAAF, and Sydney might as well be a different country. It was so far and different from her family's homestead. She had done well for herself, made new friends, learned new skills. Skills so valuable they had sent her to this tropical paradise to put them to use.

If she didn't try, she would never know.

"I think that going to Chicago might be something I could do."

Henry broke into a huge smile and leaned over to kiss her.

"Oh, my Ma is gonna love you." He kissed her again before he sobered. "I'd like to build a new life with you, Aggie. Without war and fighting."

"I'd like to build a new life with you too, Henry."

They were both bright and hardworking, they both had skills to build careers, they both loved their families, and they loved one another. She wanted to see where that love could lead them.

"I don't have a ring or anything. I don't think I want to get engaged just yet."

She looked up at him, surprised. They were talking about her going to Chicago and he didn't think he wanted to get engaged yet? She was confused.

"I know I want to be engaged to you, Aggie," he clarified. "It's only that, while the war is winding down, it's not over yet. Every time I climb into that plane, I might not come back. I don't want you tied to me; in case something happens to me. I don't want you to be a widow. And I don't want you to be stuck with me if I'm injured or crippled. I saw what happened to my Ma and Tatus. My Tatus was in a mustard gas attack during World War I that ruined his lungs. He was an invalid from his war injuries until he died. As happy as they were, it was a shadow over their marriage. I don't want that for you."

This vision of his parents' marriage touched and saddened Aggie. Then she thought of the example of her own folks. Da was so shattered by the loss of Mum that he abandoned them all. She and Henry would have the chance to learn from their parents' mistakes and build their own marriage stronger and better.

"I understand. I'll wait for you to come back. At the end of the war, we will make our plans for the future."

"For our future," he whispered to her and kissed her again.

They snuggled together on the moonlight dappled beach and whispered about their love for each other and their dreams for the future.

"So, how many kids do you want?" Henry asked with a wink.

Chapter Seventeen

April 1945
Pacific Ocean, off Okinawa

THE ENTERPRISE WAS back in action. Henry had bid Aggie goodbye with hugs and kisses on the evening of April 4, and the Big E was underway on April 5.

Before he boarded the ship, he stopped by the hospital to say goodbye to Sven. Sven was on the mend and expected to make a full recovery. However, he was in no shape to ship out with the rest of the Enterprise crew.

"I hate to leave you here," Henry said.

"Like that Aussie girlfriend of yours would say, no worries, mate!" Sven replied in a dreadful imitation of Aggie's Australian accent. "The doc says I'm going to need more recovery time. So, there's no chance I could go with you."

"Get well soon, Sven. I'm gonna need you back."

Sven looked grim. "I'll be honest with you, they're talking about shipping me back home."

Henry caught his breath, stunned. Sven shook his head.

"I'm not ashamed to say that I'm not ready to fly again. My shoulder is still killing me and they just pulled that tube out of my chest the other day. That wasn't a lot of fun. I'd be no good in your back seat right now."

Henry knew he was right, but Sven had been his back seater since the start. They knew each other's moves and communication. Having a replacement back there would be strange. Henry would miss Sven terribly. Henry bid Sven goodbye, promising to keep in touch.

"And if you're ever up for being someone's radioman and tail gunner..." Henry began.

"You're the first one I'll call," Sven finished. They shook hands, and Henry left the hospital.

When Henry returned to the ship after visiting Sven, he found a dark-haired fellow with hazel-green eyes unpacking his seabag on Sven's bunk. He stuck out his hand and introduced himself.

"Hi, I'm Jeff Berek. Nice to meet you. I'm looking for Henry Bolanski."

"You've found him. I'm Henry," he said, shaking Jeff's hand. "Nice to meet you. Welcome to the squadron. Looks like you'll be filling in as my back seater while Sven is in the hospital."

Jeff's eyes grew wide. "He's in the hospital? What happened?"

Henry recounted what had happened near Kyushu, the fire on the flight deck, Sven's injuries, needing to ditch and the rescue. As he told his tale, Jeff's eyes grew wider and wider.

"Wow, you've seen a lot of action. I just finished my training a month ago, then they shipped me off to Pearl and then a troop transport to here."

Oh, boy, thought Henry. *A green replacement.* He hoped they'd be able to keep each other alive. Henry had a lot to live for.

The Enterprise reached the waters off Okinawa on April 7 and began flight operations. The planes from Enterprise were once again flying day and night. It pleased Henry to note that Jeff was a competent radioman and a deadeye shot shooting the twin machine guns in the back seat. While he didn't know him as well as Sven, he had confidence in the replacement's skills after seeing him in action.

On April 11, Henry and the rest of the dive bombers were running bombing sorties to carpet the kamikaze bases between Okinawa and Honshu, bombing and strafing airfields everywhere they went. The kamikazes were out in strength and aiming for the Enterprise.

In the morning, gunners shot down one suicide plane so close to the ship that when the plane exploded, the blast blew a sailor overboard and he had to be rescued. In the afternoon, a bomb laden Zeke dive bomber dove on the Enterprise. The crew threw up an enormous amount of flak and the plane smashed into the water feet from the starboard bow and exploded. The forward gun crews deflected another kamikaze and as the plane turned away from Enterprise, another ship took it out.

Though there was considerable damage to the Enterprise from these encounters, she could temporarily continue her mission. However, she had a destroyed radar mount, dented hull plating, and punctured fuel bunkers. On April 14, she returned to Ulithi once more for repairs.

Henry was delighted to learn that the Navy expected repairs from the kamikaze's damage to take two weeks. To access the underwater damage to the hull, the port side tanks were flooded to induce an eight-degree list. This made moving through the interior areas of the ship challenging. The captain ordered the pilots off the ship to reduce crowding and sprained ankles as sailors negotiated the Leaning Tower of Enterprise. Henry happily moved to the BOQ (bachelor officer's quarters) with Conor, Jeff, Kowalski, and Perry.

Once again, he had plenty of free time. The pilots couldn't practice off the Big E's flight deck because of the list, so he would walk over to the WAAAFs hangar and watch Aggie work her magic on the planes. Bill had been right; she really knew her stuff and other mechanics often asked her advice on how to approach a problem. Henry sat near her workstation, passing her tools when she asked.

He laughed to himself at the flip-flop of usual expectations; the man watching the woman work and handing her tools when she asked for them. He thought it was probably easier for him to accept their switch in traditional roles because he'd had a lifetime of watching his ma defy conventions to raise her son and pay the bills.

He would join Aggie for lunch at the canteen or the mess hall. In the evenings, they would have dinner together. They settled into a similar routine as they had when the Enterprise had been in for repairs last month, and Henry thoroughly enjoyed himself. Some sailors and officers complained that the "fightingest ship" in the US Navy was spending more time in the harbor than on the seas of late, but Henry wasn't complaining. He was enjoying his time with Aggie.

He also took time to visit Sven and was happy to see his friend progressing. Henry had hoped Sven could ship out with the Enterprise when the current round of repairs was complete, although he would feel bad about dumping Jeff as his back seater if Sven came back. However, Sven had undergone surgery to remove the bullet from his chest and would return stateside for further rehabilitation to recover from his injuries.

One afternoon when he arrived at the hangar to meet Aggie for lunch, he found her reading an official-looking letter and looking concerned. She heard his footsteps as he approached and looked up.

"They're sending us back to New Guinea. "

"What? Why?"

"The letter says the US Navy has enough aviation mechanics on the base now. They appreciated our help during the crisis, but now they have adequate staffing with US Navy mechanics and our secondment is at an end. The RAAF is returning all personnel to New Guinea to start and then back to Australia as 'deemed appropriate.'"

She looked at him, stricken. "Oh, Henry, they're sending me away!"

He pulled her into a hug and held her tight. Henry started thinking fast. He couldn't lose her, not now. He had somehow found this perfect girl. Well, maybe not perfect, but perfect for him, and he couldn't let her go.

"When? When do you leave?"

"May first. They will transport us to the airfield at Aitape via airplane and then determine who will stay there and who will continue on to Darwin or Sydney."

"Okay," he said, pondering. "I heard we should wrap up our repairs around May 1or 2, so we head back out around the same time you leave. Let's go get some chow and we can talk about it some more."

"What more is there to talk about, Henry? It's April 29. We have two days."

He pulled her close and kissed her temple. "We'll think of something."

He didn't know how much longer the war would continue. From the news, it appeared action was wrapping up in the European Theater. But in the Pacific? They would have to take Okinawa, then the home islands of Japan. Given the resistance the Marines and Army had experienced throughout the Pacific campaign, it could take years.

That said, the fliers on the Enterprise were watching the calendar. The second cruise for Air Group 10 had lasted six months, from January to July 1944, and Air Group 20 also left after six months, many sent stateside as flight instructors. By his reckoning, his group was at the four-month mark of their current tour and could expect another sixty days of service in their current positions. After that, the Navy might send them to the States to train future pilots, as had happened with their predecessors. If that was the case, he and Aggie might not need to wait years.

With a jolt, Henry realized his previous opinion had changed. Before, he felt they shouldn't get engaged then married in a rush and have her end up widowed or married to a cripple. Now, he wanted to have a firm understanding between them before she left. If nothing happened to him before the end of his current tour, perhaps he could figure out a way to have her come to the United States. Of course, she would have to agree to marry him. Now he would need to work up the nerve to ask her.

They bumped into Conor and Katie in line at the mess hall and shared a subdued meal together. Katie had received the same letter, recalling her to New Guinea, and Conor was in a sullen mood. He looked as if a rain cloud was hovering over his head.

Although Henry wanted to spend every moment he could with Aggie, he and Conor needed to talk strategy. Both Aggie and Katie needed to finish work back at the hangar, so the men walked them back and then returned to the BOQ.

"We need to move our gear back to the ship," Conor said. "If we're shipping out in a few days, we need to get our bunks, and everything squared away."

"Good," Henry said. "I need to head over to Enterprise and find the chaplain."

"What do you want with the chaplain?"

"I'm going to ask him how to get a foreign national fiancé from Australia to America."

"You what?! You asked Aggie to marry you? You two are engaged?"

"Not yet, but I'm going to find out what's involved and if there's any way to make it happen, I'm gonna make it happen."

Determined, he continued shoving clothing and gear into his seabag. The sooner he spoke to Father Palazolla, the better.

Conor was looking at him, jaw slack. "You're serious?"

Henry looked him in the eye. "As serious as a heart attack."

He slung his bag over his shoulder and walked out the door. Conor shook himself and reached for his own bag.

"Wait for me," Conor called and followed him out the door.

FROM WHAT HENRY COULD tell, quite a few sailors and fliers must have enquired about bringing girls home from overseas because Father Palazolla had a stack of forms and pamphlets and a canned speech that he provided to the men. Admonishments about not rushing into marriage, as well as warnings about the sins of the flesh, were mixed in with information provided by the chaplain.

The US serviceman could apply for permission to marry a foreign national. The application would have to be approved by the man's superior and Commanding Officer. There would be a "cooling off" period once they made the application. The waiting period had been as long as three to six months earlier in the war, but as the Allied forces advanced, the waiting period grew shorter.

Henry sat down and filled out the application right there in the small chapel on the Enterprise and answered all of Father Palazolla's questions. He then took the application and went hunting for Kowalski, who would need to review and approve it. Henry found him on the hangar deck, conferring with Bill Lago.

"Hey Kowalski, can you look at this form and approve it?" Henry asked.

Kowalski took the sheaf of papers and studied them. He looked up at Henry, surprised. "This is Aggie? You asked her to marry you?"

"Not yet. I wanted to be sure I had all my ducks in a row before I asked her. What do you say? Will you approve my application and sign it?"

At that moment, Bill added his two cents.

"Good for you, Henry." He turned to Kowalski. "She's a sharp girl, sir. A real hard worker."

"Thanks for your input, Bill," Kowalski said sarcastically. "I know the young lady. I can't think of a nicer, more levelheaded girl. You'll be lucky if she says yes, Bolanski."

"I know it, sir."

"I'll sign this and send it along to the captain and fleet commander for final approval. I will add a letter of recommendation for Aggie. Given her work with the WAAAFs and her service assisting the Navy here on Ulithi, that should help grease the wheels for you kids." He slapped Henry on the back. "Congratulations."

"Don't congratulate me yet. I still haven't asked her."

"Never fear. I've seen you two together. She'll say yes." He tipped a nod to Bill and strode off, Henry's paperwork in hand.

"Good for you, Henry," Bill said, turning to him. "When are you gonna pop the question?"

"She's being transferred back to New Guinea in two days, so I'm gonna need to do it quickly. Bill, can I ask you a favor? I need a little help with something before I ask her."

"Sure. How can I help?"

THE NEXT DAY, AGGIE finished up the various projects she was working on around the hangar. She split her time between yet another Corsair engine and instructing several of the new Navy mechanics in performing oil changes. It made her laugh that she was now directing the Navy men with the basic maintenance activities that they had once relegated to her, while she was consistently working on more complex and complicated problems. She was proud of the work she was doing, as well as her ability to teach those skills to others.

Henry did not arrive at lunchtime to accompany her to the canteen for a sandwich. He had sent a note with a runner asking her to meet him at the O Club after her shift and to "wear something pretty." She snorted with laughter. Something pretty, like she had any kind of fancy wardrobe. Still, she appreciated that this would be her last night with him on Ulithi. Who knew when they would see each other again?

As she packed her coveralls and personal items and set out her uniform for the flight tomorrow, she surveyed her small collection of civilian clothes. Two pairs of shorts, a white cotton blouse, a pale blue short-sleeved blouse, a floral skirt, and a pair of canvas plimsolls. She chose the white blouse and the skirt and paired it with the plimsolls, which were easy to slip off and on if they went to the beach. Styling her hair with victory rolls, she let the back fall in loose waves, since Henry liked to run his hands through her hair. She slicked on a bit of pink lipstick and was ready to leave for the Officers Club.

Jackie was at her bunk, packing her things as Katie came through the partition, fresh from the shower, as Aggie was about to exit.

"Conor is coming to collect me in 15 minutes. He was acting funny at lunchtime, kind of anxious and secretive. Do you think he's up to something?"

"Like what?"

"I don't know. Like maybe another woman."

"Katie, there are about 30 women on this entire island. Where is he going to find another woman?" Jackie asked. "Besides, he's utterly besotted with you. He's not looking anywhere else. You have nothing to worry about."

"I suppose you're right. I had another idea about why he was acting so antsy at lunch. He said he had something serious he needed to talk to me about tonight. Something to ask me," Katie said, wrapping the belt of her robe around and around her hand nervously. "Do you think he might ask me to go to America with him? To marry him?"

Aggie paused. Maybe. Maybe Conor wanted to propose to Katie. They had been devoted to each other since they met last November in Sydney. Oh, wouldn't that be romantic?

Aggie took her friend's hands in hers and unwrapped the belt.

"If he does, he'd be lucky to have you." She gave Katie's hands a squeeze. "Good luck."

Aggie exited the hangar via the small door closest to the path to the O Club. As she stepped out into the warm, tropical night, she spotted Henry waiting for her, leaning against a lamppost and looking handsome in his uniform. He stood in the pool of light created by the lamp.

"You look like a movie star, leaning there like that. All you need is a cigarette and a fedora tipped down over your brow."

"Well, that's quite a compliment," he said, taking her hand and pulling her close. "But you wouldn't want me to be smoking and then do this." He bent down and kissed her.

This kiss seemed different from others they had shared. A little wilder, more possessive. He slid his hand up into her hair and angled her head to deepen the kiss. When they broke apart, Aggie felt breathless. He rubbed his thumb across her lower lip.

"Sorry. I messed up your lipstick. You don't usually wear it."

"That's okay. But you have some on your lips now." She pulled a handkerchief from the pocket of her skirt. She reached up and wiped his lips with the cloth.

"Come on. Let's go get something to eat."

During the meal, Aggie thought Henry was nervous. He kept repeating himself during their conversation and was frequently patting the chest pockets of his uniform shirt, like her Da used to do when he was checking to be sure he had his spectacles. Only... Henry didn't wear spectacles. It was very odd.

She thought about her conversation with Katie, about Conor's odd behavior at lunch, and her speculation that Conor might propose. Could it be possible that Henry was acting strangely for the same reason? She recalled his comment yesterday when she was upset about being reassigned and having to leave. He'd said he'd think of something. Could he be planning to ask her to come to America with him?

Aggie pushed the thoughts away and told herself not to be ridiculous. She felt such love and admiration for him and didn't want to contemplate a life that didn't include him, but she didn't want to get her hopes up only to have them dashed. They had talked about a future together after his crash, but he'd told her he didn't want to marry her until the war was over. Best not to expect him to ask.

After dinner, they went to the club to listen to the band that was playing, and they danced a bit. Again, Henry seemed nervous and, after stepping on her toes a few times, asked her if she wanted to take a stroll along the beach.

They left the club and slipped off their shoes to walk hand in hand down the shore. It was a clear evening, and the moonlight shone over the water and the ships at anchor in the harbor, almost bright as day. Henry slid his arm around her, and she leaned her head against his shoulder.

"I'm going to miss you so much when I go tomorrow."

"I'm going to miss you too," he said, leaning down and kissing the top of her head. He pulled her to a stop and turned her to face him.

"Aggie, I know we talked about you coming to Chicago and I said I wanted to wait until after the war ended before deciding anything, but I've been thinking about it a lot and I've changed my mind."

Aggie felt sick. Here she had spent her time at dinner thinking he might be about to propose and the reason he was so nervous was because he'd changed his mind. Didn't she feel ridiculous?

"Stop that," he said, lifting her chin so she met his eyes. "I've gotten to know you, Aggie Ryan, and I can tell when you're doubting yourself. I also know when I've made a hash of what I'm trying to say."

She blinked up at him.

"You had that same look on your face that night in Sydney when I said you reminded me of my Ma. I learned my lesson that night. Let me try again."

He reached into the chest pocket of his uniform and caught something in his hand. Then he lowered himself to one knee in front of her. Aggie gasped, her hand flying to her mouth. He held up a small ring that he'd taken from his pocket.

"I changed my mind about waiting to get engaged. Agnes Ryan, I love you. You're bright and fun and the best girl I could ever hope to have by my side. Will you please marry me?"

She started nodding vigorously. "Yes, Henry. Yes, yes!"

He stood up and swept her into a hug, lifting her off her feet.

"I'm so glad," he whispered in her ear.

When he set her back on her feet, he took her left hand and slid the ring on her finger. It was a band of what appeared to be braided silver and copper wire. There was no diamond, but a dollop of silver solder held the ends together in the place where a stone would be.

"Where did you get this?" She looked at the ring, marveling.

"Bill helped me make it. He uses wire for everything. I wanted to be sure you had a ring, but it's not like we've got a jewelry store here on the base. I know it's nothing special, but it's the best we could do."

"No, I love the ring. It's perfect. Thank you. I don't know that I'm a fancy diamond kind of girl."

"You're a diamond to me, Aggie. I love you."

"I love you, too." She kissed him.

"Now, we need to talk," he said. "I applied for permission to marry this afternoon."

"We need permission to marry?"

Henry explained the information he'd gotten from the chaplain and the steps they would need to take to get married.

"I hope I wasn't out of line, starting the process before I asked you. I just knew that time was running out before you were leaving and I wanted to get started."

"I'm so glad you did!"

"I don't know when we can tie the knot and make it official."

"That's okay. We'll keep writing and who knows? We keep turning up in the same places during this war. Maybe it will happen again."

"I sure hope so."

They spent the rest of the evening, sitting in the sand, kissing, and talking about their future. Making plans out of their hopes and dreams.

The next day, Henry helped Aggie and her fellow WAAAFs take down the partition around their bunks in the hangar and carried their bags out to the airstrip where the plane was waiting to take them back to New Guinea.

"Fly safe," he whispered in her ear, then kissed her.

"That's supposed to be my line," she teased him. "You fly safe, too, darling."

"I will. I love you."

"I love you, too."

With that, they kissed again, and she boarded the transport plane. As she looked down at the wire ring on her finger, she wondered how long it would be until they saw each other again.

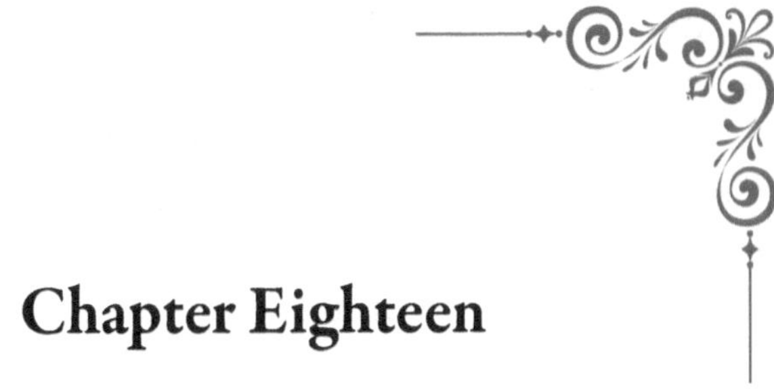

Chapter Eighteen

M ay 1945
    Pacific Ocean

HENRY AND CONOR STOOD on the fantail of the Enterprise, watching the ship's wake disappear on the horizon. They departed Ulithi on May 3 to rejoin the fleet, heading north toward Okinawa and the islands of Japan. The two men gazed out at the sea, their ship taking them further from their loved ones.

Conor, having seen the ring Bill made for Henry, cajoled him into making a ring for Katie. Knowing Katie's skill with repairing airframes and the metalwork on the planes she repaired, he asked Bill to make a ring out of a thin strip of aircraft aluminum. With no precious stone available, Bill painted a tiny US Navy roundel on the band. Katie had loved it and accepted Conor's proposal.

The women had departed for New Guinea, with some of them returning to Australia as the men returned to the fight. Before they departed the base, Henry sent a telegram to his ma, informing her he and Aggie were engaged and Ma would have a new daughter when the war ended.

The question on Henry's mind was, *How long is the war going to last?* Would they let the Air Group return to the States as flight instructors as the other groups had done? Or would the Navy keep them here in the Pacific until the bitter end?

"Are you worried we did the wrong thing?" Conor asked. "That we shouldn't have proposed yet?"

"No," Henry said. "I don't regret it at all. I had to take my chance when I could. It was a miracle that she was at Ulithi and I got to spend so much time with her. I wanted to ask her in person, and who knows when we'll see each other face to face again."

"I know," Conor said. Then he brightened. "Hey, did you see the line of guys asking Bill to make them gifts for their gals? He could open up a jewelry shop."

Henry snickered. Since word spread about the rings Bill had fashioned for Henry and Conor, fellow sailors were coming out of the woodwork, asking him to make something special for this girl or that. Bill hadn't asked Henry or Conor for payment to make their rings, but he was now doing a brisk business with the other crew members.

At their next briefing, Kowalski stood before them with the other squadron leaders, ready to share the newest plan of attack.

"Please refer to the briefing sheets," Kowalski said. "As you can see, we have a series of day and night sorties planned over the Amani Shoto islands to wear down the Japanese airfields between Kyushu and Okinawa."

The leader of the fighter squadron stepped forward to continue the briefing. "The kamikazes have been relentless while we were undergoing repairs. We will fly patrols around the clock to eliminate the impact of the kamikaze attacks."

And it begins again, Henry thought. The endless round of flight operations, planes taking off and landing at all times of the day and night. Flying out on sorties to harass airfields, to bomb them to prevent the Japanese from using them to launch kamikaze attacks.

Still, the Japanese broke through. A combination of bombs and crashing aircraft ignited horrific fires on the USS Bunker Hill, killing over 350 men and forcing Vice Admiral Mitscher off his flagship to take shelter aboard the Big E. Several of Bunker Hill's Corsairs, returning from combat air patrol to the sight of volcanic flames erupting from their flight deck, dropped into the landing pattern for Enterprise.

The Admiral, not pleased to have his flagship escorted from the area, favored a series of attacks that would extend farther afield. On May 11, Henry and Conor joined the airborne mayhem, attacking unwary airfields and military facilities on Kyushu.

As they passed over one airfield, Henry could hardly believe what he was seeing on the ground.

"Hey, Conor," he called over the radio to his wingman. "Get a look at that, down on the ground."

Below them was a mockup of an American aircraft carrier deck outlined in lights.

"That's how they know where to hit us?" Conor asked.

"I guess so. Should we demonstrate our bombing technique to them?"

"I like the way you think, sir!"

With that, the two pilots took delight in promptly bombing the fake carrier's deck to smithereens."

The next night, May 12, the Japanese expected their return and lit up the sky with dozens of searchlights. Some pilots struggled as the blinding lights spoiled their night vision. Others relished dueling with the searchlight crews and shooting and bombing any movement on the ground. On their return, over Kanoya and Kagoshima Bay, Big E's fliers claimed eight kills in the predawn. Henry could hear Jeff shouting and cheering in the back as he blasted away with his machine guns and claiming another kill.

With daybreak on May 14, the crew of Enterprise had been at general quarters for an hour and a half. Dawn revealed good flying weather, and keen-eyed sailors manning the antiaircraft guns kept their gazes on the skies.

Henry and Conor were returning to roost after a night of covering enemy airfields to keep the Japanese bombers and suicide planes grounded. It had been a successful night, with the Hellcats downing three more aircraft in the previous five hours.

Henry lined up with the flight deck and caught the center wire like a charm. All he wanted was some chow and some sleep after the night's flying. He taxied his plane to the forward elevator and waited for Conor to land so they could take their planes below. While they waited, Jeff chattered excitedly about his kill.

"I think I splashed two tonight. Three more and I'm an ace, Hank!" Jeff said enthusiastically. Henry laughed. Why were his back seaters so eager to become aces?

Conor landed, smooth as silk, and met him at the elevator. They brought their planes down to the hangar deck for post flight inspection and maintenance.

Kowalski caught them as they headed toward the mess to grab some breakfast.

"You boys might want to stay here for a while. Radar is showing bandits twenty miles out and closing. The Hellcats coming in after you guys got word from the fighter director to take up defensive positions. We may need you guys in the air as well."

Henry, Conor, Jeff, and Perry felt fatigue after a night of flying, but if Kowalski wanted them, they would stick around. They found some battle rations with the aircrews and decided that would suffice rather than a hot meal in the mess. Bill and his maintenance teams were hard at work, trying to turn around the recently landed planes.

"Head up to the flight deck, guys," Bill told them. "I'll have your birds on the next elevator going up."

The pilots and their back seaters climbed to the flight deck to await their planes and to watch the battle unfold. The flight deck crew informed them that radar had picked up 26 raiders inbound from the coast. When the hostiles met the task group's Hellcat umbrella, sixteen Japanese fell to interceptions. Six more got close enough to meet their end via the bristling antiaircraft guns. Others turned away, seeking easier targets.

The 26th would sacrifice himself for the emperor and glory.

The Zeke dropped out of the clouds and attempted to approach the Enterprise several times. The antiaircraft battery unloaded on him, forcing him through a hail of fire. He flew through the flak and tracers that flared around him, making no attempt to avoid it. Henry couldn't believe a plane could withstand such gunfire.

Henry and Conor watched as he set up his dive. Both were sure he was going to overshoot the Enterprise. As the Zeke neared the bottom of its dive, the pilot seemed to realize what Henry had seen; he was overshooting to starboard. Two hundred yards from the ship, the pilot snap-rolled inverted and pulled back on the stick, performing the first quarter of the Split S maneuver.

The suicide pilot then performed an inverted, forty-five-degree dive straight into the Big E's flight deck, splintering it just aft of the number one elevator.

Henry would have admired the skill of the pilot if he hadn't been busy shoving Jeff and Conor to the ground behind the island, yelling, "Hit the deck!"

The explosion lofted a section of the fifteen-ton elevator 400 feet into the air while the rest flipped over and fell into the elevator well. The flight deck bulged upward nearly five feet. Henry's plane, along with twenty-four other aircraft, was destroyed in the incident, as it had been waiting to be loaded onto the elevator to be taken up to the flight deck.

Henry and his friends climbed to their feet to discover they were miraculously unhurt. They peered over the side, gaping at the enormous piece of the elevator that had plunged into the sea.

There was no time for shock or standing around. Damage Control teams were already rushing into action. There was a serious fire in the forward hangar bay, threatening ammunition lockers. Destruction of the aviation fuel system had fuel lines severed and tanks leaking aviation gas. Seawater was flooding in the breaches in the hull and several water mains had broken, aggravating the flooding.

The crew fought back; fighting fires, picking up five-inch shells and powder bags and passing them hand over hand until the last man pitched the explosives overboard, rescuing the injured and carrying them out of harm's way.

They extinguished the worst flames in 17 minutes and finally put out the rest in two hours. Meanwhile, although power was out to the forward guns, other batteries remained in the fight. While the ship smoldered, Big E gunners splashed two more raiders in the next few hours.

Henry helped where he could on the hangar deck, moving ordinance away from the fires. Conor pitched in with the rescue and medical teams, putting his first aid training to good use. They found Bill, wounded but alive amidst the wreckage near the elevator. He had stepped behind a girder to grab a tool when the elevator exploded. If he'd been a few feet closer, he likely would have died.

In the end, fourteen men had died, sixty wounded. When they drained the elevator well, they found the remains of the Zeke and its pilot.

Chapter Nineteen

May 1945
Darwin, Australia

THE RAAF CATALINA WAS an amazing machine. A flying boat that was initially developed as a bomber because of its long range, the Catalinas took part in many missions during the war, including search and rescue and long-range patrols.

The RAAF Black Cat squadron flew this Catalina for night missions, laying mines in enemy waters. Now that the fighting was farther north, it was being refitted to serve as a mail plane, as its long range made it ideal for the long distances between the various Allied outposts around the Pacific. This horrified the Catalina's crew at what they perceived as a demotion. To go from an important clandestine mission to mail delivery seemed like an insult.

Aggie lay on top of the wing, working on the starboard engine, reaching into the cowling to turn her wrench. It was a good thing she wasn't afraid of heights. Right now, she was twenty feet off the ground, so different from the fighters and dive bombers she had worked on. The Catalina was a new challenge for her here in the harbor at Darwin. The corrosion from the sea air and salt water was something she had never seen before, making repairs more difficult.

She and Katie had arrived at the RAAF base at Aitape a few hours after leaving Henry and Conor and were told to continue to the WAAF squadron in Darwin. With the Pacific War focusing on the Japanese islands, the RAAF was pulling back to their home shores with little need for the WAAAFs to be so far afield.

It's nice to be home, thought Aggie as she enjoyed the sound of the broad Australian accents all around her, though she missed Henry terribly. She wrote letters every day, although it was only a few weeks since they had separated. Aggie was following the progress of the Naval campaign as best she could, gleaning information from the news. She had been so spoiled when she was working on Ulithi, where the movements of ships were easy to learn. She prayed Henry was safe.

As she climbed down from the wing, it surprised her to see Betty and Jackie hurrying along the tarmac toward the Catalina. Aggie, Katie, and Jackie had been delighted to be reunited with their friend from Sydney when they returned to Darwin. Betty worked monitoring radio traffic and assisting with myriad radio issues on the base. Betty was glamorous as ever and still flirted with any man in a uniform.

Once Aggie had climbed down and jumped to the ground from the wing strut, she met her friends, wiping her hands on a rag. Betty looked very anxious, wringing her hands together and worrying her lower lip between her teeth. She reached Aggie with a serious look on her face.

"Is Katie around also?" she asked, looking around.

"I think she was popping some rivets along the starboard side of the Catalina, near the tail. I'll show you."

They found Katie standing on a ladder and working to patch the skin of the flying boat with a new sheet of aluminum. When she spotted her friends, she climbed down and joined them. Noticing the look on Betty's face, she asked, "What's up?"

Betty looked around furtively. "I really shouldn't say anything, but I thought you should know."

Katie and Aggie looked at each other nervously.

"I was in the radio room and there was a lot of traffic about the US carriers up near Okinawa."

Aggie knew the Enterprise was in that area, having rejoined the task force after leaving Ulithi.

"What did you hear, Betty?"

Betty glanced around again, then spilled the beans. "A kamikaze hi the Enterprise. There was major damage to the flight deck and a serious fire. They said something like fifteen or twenty dead and about 50 injured."

Katie turned white as a sheet. Aggie felt like the time she'd fallen out of the hayloft as a kid and had the wind knocked out of her. She and Katie reached out for each other, clinging together for support. Jackie wrapped her arm around Katie's waist. Betty reached around to hug them both.

"I'm so sorry, girls. But I thought you would want to know."

"No, thank you for telling us, Betty," Aggie said, turning to hug her friend in return. "I would rather we hear it from you. Will you let us know if you get any more information?"

"I really shouldn't have told you what I already have. But of course, if I hear anything else, I will let you know."

"Thank you," sobbed Katie, squeezing her hand.

Betty squeezed back. "You know I'd do anything for you, ducky. Now I need to get back or Sergeant Maguire will have my guts for garters."

She turned on her heel and hurried back to the radio room. Jackie also needed to return to her work but asked her friends to let her know if there was anything she could do.

Aggie and Katie looked at each other, Katie with tears spilling down her cheeks. Aggie took the rag she'd been using to scrub her hands and wiped Katie's tears.

"Now, none of that. There are over 2,000 men on that ship and only a handful killed or injured. What are the odds it was Conor or Henry? Don't borrow trouble."

"You're right," Katie said, sniffling and wiping her eyes. "I'm glad Betty came to tell us. I just wish there was a way we could hear from the guys and know for sure."

"Me too. Let's wrap up for the day and head to the chapel. We can say some prayers and light a candle."

"I would like that, Aggie. What a good idea! Let's get cleaned up and head to church."

The women stowed their tools and went back to the barracks to wash and change their clothes. They walked to the small chapel near the base entrance and entered the cool hush of the church. Aggie lit a candle for Henry and a second for Conor, then slid into a pew, bowed her head, and prayed that Henry had survived the encounter with the kamikaze unscathed.

Chapter Twenty

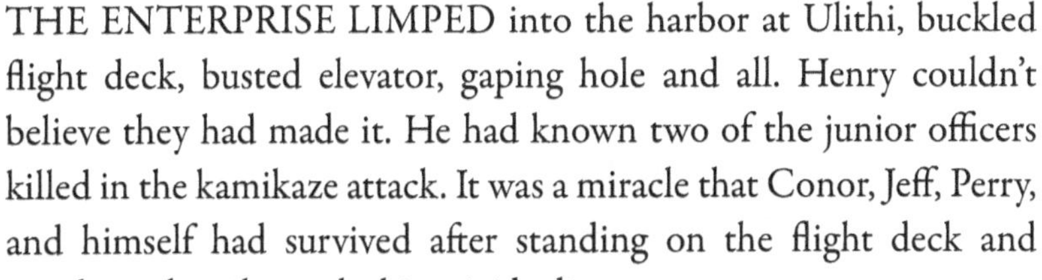

May 1945
   Ulithi Atoll, Caroline Islands

THE ENTERPRISE LIMPED into the harbor at Ulithi, buckled flight deck, busted elevator, gaping hole and all. Henry couldn't believe they had made it. He had known two of the junior officers killed in the kamikaze attack. It was a miracle that Conor, Jeff, Perry, and himself had survived after standing on the flight deck and watching the pilot make his suicide dive.

The crew were told they could head to shore while the repair crews assessed the damages and developed a strategy to get the Big E seaworthy to return to Puget Sound for major repairs.

Conor and Henry packed up their seabags and returned to their old digs at the BOQ. Upon entering the room, Henry spotted several letters addressed to him propped up on the bureau. There were two letters from Ma, as well as a letter and a postcard from Aggie. *Wonderful,* he thought. He dropped his bag and scooped up the letters.

He knew he should read the letters from Ma first, but he flipped over the postcard from Aggie first.

My Darling Henry,

Greetings from Darwin! The WAAAFs were no longer needed in NG, so they've sent us back to Oz. Reunited with our dear Betty and the obstinate Sergeant Maguire.

More later. Just wanted you to know I arrived after two more airplane rides.

I love you, darling. Fly safe.

Your Aggie

Henry smiled and held the postcard to his chest. He was glad she was back in Australia. Next, he read the letters from Ma, full of chatty gossip about the ladies in the neighborhood, which boys were already back from service, and her opinion that it was terrible Mr. Hitler had killed himself after causing everyone so much trouble. He had to smile. His Ma was one in a million.

He then read Aggie's letter in which she shared her memories of their time together and her dreams of the life they would build together. He couldn't wait to make those dreams come true for her.

Connor and Perry popped their heads in the doorway.

"What's up?" Henry asked.

"Latest report is that we're going to be stuck here for a few weeks so they can plug the leaks and get her safe enough to make the voyage back to Seattle."

"Weeks? Ugh. What the heck are we going to do here for two or three weeks?"

"I didn't hear you guys complaining about being here for two weeks the last time. Maybe that's because your girlfriends were here then. No girls to squire around this time. Poor you," Perry joked.

He's not wrong, Henry thought. Two weeks on this tropical island with Aggie had been fabulous, even if they were stuck at a giant Navy base and not on vacation. There had been sun, surf, Coca-Cola, and kissing. This time, he was on his own. Well, on his own with the rest of the Enterprise crew. No one was sure what came next. Pilots like Henry and Conor were on the tail end of their tour and might be reassigned to another carrier or transferred to their next duty station. The powers that be in the US Navy had yet to decide their fates.

At that moment, Kowalski strode in and handed Henry a sheaf of papers.

"Your permission came through. I thought I'd deliver it myself," he said cheerily.

"My permission?" Henry asked.

Kowalski gave him a look of displeasure and shook his head.

"It's really a wonder you managed to catch a girl, Bolanski. The marriage permission, you knucklehead. Remember handing me a stack of paperwork a while back? Needed to go to the fleet commander?"

Henry looked shocked, then stared down at the paperwork in his hands. He flipped through the papers. There were the signatures, Kowalski, the captain, and on the last page, Admiral Halsey. Holy cow! In the middle of a war, Admiral Halsey had taken the time to sign Henry's permission to marry Aggie. Amazing!

He looked up at Kowalski with a huge grin on his face.

"Thank you! Thank you so much!" He pulled Kowalski into a bear hug. Kowalski immediately pushed him away.

"Enough of that! Sheesh," he muttered before giving a small smile. "And you're welcome. She's a great gal. I still don't know how you snagged her."

He turned to Conor with another stack of papers.

"Here's your permission paperwork, too. You boys can have a double wedding," he said with a wink.

Kowalski bid them farewell, letting them know he would be at the O Club if he was needed.

"What's next?" asked Perry from the doorway.

Henry looked down at the paperwork in his hands and then back at his friends.

"I don't know about you, but I'm gonna write to my girl and let her know I'm safe."

TWO DAYS LATER, THE pilots and back seaters from their flight group received orders to report to the briefing room on the ship. There was news about the Navy's decision regarding the disposition of the Enterprise's flight crews.

Squeezing into the back of the crowded space, Henry looked around at the anxious faces surrounding him. Some of the younger, newer pilots wanted reassignment to other carriers while others were hoping to move on to their next assignment, knowing it might be their ticket home.

Kowalski stepped to the front of the room.

"Listen up," he barked. The room quieted, and all eyes turned to him.

"The Navy has decided what to do with us. As you know, we cannot unload the aircraft off the ship. With the forward elevator destroyed and the buckling of the flight deck, we'll have to wait until the ship is back at Pearl or Bremerton to offload the planes."

There was a collective groan. Pilots hoping to be transferred to other carriers had hoped to do so with their own planes.

"Several of you are nearing the end of your current six-month tour. The Navy has decided that, with only a month left on this tour, it's not worth transferring you to another ship temporarily if that will not be your duty station for the next tour."

He held up a stack of envelopes.

"I have the assignments for your next postings here. If your new assignment is here in the Pacific theater, there will be instructions for transport to your next ship or post. If your next posting requires a return to the States, you will travel back to Seattle on the Enterprise.

Once in Seattle, you will have transportation to your next duty station."

There was murmuring around the briefing room. Kowalski and the other squadron leaders moved amongst the pilots, distributing their envelopes.

As Kowalski handed Henry his envelope, he held onto his side of the envelope for a moment longer than was necessary and looked Henry in the eye.

"This ought to make you happy, Bolanski." Then he winked.

Henry looked at him quizzically, then caught his breath. Did they station him in Australia? Somewhere near Aggie? Henry didn't think the Navy had any air stations in Australia, but since he'd been aboard a ship since leaving Puget Sound, he wasn't aware of what ground-based locations the Navy had in the Pacific. He tore open his envelope.

Flight instructor, Glenview Naval Air Station, Glenview, Illinois.

Henry stared at the assignment, dumbfounded. Glenview was just north of Chicago. He was going home. And not just 'back to the States' home, but 'his own backyard' home. He blinked in shock. He looked up at Conor, who was staring at his own assignment.

"What did you get, Conor?"

"Glenview. They're sending me to Glenview as a flight instructor." Conor seemed as dazed as he was. "They're sending me home."

"Yeah. Me too."

They looked at each other and broke into broad grins, grabbed each other in a hug, and began pounding each other on the back. They looked around for Kowalski, knowing he must have had a hand in this.

When they cornered him, Kowalski admitted he recommended the two for the positions at Glenview.

"You boys have done enough fighting. It's time you share everything you've learned with the next crop of pilots we're training," Kowalski said. "If we need you for that task, I thought it might be nice for you to be a little closer to home, if possible. Why send some guy from Texas to Glenview and a guy from Chicago to Corpus Christi?"

"Thanks, Kowalski," Henry said, shaking his hand. "Ma is gonna love you forever for this."

Kowalski laughed. "Well, that's good to hear. If I'm ever in Chicago, I want her to make me one of those delicious Polish feasts you're always talking about. Kielbasa, pierogi, kapusta, the works!"

"You've got it!" He looked down at the assignment sheet. "I can't wait to tell Aggie."

"Hey, speaking of that," Kowalski began, his mood becoming serious. "I know you got your permission to marry. I heard from some friends in the European theater that it has been challenging to get wives and fiancees to the States, but it is considerably easier to bring over a wife than a fiancé."

Henry and Conor exchanged a look. How were they supposed to get married when they were stuck here Ulithi with a broken aircraft carrier and the girls were in Darwin? With the timetable for proposed repairs to the ship, they were going to have a few weeks to figure something out.

THEIR POSSIBLE DELIVERANCE arrived the next day in an RAAF Catalina flying boat with a load of mail for the Navy base. Henry and Conor had been lounging along the dock as they watched the Catalina swoop in for a landing in the harbor, like a Canada goose coming in to land on a pond. As it puttered to the dockside to be tied off, the friends wandered over to check out the plane up close.

The crew had opened the hatch and were tossing out bags of mail and parcels.

"Got anything for us?" they quipped.

The pilot from the Catalina turned to them. "I dunno, Yank. I just know this mail run is a real letdown after our last assignment."

He explained their previous mission, laying mines under the cover of night. The friends agreed that running mail must be significantly less exciting.

"Say, the gal who worked on our plane gave me something to deliver." He reached into his pocket and fished out an envelope. "D'ya know a Henry Bolanski? Off the Enterprise?"

"That's me!" Henry said, snatching the envelope out of the man's hand. "It's from Aggie."

"That's the one," the Cat pilot smiled. "Lovely girl. Really knows her way around an engine."

Henry grinned. "That's my girl." He tore open the envelope.

"We're flying back this afternoon, after some chow, and refueling the Catalina. I can bring back a response if you like."

"Really? That would be fantastic. Thank you."

"No worries, mate."

Henry read through the letter. Aggie had heard about the kamikaze attack and was praying for his safety. Clearly, she hadn't received his letter assuring her he was okay. He looked at the sacks of mail waiting to be loaded onto the plane, replacing those that had been removed earlier. No doubt his letter was in one of those mail bags.

Henry paused, looking at the mail bags that were going to be flown to Darwin later that day.

A plan took shape in his mind.

"Come on," he said to Conor, taking off at a trot. "We need to find Kowalski."

"YOU WANT TO TAKE A week of leave?" Kowalski asked as the men stood before him. "Now?"

"Yes, sir," barked Henry and Conor in unison.

Kowalski's eyebrows rose nearly to his hairline at their emphatic response. "Explain."

Henry looked at him pleadingly.

"The ship will be here for repairs for another week or two, then we will need to be aboard to go to Seattle and our posting at Glenview. This could be our only chance to get to Australia and get married before we ship out. There is nothing to do here but cool our heels. The explosion destroyed my plane. Conor's plane is stuck inside the ship. We haven't had a proper leave in the past two years. We could easily go for a week and get back."

"How long have you been practicing that speech?"

"As long as it took to run from the Catalina and find you here at the O Club."

Kowalski looked at them skeptically, then smirked. "I'll talk to the captain, but I think we can probably make it happen. Let's see if I can talk him into it."

While Kowalski spoke to the captain, the friends rushed back to the BOQ to pack their bags. Henry carefully folded his dress uniform, figuring he would want it neat if they were going to have a wedding. They returned to the Enterprise to see Kowalski strolling down the gangway, waving a set of papers over his head.

"Looky what I have here. Two seven day passes for leave in Australia for one LT Bolanski and one LT McLean. You need to be back on time. This ship will not wait for you, if you are not on it when we pull away, you'll be AWOL."

"Roger that!" Henry saluted as he took the pass with his other hand. "And thanks – thanks for arranging this."

"Get out of here," said Kowalski. "You better go catch a ride on that Catalina."

Henry and Conor hurried back to where the Catalina was bobbing on the waves, moored to the pier near the Enterprise. The RAAF pilot was leaning against the gunnel, having a smoke when they stopped in front of him, out of breath. He eyed them and the bags over their shoulders.

"Hey, mate, you're the fella with the letter, right? You have a response for your girl?"

"I do, but I'd like to deliver it in person. My buddy and I have a pass for seven days' leave in Australia. Do you think we could catch a ride to Darwin with you guys?"

The pilot crushed out his cigarette. "I suppose we could come to an arrangement. What do you have to offer?"

Henry figured the Aussies might not give them a lift out of the kindness of their hearts. He had taken the time to stop at the exchange during all the running around this morning. He reached into his bag and pulled out a carton of Lucky Strikes and held them just out of the pilot's reach.

"American cigarettes," the man whispered, as if viewing the Holy Grail.

"That's right, my friend. A carton from each of us now, and another carton when you bring us back in seven days."

"Deal! Throw your stuff in the back and grab a seat. We're taking off in about fifteen minutes."

"Thanks! You don't know how much we appreciate this."

As the Catalina taxied out over the waves and gained speed for take-off, Henry and Conor sat back in the seats of the flying boat and sighed with relief. Their plan had come together. Now they hoped the girls would like their surprise arrival in Darwin and the prospect of a very speedy wedding.

Chapter Twenty-One

M ay 1945
Darwin, Australia

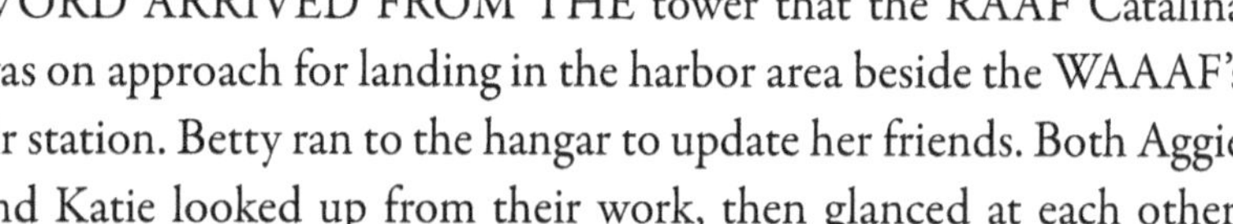

WORD ARRIVED FROM THE tower that the RAAF Catalina was on approach for landing in the harbor area beside the WAAAF's air station. Betty ran to the hangar to update her friends. Both Aggie and Katie looked up from their work, then glanced at each other. Aggie had spoken to the Catalina's crew before they departed on their mail run to Ulithi and asked the pilot to hand deliver a letter to Henry if they could find him. If he hadn't died in the attack on the Enterprise.

Sergeant Maguire, aware of the drama regarding the damage and death on the carrier and how it might affect his mechanics, overheard Betty's announcement and sighed. The ladies had been doing their usual high-quality work, but he found them distracted and worried about their fiancées. He was tough on his maintenance team, but he had sympathy when he saw the tired circles under Aggie's eyes and that tiny Katie was not eating. He inspected the hangar to assess the progress on the aircraft being repaired and saw everything in order. Nodding to himself, he called over Aggie and Katie.

"Ryan! Larkin! Over here, now!"

The women hurried to him, concerned they had displeased him.

"Yes, Sergeant?" they asked in unison as they stopped before him.

"Take the jeep and make a run out to the harbor. You need to talk with the Catalina crew, make sure she flew well, that there were no issues on the flight out to Ulithi and back."

"Really?" Aggie asked in disbelief. Sergeant Maguire never asked them to follow up with a flight crew after a repair. If there were issues with the airplane, the crews communicated with the maintenance crew via the flight log, reports, and forms.

"Yes, yes. See how the engines performed and ask if the plane needs any more work. And, um, they were supposed to be bringing back some mail. You can bring the mail bags back, in case there is any, uh, important correspondence."

Aggie felt tears prickle the back of her eyes. Sergeant Maguire might act like a tough guy, but he had noticed their distress and was offering them a chance to get word about the fate of Henry and Conor.

"Yes, Sergeant," she said, blinking to keep tears from falling. "Thank you, Sergeant."

"You're welcome," he said. "Good luck."

Aggie thanked him again, then she and Katie dashed to the jeep. As they moved away, Betty approached the sergeant.

"That was very nice of you."

"I don't know what you're talking about. I gave them an assignment."

"Of course you did," agreed Betty, before she nudged him with her elbow. "You big softie."

Sergeant Maguire turned to her, his glare glacial.

"Don't you have work in the radio room, Miss Diamonds?"

"Oh, I do," she responded sweetly. She turned on her heel and shot him a saucy look over her shoulder as she walked away. "Don't worry, I won't tell anyone what a teddy bear you really are."

Sergeant Maguire looked after her, thunderstruck at his first experience of being on the receiving end of Betty Carter's considerable charms.

AGGIE PARKED THE JEEP as close to the pier as possible and she and Katie hurried to the Catalina's mooring. She had her fingers crossed and was pretty sure Katie had been whispering prayers under her breath the entire ride to the harbor.

As they approached the flying boat, the hatch opened, and the gangway extended from the plane to the pier. Two members of the RAAF flight crew emerged with sacks of mail over their shoulders. At the sight of the women approaching, they broke into broad grins.

"G'day, ladies. I think the captain might have a surprise for you."

Aggie breathed a sigh of relief. The men were smiling and saying the captain had something for her. He must have found Henry and brought a letter in response to hers. She closed her eyes and offered a brief prayer of thanks.

Her eyes popped open when she heard Katie shriek. Looking toward the Catalina, she saw two American Navy officers stepping off the gangplank to the pier. And not just any two naval officers, but Henry and Conor. She stood, stunned, as Katie took off running into Conor's open arms.

"Oh, my goodness," she breathed as Henry approached her. He looked tanned and healthy, all in one piece. She had never been so happy to see someone in her entire life.

"Surprise," he whispered into her hair as he drew her into his arms.

Aggie burst into tears. She had been so worried for Henry but had tried to keep her emotions in check to keep Katie's spirits up. In that moment, the days of fear and worry released as she clung to Henry, finally knowing he was safe.

He held her tight and stroked her hair while whispering gentle endearments in her ear. She didn't even know what he was saying. She simply enjoyed the feeling of her body pressed to his and the sound of his voice. He was safe. He was here.

Wait, she thought, pulling back from him.

"What are you doing here?"

He held up some papers. "We have seven days of leave here in Australia and permission to get married."

"Wait, what?"

Henry laughed at her surprised expression. "Let's go somewhere other than the pier to have this conversation."

He pulled out his handkerchief and used it to mop the tears from her face, then stuck the handkerchief in her hand. He took her face in his hands and kissed her forehead.

"We have a lot to talk about and not a lot of time."

At that moment, the Catalina's pilot opened the flight deck window and shouted down to Henry, "I see you found your girl!"

"Sure did! Thanks for the ride. We'll see you in a week."

"Enjoy your wedding, but don't be late!"

Henry shot the man a jaunty salute. Aggie followed this exchange in disbelief. Henry looked at her with a roguish grin.

"Let's find you a cup of tea, young lady. You look like you've had a shock." He winked at her and took her hand. "We need to talk."

The couples found a small café near the harbor for some tea and conversation. The men told them about the experience with the kamikaze, the damage to the Enterprise, the time at Ulithi to make the temporary repairs needed to get back to Bremerton. They explained they had received their orders for their next duty station back home in the States. Further, they would ship out when the Enterprise left for her repairs.

Aggie's heart sank. Henry would be returning to America. She spun her ring around her finger as he spoke, her thumb rubbing over the little dollop of solder as it spun. He noticed what she was doing and took her hand, stilling the motion.

"Kowalski received our permission to marry from fleet command the day we returned to Ulithi. There is nothing for us to do there while they complete repairs on the ship, so we requested a week of leave to come to Australia and see you."

"I still can't believe you're here," Aggie said. She squeezed his hand.

"I know we had talked about waiting until the war was over to marry but being reassigned back to the States changed things. I don't want to rush our wedding, but it seems the Navy isn't giving us a choice. Either we marry now while I'm here on leave, or we will have to wait until after the war is over."

Well, Aggie didn't like the idea of that. Who knew how much longer the Japanese would continue fighting?

"But a wedding without your mum? Or my family?"

"It's not ideal, but Ma will understand. Maybe your family could come. Do you think we can arrange a wedding in a week?"

Aggie considered. It was Friday and Henry and Conor needed to be on the Catalina, heading back to Ulithi the following Friday morning. Both she and Katie had some time off coming. Neither of them had taken much leave since they transferred from Darwin to New Guinea and beyond.

They could go to City Hall and have a simple civil service, but both were Catholic and she would like to have the blessing of the church for their union. She could telephone the Ryan family homestead and see if they would make the trip to Darwin. They had a great deal of planning to do in a very short time frame, but she thought it would be possible.

"Yes, I think we could manage it. It won't be anything fancy."

"I don't need fancy. I just need you," he said, kissing her gently and looking into her eyes.

She looked back intently and nodded. "I just need you, too. Now, let's get to work."

The first stop was the WAAAF headquarters to request a week of leave so Aggie could spend every moment with Henry. Jackie and several other mechanics offered to take extra shifts to cover for the girls. Sergeant Maguire grumbled and grouched about approving leave for two of his best mechanics as he filled out the paperwork, but his protests seemed pro forma to Aggie. After signing and stamping the multiple forms, he shook Aggie's hand, then Henry's, and wished them well.

"Softie," singsonged Betty from behind her desk.

"That's enough out of you, Carter!" barked the sergeant, but Betty just winked at him. She was pushing her luck with the sergeant.

Next was the Catholic chaplain at the base. They hoped he could provide information about a local church and a priest who would perform the ceremony. He agreed to make some calls and keep them updated.

They planned until evening fell and all the businesses and churches were closed. The two couples went to the mess hall to plot strategy for the following day. They started a list of what they needed to plan the wedding; a church, a priest, and dresses for Aggie and Katie seemed to be the priorities. Maybe some flowers for the ladies if they had time. Phone calls to the Ryan and the Larkins to see if any family members could join them for the wedding would have to wait until they had a date and time.

Betty arrived at the mess hall and joined them in their planning. She was not on duty the next day and volunteered to help with the wedding dress hunt.

"There are plenty of nurses, WAAAFs, and WRANS around Darwin. We are constantly having clothing swaps to update our wardrobes with 'new to us' frocks. I will put out some feelers and see if we can find something that would work for a wedding. If not, we can try the shops in town."

Aggie hesitated. She wasn't sure she wanted to use all her clothing ration coupons for a wedding dress. That said, she wanted to look pretty for Henry on their wedding day and she didn't fancy being married in her WAAAF uniform.

"I can see you fretting already," Betty admonished. "Just stop. We'll work something out."

With that, Betty left to place calls to the Nursing barracks at the Navy hospital and to the WRANS (Women's Royal Australian Navy Service) barracks to ask if anyone had a wedding appropriate dress they would donate to the cause.

"She's a force of nature," Henry said as Betty breezed away.

"She is," Aggie chuckled. "I'm just glad she's on our side."

The foursome left the mess hall and walked to the WAAAFs barracks. Conor and Katie excused themselves and drifted off for a private moment to say goodnight. Aggie turned to Henry for an embrace and a kiss.

"What a whirlwind today has been! I woke up worrying whether you were alive or dead and hoping to get a message from the Catalina crew. Now I'm going to bed planning our wedding."

"I know," Henry smiled down on her. "It's been wild, but I'm so glad that we'll have time together. I hope we can get everything finished before next Friday."

"So do I, darling." She lifted up onto her tiptoes to kiss him. "I'm so glad you're okay and that we're getting married, even if it's rushed."

"Never fear. The wedding might be rushed, but we'll have the rest of our lives together to take our time."

They kissed and bid each other good night. They had a busy day ahead of them the next morning.

Chapter Twenty-two

May 1945
Darwin, Australia

IF FRIDAY HAD BEEN a whirlwind for the couples, then Saturday was a tornado. What had begun with a vague plan to get married yesterday morning in Ulithi had morphed into a battle campaign in full force on Saturday in Darwin.

Henry and Conor were at the BOQ when they received a call from the chaplain early in the morning. Both couples were to present themselves at his office at 0900 hours. The men debated picking up the ladies right away but ate breakfast first.

"If today is anything like yesterday, we are going to need to eat. Who knows when our next meal will be?" Henry said.

"That's my boy," Conor teased. "Always thinking with his stomach."

Henry laughed. Waleria Bolanski didn't raise a fool. When you can eat, you eat. They hit the mess hall for a hearty breakfast of eggs and bacon and plenty of coffee before setting off to meet Aggie and Katie.

Henry's heart swelled when he saw her. She looked so crisp and pretty in her Class A WAAAF uniform with its neat skirt and pale blue blouse and necktie. He was so used to seeing her in her coveralls or casual beach clothes from their time on Ulithi, he now appreciated her more formal uniform. She had her hair pulled back into a tidy chignon and a bit of lipstick was her only makeup. He thought she was the loveliest thing he'd ever seen. He hopped out of the jeep, offering her a hand to climb into the passenger's side. As she stepped up, she also leaned in to give him a kiss.

"Oh, I'm sorry! I left lipstick on you." She reached up and swiped her thumb over his lips, then held it up for him to see the lip color she had left behind.

"No worries, as you Aussies say," he replied and kissed her thumb. "I don't mind a bit of lipstick if I get to start my day with your kiss."

Arriving at the chaplain's office at 9:00 sharp, Father Gilbert greeted them and escorted them into his office. He had a jolly face with a blinding grin and crinkled laugh lines around his eyes. The priest was bursting with excitement.

"Come in, come in," he urged as the foursome took their seats. "I have good news! Wonderful news!"

The four young people leaned forward in their seats in anticipation.

"St. Mary Star of the Sea Cathedral is HQ of the garrison of the military chaplaincy in Australia. We train and prepare all the chaplains serving the troops. We have plenty of priests available to perform your wedding service."

There was a collective sigh of relief amongst the group. Henry was the first to speak up.

"That's wonderful news, Father. We haven't gone to City Hall for marriage licenses yet, I doubt they'll be open on a Saturday."

Father Gilbert waved away Henry's concerns. "We don't need a marriage license here in Australia. You shared your permission to marry paperwork yesterday that the US Navy has approved, so I know this isn't a whim for you, my children. I would like to conduct a brief interview with each of you to ensure each party is entering the marriage willingly. But other than that, we can get the wedding on the calendar today."

"How soon can we schedule the wedding?"

"Assuming you answer my questions satisfactorily, we can probably get you folks on the calendar for…" At this, Father Gilbert began flipping through papers on his desk. "I can get you on the calendar for Monday."

"Monday? As in the day after tomorrow Monday?"

"Well, yes," Father Gilbert said. "We won't have time today and we rarely hold weddings on Sundays because we are so busy with the regular Mass schedule. I apologize for the delay, I know you said as soon as possible." He broke off with an apologetic look.

The four of them looked at him, astonished. Henry jumped in. "No, sir, Monday is fine. We thought it would take longer."

"I understood from our conversation yesterday that time was of the essence because of your leave schedule and shipping out. I could tell you kids were anxious to have everything taken care of as soon as possible."

"Yes, thank you, Father."

"Good! Now, who wants to face the Inquisition first?" Father Gilbert asked, chuckling at their shocked faces. "No, no. Just a little priestly humor. It won't be that bad. Who's first?"

Henry raised his hand as a volunteer. Aggie squeezed his other hand and left with Conor and Katie to wait in the hall for their turn to be questioned by the priest.

"Now, let's have a little chat, shall we?" Father Gilbert said seriously, looking Henry in the eye.

Henry gulped. Father Gilbert didn't look so kind and jolly anymore. He was reminding Henry of Father Parkolewicz back home now that he suddenly had a steely glint in his eye.

He questioned Henry about where he had received his sacraments of baptism, communion, and confirmation. Asked about

Henry's home life, about his parents, whether they were practicing Catholics. He questioned if he had siblings, had he served as an altar boy. Then he started asking about his relationship with Aggie. Did they have to get married because she was pregnant? Was he coercing her to marry him? Was she coercing him? Were they entering the marriage of their own free will?

Henry was sweating by the time the questions stopped. He knew he had answered truthfully, and his answers were all the "right" answers, but he still felt like he'd been through the wringer. Father Gilbert hadn't been entirely joking about an inquisition. As the Father stood up and reached out to shake Henry's hand, the priest's cheerful mien returned.

"Thank you for your honesty, Henry," Father Gilbert said, grinning as they shook hands. "I look forward to talking to your young lady. But for now, send in Mr. McLean next."

As the priest returned to his chair, the steely glint returned to his eyes. *Poor Conor,* thought Henry.

As Henry went out into the hall, he explained that the priest wanted to talk to Conor next before flopping down into the chair next to Aggie. She raised a skeptical eyebrow.

"That bad?" she asked.

Henry shook his head and wiped the sweat from his brow.

"He should run interrogations for military intelligence. He broke me like a china dinner plate. Every youthful misdeed as an altar boy at Holy Trinity laid bare."

Henry shuddered.

Aggie laughed and gave him a playful shove. "I cannot wait to hear all the stories about your naughty childhood antics."

"They are legion."

The friends finished their interviews with Father Gilbert by 11:30, then went to the mess hall for lunch and to plan what needed to be done next. There was much discussion about whether Aggie and Katie's families might get to Darwin in time for the wedding on Monday morning. It seemed unlikely, but each woman planned to place a call home to let their family know about the impending nuptials.

As they were finishing their meal, Betty appeared in a state of agitation. She came bearing news about wedding dresses.

"The local population of servicewomen have made an exhaustive search of their wardrobes for wedding dress options and I think we have a few promising possibilities. Gentlemen, I would like to borrow your brides for a bit to see if we can find something that works for them."

Aggie looked at Henry hopefully. "If I go back to the barracks, I can place the call to my family while I see what Betty has found for us."

Henry didn't want to spend any of his limited time this week away from her, but she needed to contact her family and, at some point, find a dress for the wedding. He didn't want her to get married in her WAAAF uniform.

He pulled her into a hug.

"Go," he said. "Find something pretty. Conor and I will work on finding a restaurant for the wedding lunch and hotel rooms for after the wedding. We won't be able to stay at the BOQ with our wives."

Aggie blushed pink at the mention of sharing a hotel room together, which he found charming and adorable. He gave her a kiss.

"See you soon."

"WHAT SHOULD WE DO FIRST? Telephone calls or dress shopping?" Katie asked as they strolled back toward the barracks with Betty.

"I think we should call home first," Aggie said.

She wanted to let her family know she was getting married, although she didn't have hope that they could come to Darwin in time. Working with the cattle, they couldn't leave home on a whim. Someone had to be there to look after the livestock. Katie's family might come. The Larkins didn't work on the land like her family.

Once in the office, she dialed the operator and requested a line for her family's cattle station. Her brother Chester had finally agreed to have a telephone installed when Joe left for the service; he wanted to be sure their brother could reach them. When she heard the line ringing, she clutched the handset tighter and held her breath. *Please let them pick up.*

"G'day?" She heard her brother's voice down the line.

"Chester! It's Aggie."

"Aggie? What are you doing calling? This must be costing you a fortune."

Leave it to her brother to always worry about the price of things.

"I know, Chester. I'll be quick. Chester, I'm getting married on Monday, here in Darwin."

"Married?! To who? To that Yank who proposed?"

Aggie rolled her eyes.

"Yes, to the Yank who proposed. We're engaged. Who else would I be marrying?"

"Well, I dunno. I dunno how it's done in the big city."

"In the big city, it's done just like back home, Chester. One proposal, one marriage. Sheesh."

"I love riling you up, Aggie," Chester laughed.

Aggie shook her head. Her brother was an idiot, but she loved him.

"I wanted you to know the ceremony is on Monday morning. Henry is here on leave until next Friday. I was wondering if any of you could come. I know it's short notice."

"Oh, Aggie, I don't know." Chester sounded crestfallen. "You know we'd love to be there, but the livestock…"

"That's what I thought. I understand."

"Wait. Joe's home on leave and Casey just got back to Oz and is supposed to be coming for a visit this week. What if you and your new husband come to us for a few days? A little honeymoon in the bush? A chance for him to meet your family?"

Aggie paused to think; that could work. The wedding was early on Monday. They could catch an early afternoon train and be in Birdum by Monday evening and the cattle station by bedtime. They could then reverse the trip on Thursday to ensure Henry was back in time for his flight back to Ulithi on Friday. It would be a rush and might not be the most romantic honeymoon, but she liked the idea.

"Let me talk to Henry," Aggie said. She wasn't sure that he would want to share his new wife with her family, but she wanted him to meet them and see the place that had formed her.

"Good. Keep me posted. We'd love to have you. Mary and my Lily could plan a little party. We could do a barbecue and Mary could bake a cake."

Aggie's eyes filled with tears. That sounded so lovely. A wedding reception at the homestead. She hoped Henry would agree.

"I would love that. I'll talk to Henry and I'll let you know our plans."

"Please do. We'd all love to see you, Aggie, and meet your young man."

"Thank you, Chester. I'll let you know as soon as I can."

"We love you, Aggie. We're all so proud of you and happy that you met someone."

"I love you, too. Give my love to everyone. Talk soon."

Not a moment after she had hung up with her brother and wiped her eyes, Betty whirled into the office.

"Enough jibber jabber on the phones. You girls have wedding finery to try on!"

She dragged Katie and Aggie to their bedroom in the barracks. On the rail of the upper bunk's footboard hung several dresses and suits, in colors from white to a blush peach. It amazed Aggie that Betty had found any wedding appropriate dresses in less than twenty-four hours – and with a variety of choices, at that.

"You are a miracle worker," gushed Katie. Betty waved her hand dismissively.

"Who on Earth owns clothes like these after five years of war?" Aggie wondered.

"It was a matter of calling on my resources. Several of the nurses are from well-off families. One of the WRANS, her father is an industrialist. Plenty of money for pretty frocks for dancing and evenings out. Besides, everyone was eager to help make your weddings special. Now, let's see what will work for you two."

The women began trying on dresses. They thought that finding something to fit Katie's tiny frame would be a challenge, but there was a pale pink evening dress that fit her well. Meant to be knee length, on diminutive Katie, it was tea length with a flowing skirt and ruching around the hips that gathered into a bow and flowed down the back. One of the nurses had offered a pair of pale pink dancing shoes that mostly fit Katie and worked well with the dress.

Aggie chose a cream-colored suit of silk shantung. The jacket of the suit had a charming peplum and there was lace edging the lapels. The straight skirt fit like a glove and fell just below her knee. Also in the pile of proffered finery was a pair of cream color T-strap heels, made of the softest leather she had ever felt. She felt like a princess in a fairy tale in such lovely clothes.

Betty bounced up and down, clapping her hands as she took in the women in the wedding ensembles. It delighted her to find such beautiful outfits for her friends.

"Well, that takes care of something borrowed. Each of you has a linen and lace handkerchief, don't you? That will suffice for something old."

She looked around and grabbed a hat that was off to the side. It was a smart hat of cream-colored straw with a rolled brim and a pale blue ribbon circling the crown. Betty popped it on Aggie's head with the brim tipped down over her right eye.

"There! Something blue!"

She grinned, then dove into her own dresser and presented Katie with a set of blue satin and lace garters. Katie's face flamed red, causing her friends to burst into laughter.

"You girls are on your own for 'something new.' I've taken you as far as I can."

Betty beamed at them. The girls hugged her and thanked her for finding them such perfect wedding dresses with barely any notice. Katie said she would like to stop in town for a new pair of gloves, and Aggie agreed. New gloves would be the perfect finishing touch to her wedding suit and would serve as her 'something new.'

They carefully took off the dresses and hung them in the wardrobe to wait until Monday. Aggie set her hat on the dresser. It was four in the afternoon and they had somehow organized a double wedding in a day. Unbelievable!

They met Conor and Henry at the mess hall for tea and to determine if there was any further planning to be done the next day. It seemed they had ticked all the boxes on their list of wedding necessities in a day. The men booked the last two available rooms at the Hotel Darwin, an elegant hotel on the Esplanade and a short walk from the cathedral. They also reserved a table at the Green Room restaurant at the hotel for their wedding luncheon.

"How were the phone calls home?" Henry asked.

"My parents are coming!" Katie exclaimed. "They're getting on the train in Alice Springs first thing tomorrow and will be here for the wedding on Monday. I can't wait for them to meet you." She gave Conor a kiss on the cheek.

"I'm so glad for you," Aggie said, squeezing her friend's hand. She felt a little melancholy that no one from her family would be there.

"No luck with your brothers and sisters?" Henry asked quietly, reaching up to stroke her cheek.

"No, but I'm not surprised. They can't leave the livestock unattended and the cost of all those train tickets? Chester would have a fit." She tried hard to joke, but it felt forced. Then she remembered her brother's suggestion.

"Chester invited us to the homestead for a few days. They'd like to meet you and have a small reception for us at the station."

"A wedding reception on the ranch? Sounds great."

"Really? You wouldn't mind going? It will be a lot of travel and probably not a lot of privacy for a honeymoon."

"Really, I'd love to go. I want to see where my Aggie grew up."

Aggie threw her arms around his neck and kissed his cheek. "Oh, thank you, Henry!"

He laughed. "We'll have to call your family and let them know we'll be coming. We should go to the train station in the morning and arrange tickets."

"Perfect. I need to stop in town for a pair of gloves tomorrow. We can do that at the same time."

With a plan for the next day, the couples said good night and parted after their busy day.

SUNDAY WAS ANOTHER busy day with honeymoon preparations.

Henry and Aggie met for Mass to start their day. Then, they went to the train station to review the train timetables, making sure they could travel to the family cattle station and back before Henry's return flight on Friday. Satisfied the trip was possible, they booked their tickets. The couple placed a call to the homestead to inform them the honeymoon couple was coming to see the family.

Henry reserved a hotel room in Birdum for Monday night with help from the information desk at the station. Though Aggie wanted to see her family, Henry wouldn't spend his wedding night in twin beds at her brother's homestead. While embarrassed by his insistence on having their first night of married life to themselves, Aggie agreed.

They stopped at a shop to purchase a new pair of cream-colored gloves for Aggie's wedding ensemble. They found a small pawnshop and bought a pair of simple, gold wedding bands. Aggie's ring would nestle alongside the copper and silver engagement ring Henry had given her. After paying, he slid both rings into the inside pocket of his jacket, where they rested over his heart.

Most importantly, they telephoned Henry's ma in Chicago. He had written to her about Aggie and even sent a telegram when they were engaged. But he was getting married, and she wouldn't be there. He needed to hear Ma's voice and have her meet Aggie, even if only over a long-distance phone line. The call was brief and expensive, but worth every penny.

"Hello?"

"Ma! It's Henry!" he yelled into the phone. The line was full of static and difficult to hear.

"Heniu? You sound very far away."

"I am, Ma. I'm in Australia. I'm here with my Aggie."

"Australia! Oh, your girl Aggie. Is she being nice to you?"

"Yes, Ma. We're getting married tomorrow, on Monday."

"You're mixed up, Heniu. Tomorrow is Sunday."

"I know. In Australia, it's already Sunday. It's the time zones."

"Bah! What do I know about time zones? Let me talk to your girl."

Henry paused. This was why he'd wanted to call, so that his ma could meet Aggie. Now that the moment had arrived, he was a little nervous. Who knew what his ma might say?

He looked at Aggie and handed her the receiver. "She wants to talk to you."

Aggie gave him a nervous look as she took the phone.

"G'day, Mrs. Bolanski."

Henry watched as Aggie listened to his ma. He could see her squint and tilt her head; Aggie must be struggling with his mother's Polish accent. She nodded and murmured "yes" several times. She then gave Henry a funny look out of the corner of her eye and burst out laughing. What in the world had Ma just told her? No doubt some horrifying, embarrassing story from his youth.

"Yes. Thank you. Yes."

He glanced at her again; it sounded like the call was wrapping up.

"Yes. How did you pronounce that? *Matka?* Yes, *Matka.* Thank you. I look forward to meeting you, too." She smiled brightly at Henry. "She wants to finish talking to you now."

He took the receiver. "What did you tell her?"

"Stories to keep you on your toes. I told her about the time you came in drunk and I punched you in the nose. It made her laugh. Plus, she should know not to let you get away with things. I like her, she sounds nice. A funny accent, but nice."

He looked at Aggie. "Yes, she's very nice. I love her very much."

"Good, then you bring her home as soon as you can so I can love her, too. I will like having a daughter."

"I will, Ma. I gotta go. This call is costing a fortune. I'll call you with my travel plans when I get to Seattle."

"I love you, Heniu. I will pray for your marriage and that it is as happy and loving as my marriage to your Tatuś."

"Thanks, Ma. I love you, too."

He hung up the receiver. He had last spoken to his ma on the phone while in Hawaii in December. Now it was six months later, and he was getting married.

They joined Conor and Katie at the train station to meet Mr. and Mrs. Larkin's train from Alice Springs, then shared a meal with them at a restaurant near the base. Katie was going to spend the night in her parents' hotel room while Aggie would spend the night with Betty and Jackie at the barracks.

Chapter Twenty-Three

M ay 1945
       Darwin, Australia

MONDAY DAWNED WITH clear blue skies as Henry rose from his bunk at the BOQ. It was the morning of his wedding day; it amazed Henry how well he slept.

Getting ready for church, Henry took his dress uniform from the closet, carefully pressed the dress shirt, and brushed any lint off the jacket. After a shower and a shave, he pulled on the uniform, carefully buttoning the golden buttons to his throat.

Straightening his epaulettes, he affixed his golden aviator wings over his chest, above his ribbons. He inspected himself in the mirror and nodded at what he saw. He hoped Aggie would be pleased. She had never seen him in his service dress whites before.

Conor knocked on his door, inquiring if he was ready to go. Henry picked up his uniform hat and hefted his bag in the other hand. He would not be returning to the BOQ. Henry felt calm as they drove through town. He'd slept like a rock and woken up refreshed. No jitters. No nerves.

They arrived at the church to find the Larkins had already arrived. Katie was waiting in the bride's room. Aggie was driving to the church with Betty, Jackie, and the other girls in the latest iteration of the WAAAF Mobile. Father Gilbert came out to greet the men and hurried them to the front of the church. He didn't want to risk having the grooms catch sight of the brides before the start of the ceremony.

Henry checked his watch. It was 0900; the ceremony would start at 0930. The train left at noon. Henry was mentally back timing how long the ceremony and lunch would take to allow them to get to the train on time. A young man in an Australian Army uniform interrupted his thoughts.

"Excuse me. Is one of you fellows Henry? Something Polish with a B?"

"Uh, that would be me. Henry Bolanski," he replied. He ran a mental inventory of all the Australians he'd met while in the Pacific, but this soldier didn't ring a bell.

The Aussie thrust out his hand.

"Casey Ryan," he introduced himself. "Aggie's younger brother."

Henry broke into a wide grin as he shook the man's hand.

"Oh wow! It's great to meet you! We didn't think anyone from the family was going to be here."

"Well, I got in on Friday night and was supposed to head to the station yesterday. When I called to tell Chester my travel plans, he let me know about the wedding. I reckoned I could make a detour and represent the family at Aggie's wedding."

"Does she know you're here?"

"No, sir. Should be a big surprise."

"Well, I should say so. You should go to the back, they're in the bride's room or something. Let her know you're here."

"Nah, if she sees me, she'll get all weepy and blotchy. You don't need her with a red nose in your memories. I'll have a seat and surprise her after it's over."

"Are you sure? You could walk her down the aisle."

"No one needs to walk Aggie down the aisle. She's her own person. I reckon she can give herself away."

The men shook hands again and Casey wandered off to find a spot in the front pew.

At that moment, the doors opened and Betty, Jackie, and a contingent of WAAAFs clattered in, chatting and laughing. Betty waved to Henry and Conor as the ladies slid into the pews. Henry was surprised to see even the gruff Sergeant Maguire slide into a pew toward the back of the church. Henry was so happy that so many folks came to celebrate.

He looked at Conor, who was chatting with Katie's mom in the front pew. Henry was glad to have Conor here as his best man and fellow groom. He sighed, wishing Ma could have been there for his wedding day.

The organist began playing the prelude and the chatting and shifting in the pews halted. Father Gilbert stuck his head through the doors at the back of the church and nodded to Henry. He and Conor stepped to the end of the aisle, just in front of the altar rails. The doors opened to the nave, and Father Gilbert started down the aisle, preceded by an altar boy carrying a cross and flanked by two other altar boys carrying candles. As Father Gilbert reached the front of the church, the music changed to the Wedding March. Everyone stood from the pews and turned to watch the brides enter the church.

Henry elbowed Conor as Katie walked down the aisle on her father's arm. His breath caught as he saw Aggie begin her walk toward him. She looked so lovely in a slim cream suit and a hat perched at an angle on her dark hair, holding a small bouquet. She looked like a proper bride. He felt like the luckiest guy in the world to have this beautiful woman walking up the aisle toward him, ready to pledge their lives to one another.

AGGIE'S MORNING HAD been busy. She had risen early to pack her small suitcase for the trip out to the homestead. Betty had thoughtfully brought some breakfast to her room, knowing Aggie wouldn't want to go to the mess hall on her big day.

Betty helped her with her makeup, then styled Aggie's hair so the hat sat perfectly amidst the tresses. She dressed carefully, making sure not to snag her stockings or scuff the soft leather shoes. Betty proclaimed her a vision, then hurried off to get dressed herself.

There was a soft tap on her door. She opened it, surprised to see Sergeant Maguire standing in the doorway.

"Yes, Sergeant?"

"I would like you to please meet me in the barrack's lounge, Miss Ryan. Bring your suitcase."

What could the sergeant possibly want? He knew Aggie was on leave and must know she was leaving for the wedding soon. Everyone in the squadron was talking about it. She picked up her handbag, gloves, and suitcase before following him to the lounge.

When she arrived, Sergeant Maguire was standing there with a small bouquet in his hands.

"Miss Ryan, I wanted to wish you felicitations on your wedding day," he said formally.

"Why, thank you, Sergeant Maguire."

"These are for you." He thrust the flowers toward her. "My contribution to your wedding."

Aggie flushed, touched by the gesture. "Thank you so much, Sergeant."

"I understand you were planning to drive to the church with the other girls in the truck?"

"Yes, it made sense to ride together. Katie spent the night at the hotel with her parents, so she will go to the church with them."

"Captain Dempsey granted me permission to borrow his staff car. Allow me to drive you. I wouldn't want anything to happen to your wedding dress in the truck."

Aggie was so moved by his kindness. She sniffed and blinked rapidly to keep from crying. The sergeant saw her trying to hold back her emotions.

"Enough of that," he barked. He took the suitcase from her hand. "The car is this way." He walked from the lounge toward the parking lot.

Aggie laughed; typical of Sergeant Maguire to switch back to being a grouch. Aggie let Betty and Jackie know she had a different ride to the church and headed to the staff car.

She climbed into the passenger seat. The sergeant started the car, and they pulled away. It was a quiet ride to the church. Aggie was grateful the sergeant had given her a ride; she was positive she was much more comfortable than if she had ridden in the truck.

As they approached the church, she turned to the Sergeant. "Thank you so much, Sergeant. I appreciate the flowers and the ride in such a nice car. Thank you for helping to make my wedding day special."

"You're welcome," he said, clearing his throat several times. "I remember my older sister's wedding. She and my mother spent months planning to make it the perfect day. I know you had to plan your day quickly, I wanted to help if I could."

It took all of Aggie's self-control to keep from reaching across the car and hugging him. That would have been terribly inappropriate, and the sergeant would probably revoke her pass for leave on the spot.

"Thank you. I hope you will stay for the ceremony and join us for luncheon afterward."

"Oh, I don't know. I need to get back to work. And make sure the WAAAFs get back to work as well."

"Of course. Please know we'd love for you to attend."

He pulled the car to a stop outside the cathedral. He hopped out, racing around to open the door for her. She stepped out, brushing down her skirt. The sergeant reached into the backseat to take out her suitcase and carried it up the church steps for her. He held the door open for her and followed her to the bride's room, setting down the suitcase.

Aggie held out her hand. "Thank you again, Sergeant."

Sergeant Maguire shook her hand. "You're welcome. Best wishes, Miss Ryan." Then he turned and left.

Katie rushed over to give her a hug. "What was that all about?"

"I think I remind him of his sister," Aggie said, uncertain how to explain the sergeant's actions. She lifted the bouquet to her nose and sniffed. The flowers smelled lovely.

"Where did you get the bouquet?"

"From the sergeant."

"You're joking!" Katie exclaimed. Aggie simply shook her head.

Katie's father popped his head into the room.

"The grooms are here, and your friends have arrived. Father Gilbert says we are ready to begin. He's cued the organist to play. Shall we?"

They walked to the vestibule. Mr. Larkin offered to walk Aggie down the aisle on his other arm, but she demurred. She was embarking on this new life on her own. Traveling to America to live with Henry on her own. She would begin as she meant to go on.

As the doors of the sanctuary opened and the music swelled, she was happy to see that her friends were there to celebrate with them. She was delighted to spot Sergeant Maguire in a pew to the rear of the church. Katie and her father started down the aisle ahead of her. Aggie took a deep breath and followed them to the front of the church.

When she caught sight of Henry at the end of the aisle, tall and handsome in his white dress uniform, she felt her heart swell. He was a good man, brave and kind. She knew he had a tough childhood like she'd had, but he had come through it strong. Together, they would face whatever life sent their way.

As she reached the head of the aisle, she had eyes only for Henry and he gazed back at her steadily. He took her hand and led her to the kneeler they would share during the Mass. They knelt, side by side, as Father Gilbert began the prayers.

When the time came to say their vows, they stood to face each other, still holding hands. Father Gilbert asked Henry to begin.

"I, Henry Daniel Bolanski, take you, Agnes Rose Ryan, to be my wife. I promise to be true to you in good times and in bad, in sickness and in health. I will love you and honor you all the days of my life."

Aggie felt the smile on her face growing wide. Henry smiled back at her. Then she started giggling. Henry arched an eyebrow in her direction.

"I'm sorry," she whispered. "When I get nervous, I either laugh or cry. I guess today it's going to be laughter."

He smiled and shook his head. He then lifted her hand to his mouth and kissed her knuckles.

"Life with you will never be dull, Aggie."

Father Gilbert smiled at them indulgently, then cleared his throat. "Shall we continue?"

They nodded; it was Aggie's turn to recite her vows. To promise to love, honor, and cherish Henry, in sickness and in health, in good times and in bad. They looked into each other's eyes as they pledged their lives to one another. They continued to share their gaze as Conor and Katie made their vows.

Henry produced the rings and placed them on Father Gilbert's prayer book to be blessed. He took her ring and placed it on her left ring finger, nestling it next to her engagement ring. She then slid the simple gold band on his finger, binding them to each other.

At the end of the ceremony, Father Gilbert announced they were husband and wife and asked Henry to kiss the bride. He swept Aggie into a breathless kiss.

"I love you," he whispered in her ear.

Oh, how she loved him back.

The members of the congregation burst into applause. Henry and Aggie turned to move back up the aisle when a soldier in the front pew caught her eye. Aggie blinked, shocked to see her brother, Casey. Stunned, she stopped in her tracks. He gave her a chirpy salute.

"Surprise!"

With that, she promptly burst into tears.

"Now you cry?" Henry asked.

She turned to him, asking if he had arranged for her brother to be here for the wedding.

"I wish I could take the credit. Your family worked this out on their own."

Aggie rushed over to hug her brother. It delighted her that one of her family could be there to see her married. She wished that Henry's mum could have been there as well.

"Casey! I'm so happy you're here. Thank you for coming!"

"I wouldn't have missed it, sis. You look so happy. I'm glad."

She attempted to introduce Henry, but the men waved her off. They had made their own introductions before the service. Henry explained Case wanted to surprise her.

Casey held up a small brownie camera.

"Can I take some wedding photos?"

The couple posed for several pictures in the church and on the steps outside under the wide blue Aussie sky. They took pictures with Conor and Katie as well.

The WAAAFs stopped to give them their congratulations, then explained that they needed to return to the barracks and their work at the airfield. Aggie looked around to see that Sergeant Maguire had already departed with the captain's staff car.

"Are you going to toss the bouquet, Aggie?" asked Betty. "Maybe give one of us other girls a little good luck in finding a husband."

"I hadn't thought about it," Aggie said, looking down at the pretty bouquet from Sergeant Maguire. "I think that would be fun. You girls line up at the base of the church steps."

The women scurried to get into place. Betty was front and center, while Jackie stood well back in the group of ladies.

Aggie stood halfway up the church steps, then turned her back and pitched the bouquet over her shoulder. There was shrieking and laughter and when Aggie turned back around, she was unsurprised to see Betty wrangling the bouquet from another girl's hands. Jackie was leaning away from the bouquet with her arms stick-straight at her sides, laughing at the tussle.

"Congratulations, Betty!" Aggie said. "You're next!"

Casey asked the WAAAFs to gather around the brides for a group photograph and then there was laughter and hugs as the women wished the wedding couples all the best. The girls bundled into the truck and waved goodbye.

The group had dwindled to Henry, Aggie, Conor, Katie, Mr. and Mrs. Larkin, and Casey. As they prepared to depart for the Green Room for the wedding luncheon, they invited Father Gilbert to join them. He declined, stating he had training sessions with several new chaplains. He gave them a final blessing and they were on their way.

The wedding couples and their family members enjoyed an elegant lunch at the restaurant, but Aggie noticed Henry frequently checking his watch.

"Is something wrong?"

"Not at all. I just want to be sure we leave early enough to get to the train station. If we miss the train, we won't be able to get to your family's ranch until Tuesday night."

She nodded. The meal had ended, everyone was now relaxing over coffee and slices of cake. Conor and Katie were staying in Darwin for their honeymoon, and Mr. and Mrs. Larkin wouldn't depart for Alice Springs until later in the week. None of the others were in a hurry.

Aggie turned to Casey. "Are you on the train with us today?"

"No! Heaven forbid I should have to watch the two of you all lovey dovey on the train for hours. Yuck!"

Henry and Aggie laughed.

"I have a certain young lady I plan to see here in Darwin; a nurse I met abroad. I'll try to see her today and then I'll head home tomorrow for the party at the station."

"Party?" Aggie asked.

"Oh, Chester and Mary have lots of plans for you. If you two can pull together a wedding in a few days, the Ryans can certainly plan a party."

Henry checked his watch again while Aggie gathered her things.

"We should be going. We don't want to miss our train."

There were goodbyes and hugs all around.

"You better not miss our flight back to Ulithi!" Conor teased Henry. Henry assured him he would be back in time.

They departed the restaurant and Henry hailed a cab outside the hotel to take them to the station. The pair sat in the back of the cab, their first moment alone since they were married. Henry leaned over and kissed Aggie, then smiled.

"Hello, wife."

She broke into a dazzling smile.

"Hello, husband," she replied, and he kissed her again.

They arrived at the train station forty-five minutes before their train was due to depart, allowing them to find their seats and get comfortable. The train ride would take about eight hours, so they would have hours to talk and settle into married life.

Chapter Twenty-Four

M ay 1945
Northern Territories, Australia

IT AMAZED HENRY HOW open and desolate the land out the train window appeared. He had ridden the train across the United States from Chicago to Seattle, but this land was even more wide open and unpopulated, with sparse trees and rusty red soil.

The train was quite full. The RAAF and American Army Air Force had established the town of Larrimah with an airfield and training facilities just north of where they would get off the train. If he had known that he would have tried to catch a ride with the Army Air Force, skipping the train altogether.

Hindsight aside, Henry was enjoying riding the rails with Aggie. She was dozing with her head on his shoulder. They had passed the time playing cards and talking about their future. She would come to live with him in Chicago once the war ended unless they could find a loophole for her to move sooner. He would work with the Navy to see what could be done. Now that they were married, he didn't want to be apart more than necessary.

He hoped she would like Chicago. He looked out the window at the vast tracts of emptiness outside. It would be so different for her, compared to where she came from.

As the train slowed again, Henry consulted his watch. Soon they would reach their stop. Many of their fellow travelers had disembarked at the last stop in Larrimah. There were still several nurses on the train, bound for the Army evacuation hospital in Birdum. Henry shook Aggie awake.

"Aggie, sweetheart. We are coming into the station."

Aggie's eyes fluttered open and she looked out the window. Henry could see her shoulders relax as she took in her homeland. She turned to him with a smile.

"I'm so sorry I fell asleep on you. I could have told you about all the sights."

The sights, Henry mused. All he could see were dusty tracks, brush and scrub, and the occasional stream meandering through the vastness. Nevertheless, Aggie seemed excited, and he was happy to see her happy.

The train pulled into the station, a small building along the railway platform. They departed the train with Henry carrying their bags. They crossed the dusty main street, the only street as far as Henry could tell, to the small hotel where they would spend their wedding night. It was already late, almost nine o'clock, and they needed to get checked in. He was glad that he insisted on having dinner in the dining car. The town did not appear to have a restaurant, or at least not one that was open this late in the evening.

The pair proceeded up the steps, into the hotel, and approached the welcome desk together, ringing the bell for service. The clerk appeared from the office off the lobby.

"G'd evening. How can I help you?"

"Yes, a reservation for this evening. Mr. and Mrs. Henry Bolanski," Henry said proudly. It was the first time he had introduced themselves as Mr. and Mrs.

"Yes, right here," the young lady said, consulting the reservation book. She glanced up, cheeks a deep shade of pink. "I'm afraid I will need to see proof of marriage before I can give you the key. Between the airfield up at Larrimah and the hospital here, we need to be careful. I hope you understand."

Henry absolutely understood. He could easily imagine the shenanigans some of the Army fliers and the nurses might get up to.

Aggie produced the copy of their marriage certificate that Father Gilbert had provided. The woman looked at the document, then met Aggie's eyes in surprise.

"You were married today!"

"Yes, we were," Henry said, wrapping an arm around Aggie's shoulders. "We're traveling to see my wife's family – stopping here for our wedding night." He noticed Aggie's cheeks flush bright pink.

"Of course," said the clerk. "Let me offer my congratulations. You'll be in room 20, just up the stairs and on the left." She offered Henry a key. He took it with alacrity.

"Thank you," he replied. "Have a pleasant evening."

"Not as pleasant as yours," he heard the clerk mutter as they walked away. Henry blushed to the tips of his ears. He glanced toward Aggie, who was looking down with bright pink cheeks.

At the door of the hotel room, Henry set the suitcases down and unlocked the door. As the door swung open, Aggie stepped forward, but he caught her by the arm.

"Not so fast," he said, as he swung her up in his arms and carried her across the threshold. Aggie began giggling as he swept her into the room. Before setting her down, he gave her a thorough kiss. When he put her back on her feet, she was breathless and the giggles had stopped. He stepped out into the fall to collect their bags, then shut the door and slid the lock closed.

They stood looking at each other for a moment, unsure what to do next. Aggie broke the tension.

"May I have my bag? I'd like to brush my teeth and wash my face."

"Of course."

Henry put her small suitcase on the luggage rack across from the bed. She stepped over, popped it open, and began rummaging through the contents. She paused briefly, then turned to him with something pink and lacy clutched in her hand.

"Betty gave me this," she said, blushing fiercely. "She said my cotton nightgowns wouldn't be appropriate for our wedding night. But it's been a long day, I didn't know if you might want me to save it for later." She looked at him inquiringly.

Henry looked at the shimmery satin fabric in her hand and his imagination took flight.

"No, nope. No need to save anything for later." He paused. "Unless you want to?"

She gave him a nervous smile and brushed past him on the way to the bathroom, clutching her toiletry bag and the pink creation. Henry shrugged off his suit coat and removed his tie, having changed from his dress uniform after the wedding ceremony. He kicked off his shoes and was halfway through unbuttoning his shirt when Aggie emerged from the bathroom.

She had scrubbed her face clean and pink and brushed out her hair, so it hung soft and loose to her shoulders. The nightgown was a pale pink satin with lace edging the neckline and hem. The thin straps over her shoulders and low neckline showed off her delicate collarbones and an expanse of creamy skin, as well as a hint of cleavage. She looked beautiful, better than any pin-up girl he'd ever seen.

"You're gorgeous."

She looked down, shyly. He stepped toward her and tilted her head up for a kiss, looking her in the eye.

"I want to warn you, I don't know what I'm doing. I've never done this before," he said.

"And you think I have?" she squeaked.

Henry laughed. "No, I know neither of us is very experienced. I'm just trying to, you know, set expectations."

Now it was Aggie's turn to laugh.

"I'm sure we'll figure it out. I'm mechanically inclined after all," she teased.

Henry pulled her into another breath-stealing kiss.

"Yes, we'll figure it out together. Like we will with everything else."

AGGIE AWOKE TO THE soft light of morning drifting through the curtains of their hotel room. She was warm and cozy, with Henry's strong arm wrapped around her waist. She grinned to herself. What a pleasant experience, to wake up with him next to her, holding her close.

The previous night had been lovely, with kissing and cuddling. She thought Henry had probably enjoyed it more than she had. There had been some discomfort, but Henry had been equal parts endearingly awkward and awkwardly endearing through the venture. *It will get better with practice,* she thought with a self-satisfied smile.

Henry stirred beside her, and Aggie glanced at his little travel alarm clock on the bedside table: 6:30. She had never been one for sleeping in. Between growing up on the cattle station and her time as a cook at Sullivan's, she was used to being up with the dawn. Even her work with the WAAAFs had her rising early. She wondered what her life would be like in America, living in a city with no livestock to manage, hungry drovers to feed or airplanes to repair. What would she do with her days?

Henry's eyes blinked open, giving her a sleepy smile. Her heart gave a little thrill at the sight of him, hair tousled from sleep and a dark wash of whiskers across his chin and cheeks. He squeezed her tight, then relaxed back with his hand and wrist draped over the curve between the flare of her pelvis and her ribs.

"I'm declaring this 'my spot.' This spot where my hand fits perfectly over your hip," he said, patting the area to show what he meant. "This is where I want my hand to rest every night when I go to sleep."

Aggie smiled. What a lovely thought, in a romantic sort of way. She leaned over to kiss him.

"Good morning, husband," she greeted him.

He smiled back and wished her a good morning. Then his face grew pensive as he asked, "How are you this morning? Did you sleep okay?"

"I'm grand," she assured him. "Slept well. I loved waking up next to you."

He grinned and seemed to relax.

"I slept like a rock," he said while smothering a yawn. "It's amazing how much better I sleep curled up with my wife like spoons in a drawer, and not on a ship surrounded by snoring men and the sounds of planes being launched off the flight deck at all hours."

She snuggled in closer to him.

"I'm sorry if I woke you up. I'm used to getting up early."

"It's fine. I'm an early riser too. All those years of getting up to serve early Mass with Father Parkolewicz. Mass started at seven, and if you weren't fifteen minutes early, you were late."

"My brother is supposed to be here at 8:30 to collect us and take us out to the homestead. I guess we could go downstairs and have some breakfast while we wait."

Henry slid even closer and started dropping kisses along her neck, from her earlobe to her collarbone.

"Oh, I can think of another way to pass the time until we need to go," he whispered in her ear. He pulled her underneath him and kissed her deeply.

"Now? In the morning?" she asked breathlessly, between his kisses.

"Whenever we want, sweetheart," he breathed against her skin as he slid his hand up her thigh under her nightgown.

In the end, they were very nearly late for her brother's arrival. Her pondering of the early morning had been correct. *That experience was much more satisfying,* she thought smugly. *Practice makes perfect.* The busy day yesterday, followed by a long train ride and the late night, as well as their mutual inexperience and nervousness, had been an issue. In the languid morning light, though, both had enjoyed the encounter immensely.

Afterward, they rushed around the hotel room, taking turns in the bath, packing up their belongings, and preparing to head out to the homestead. Henry had run down to the dining room of the hotel for coffee and toast for their breakfast and brought it to the room so they could eat while they washed up and packed.

Miraculously, they arrived in the lobby at 8:30 on the dot, dressed, packed, and ready to depart. When they caught sight of the clock over the front desk, they shared a knowing glance and started laughing. They were returning their room key and signing out when Aggie heard a familiar voice behind her.

"Well, if it's not my favorite sister, returned from the city with her new husband."

Aggie whirled around to see her brother, Chester. His nose was red from sunburn and his dark hair flopped over his brow from when he'd removed his wide-brimmed hat. Aggie broke into a wide grin and threw herself at him.

"Chester!" she cried as he caught her, lifting her off her feet and swinging her in a circle. They laughed together, and she shed a few tears as they hugged. He set her back on her feet, and she turned, reaching out a hand to Henry.

"Chester, this is my new husband. Henry Bolanski, United States Navy. From Chicago."

Henry reached out to shake Chester's hand. "A pleasure to meet you, Chester."

Aggie could see the hard glint in her brother's eye as he surveyed Henry from top to toe as the men shook hands. She thought she saw Henry wince and she shoved Chester's shoulder.

"Stop that!" she bossed her big brother.

"Stop what?"

"Trying to crush his hand."

She looked at Henry as he extracted his hand from Chester's grip and shook it out. Aggie shook he head at her brother.

"What's wrong with you?"

Chester simply shrugged. "Needed to see what he's made of, didn't I?"

He looked at Henry. "You okay there, mate?"

"Yeah, I'll do," Henry said, flexing his fingers, trying to get the feeling to return. "I checked us out. Shall we get going?"

They followed Chester out into the dusty sunlight and he led them to a battered Model A Ford. Henry opened the door for Aggie and gave her a hand in the car. Aggie saw her brother nod in approval at Henry's good manners. She rolled her eyes. As if she would marry someone with bad manners.

As they drove out of town and into the countryside, Aggie asked Chester for the latest news from the family. Chester and Lily's children, a son and daughter, were healthy and growing strong. Mary and Louis's little girl had just turned two and Chester thought they were expecting again but hadn't made the announcement. Joe was home for a while. Injured overseas, the Army shipped Joe home to convalesce. Aggie was concerned about his injurie, but Chester simply waved off her concerns. She would find out more when she talked to Joe.

Aggie looked out at the landscape as they rolled along the dusty road, remembering all the places they had played when they were little. The trees they'd climbed and the creek they had splashed in. So many memories. After an hour, they turned onto the track that led to the homestead. As the house came into view, it amazed Aggie again how little it appeared. She had the same thought the last time she had been home.

As they pulled to a stop in the dooryard, Lily and little David came out of the house, with baby Colette cradled in her arms. Mary, Louis, and their toddler, Natalie, came up the path from their small house. There was hugging, laughter, and tears as everyone said hello and met Henry. Eddie was eager to hear Henry's stories about flying and fighting the Japanese. Edith, the youngest of the Ryan siblings, chatted about the animals at the station and offered to take Henry for a tour on horseback.

Aggie looked around for her brother, Joe. Chester had said he was home, but she had yet to see him.

"Where's Joe?"

"Joe had to go up to the hospital today," Mary explained. "He'll be back this afternoon, hopefully after picking up Casey from the train. I think Joe might bring his girlfriend. She's a nurse at the hospital."

"Was he badly injured? No one sent me any details, just that he was wounded and sent back home."

Henry stepped closer to her, lending her quiet support as he knew her concern about her brother.

"He was shot in the arm and chest. There was damage to his lung, but he seems to be getting around just fine," Mary reported. "He's not able to ride a horse yet, but he's been helping Chester and Louis with some simple chores. And going up to the hospital to see that girl."

Lily welcomed them into the house, showing Aggie and Henry to the small bedroom Aggie used to share with her sisters. Aggie looked at the double bed she used to share with Mary and spotted Edith's old trundle bed under the bed. Edith scooted past them to gather up some of her things.

"I still sleep in this room. While you're here, I'll sleep on one of the bunk beds in the boys' room," Edith explained.

She turned brightly to Henry. "Let me know when you're ready to go on our horseback ride to see the cattle."

He nodded and agreed as she skipped out with her bundle of clothing. Lily said she would let them get settled and to let her know if they needed anything. With that, she left them alone.

"I don't know how to break it to your kid sister that I really don't know how to ride a horse," Henry confessed.

Aggie laughed. "You'll be fine. I'll be sure you get the gentlest, most docile mount in the barn. I'll take care of it. Don't trust any horse offered to you by one of my brothers."

"No way. I've only just had the circulation return to my hand after your brother's handshake."

He pulled her into a hug.

"So, this is where you grew up?"

"For what it's worth. Would you like a tour?"

"Of course!"

Aggie rummaged in the wardrobe and found a pair of her old work pants and a cotton shirt. She changed out of her skirt and blouse and pulled on an old pair of work boots. They had worn down heels and there was a hole in the sole, but they would do for a knockabout the land. She turned to Henry. He was wearing a pair of khaki trousers and a blue denim shirt and looked very handsome. She reached for his hand and led him out to see the homestead.

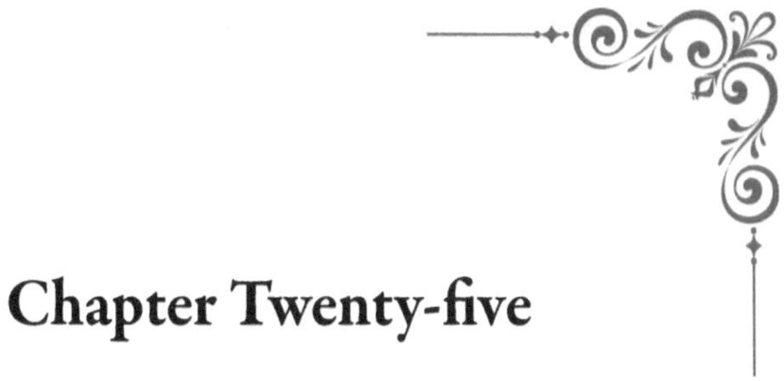

Chapter Twenty-five

M ay 1945
   Northern Territories, Australia

HENRY THOUGHT HE'D acquitted himself well on the tour around the ranch. Aggie had saddled an ancient, gentle mare for him and taught him how to kick her to start and pull on the reins to stop. Mostly, the animal just followed the horse ahead of her, which was fine with Henry.

Edith talked a mile a minute as she showed them around the barn and paddocks. They toured the property, exploring some of the outlying areas where the cattle were grazing. Henry enjoyed Aggie's chatty little sister and hearing her stories about how Aggie would take care of her when she was little, making up fairy tales and playing games with her as they worked around the ranch.

After their tour, Lily and Mary were preparing to serve supper in the yard at a table set up under an acacia tree because the kitchen was not large enough to hold all of them. As Henry helped Aggie and Edith set the table, Chester pulled up with two men and an auburn-haired woman in the back seat. Aggie raced to the car to greet Casey and hug the other man, who Henry assumed was her brother Joe.

Henry marveled at such a large and loving family. After Tatus had died, it had been him and Ma. Ma had a few cousins who they would see for the holidays, but nothing like the crowd of people surrounding Aggie with their teasing and hugs. He felt a little envious, if he was honest, though the Ryan clan did all they could to include him.

Aggie introduced him to Joe, who seemed quieter and more reserved than Casey, but still friendly. Joe then introduced his girlfriend, a nurse from the nearby convalescent hospital named Alicia Harper. A charming girl, quick with a joke and a smile, Henry could tell she was keeping a close eye on Joe to be sure he was okay.

The family gathered around the table for the meal as the women brought out platters and bowls of food.

"This feels like Thanksgiving," Henry said. When the Ryans looked baffled, he explained the American holiday of Thanksgiving.

"That sounds like a wonderful holiday," Joe said. "Time with family to share a meal and give thanks."

He reached over and took Alicia's hand.

"I'm thankful to be here with all of you."

As the meal ended, the women cleared the table. Aggie kissed Henry on the cheek as she rose to help carry dishes into the house. He squeezed her hand, thankful he had this opportunity to meet her family.

Joe and Henry fell into a quiet conversation about their combat experiences. Joe described his injuries, which sounded very similar to the wounds Sven had sustained. Henry told him about what happened when Sven was injured, and Henry had to ditch the plane.

Joe nodded and looked around the table.

"Some people will never understand."

He then looked Henry in the eye.

"You seem like a good man. Take good care of Aggie. And take her away from here. She deserves more than to be trapped here at the cattle station."

This surprised Henry. He thought Aggie's family would want her near and would resent him for taking her away to America.

"Aggie gave up so much for the family. She loved going to school, but she left to go to work to support us. When she wasn't breaking her back cooking for those louts over at Sullivan's, she was here helping Chester hold the place together with chewing gum and baling twine. I honestly don't know how she kept the well pump equipment running. If it weren't for her, we would have run out of water at the homestead years ago.

"And we were so terrible to her." Joe continued, shaking his head. "Casey and I used to tease her mercilessly. Eddie, too, once he was old enough to join in. We made fun of everything she did. She would usually just take it or tease us back. But I'll warn you, she's got a hell of a right hook."

Joe smiled.

"We didn't appreciate her sacrifice. I didn't understand it until I went away and saw similar kinds of sacrifice with the men in my unit. Mates willing to share the last of the water in their canteen, share their last cigarette. Take duty for another fellow and end up getting shot."

His gaze became unfocused, as if he were seeing a desert landscape a half a world away.

"She deserves better than a life in the middle of nowhere."

At that moment, Alicia put her hand on Joe's shoulder and he turned to her. She took his hand as they stood from the table and walked toward the barn.

Henry looked out at the desolate space surrounding the homestead and realized what a hard life Aggie had lived. Working night and day to keep their family together after their mom had died and their father abandoned them.

He thought about the reading at the wedding yesterday, saying there was no greater love than to lay down one's life for his friends.

Aggie had done that for her family; given up school, worked a job she disliked, all for the love of her family. He vowed to make those kinds of sacrifices for her, to give her the best life he could, and to always let her know he appreciated her. That he thought she was extraordinary.

"What was that about?" Aggie asked, nodding toward Joe as she sat down next to Henry.

"We started talking about our experiences in the war and finished by talking about how special you are."

"You were telling Joe I'm special? I'm sure he got a big laugh out of that. He and Casey were dreadful when we were kids. They were always teasing me. Luckily, I was just older and bigger to make them regret it."

"He warned me about your right hook," Henry chuckled, then he grew serious. "Joe was the one who said you're special. He admitted they were awful to you sometimes. That they didn't appreciate the sacrifices you made for your family."

"I did what needed to be done. I took care of my family."

"I know. That's what makes you special."

She smiled and took his hand.

"I'm worried about Joe. Physically, he's healing, but he isn't himself when I talk to him."

"Battle fatigue," Henry said, knowingly. "He's seen a lot and been through more. Experiences that most people won't understand unless they've been through it themselves. He's probably trying to shelter you as well, not telling you what really happened to him."

"Do you think so?"

"Sure. Think about those first letters I wrote to you. I didn't tell you how bad it could be, about the planes that were shot down and the men we lost. I didn't want to scare you."

Aggie nodded. "Was he able to talk to you?"

"A little. I told him about Sven and having the plane shot up, but my experience is so different from his. Dropping bombs from a hundred feet off the deck of a ship and evading dogfights is a world away from crawling through the desert with Rommel and his tanks on your tail."

Aggie shuddered at the thought. "Do you think he'll be okay?"

Henry shrugged. "He's doing that stiff upper lip thing. It seems like Alicia is watching out for him. She sensed he was drifting into dark memories and came over and took him for a walk. She's probably seen some terrible things as a nurse at the convalescent hospital. She'll understand him better than most."

The sun had set and the air was cooling. Aggie rubbed her arms against the chill and Henry put his arm around her to pull her into his warmth.

"Let's head in and help with the dishes. Your sister and sister-in-law worked hard on the meal. The least I can do is help clean up."

"You're going to help with dishes?"

"Of course! Ma would have punched me in the head if I didn't help with dishes. She worked too hard. She didn't raise a son who wouldn't pull his own weight."

"Well, you're going to put my brothers to shame. I don't think any of them have washed a dish in their lives."

Once in the kitchen, Henry rolled up his sleeves, pushed his way to the sink, and began scrubbing plates and pans. Lily tittered at the sight of a man elbow deep in a sink of dirty dishes and Mary commented that perhaps she would have Henry give Louis some lessons. Aggie worked beside him drying the dishes and putting them away. He liked working as a team. That's what he wanted their marriage to be, a team, a partnership.

While they finished tidying the kitchen, Lily let them know the plans for the next day. The Ryan family had invited the other local families and ranch hands to the ranch for a cookout and wedding celebration. The neighbors would arrive around noon, as everyone had to be home for morning chores and return in time for the evening care of the livestock. Also, Henry and Aggie would have an early departure on Thursday morning for the train back to Darwin and Henry's Friday flight back to the Enterprise. Henry didn't even want to think about leaving Aggie on Friday.

Night had descended on the homestead with the littlest children tucked into bed already. Henry and Aggie bid her siblings good night and retired to their room. They washed up and climbed into bed together.

Tonight, Aggie was wearing a simple cotton nightdress, not the silky, lacy confection she had worn the night before. While she had been gorgeous in satin and lace, Henry thought she looked beautiful in her simple white nightgown. It suited her better than the fancy one. He reached over and pulled her close.

"Henry, I don't think we should do anything tonight. The walls in this house are paper thin."

He snuggled her closer.

"No worries," he said, using the Aussie idiom. "I'm still recovering from the horseback ride. And I'm afraid your brother will come in her and clobber me if he thinks we're up to any funny business."

"We're married! It's not funny business if you're married," she said indignantly.

"I'm pretty sure most guys consider it funny business if it involves their kid sister."

Aggie giggled. "You're probably right. I think they like you though. You definitely won over Mary and Lily by helping in the kitchen."

"Probably didn't help my case with your brothers with that move, though. Ah, well, Ma would have been proud that I helped."

"I'm so glad you've met my family. I can't wait to meet your mum."

She grew quiet. Henry reached out and touched her cheek, turning her to face him.

"Is everything okay?"

"Tomorrow, there will be a lot of people here. I wasn't expecting my family to invite everyone from the surrounding area, just a few families from the neighboring stations. Not every drover in the territory. The people I worked with at Sullivan's, not all of them are...pleasant. I'm dreading seeing some of them."

Henry wasn't sure what to say. He knew she had gone to work in the kitchen at the Sullivan ranch when she was only 13 or 14. Had the Sullivans been unkind to her? Cheated her out of her wages? He tried to probe the issue, but she demurred, stating she was tired and didn't want to talk about it. Holding her close, he felt her body relax as she drifted into sleep. He might not understand Aggie's hesitance about seeing her former coworkers, but he would stay close to her tomorrow.

ALL MORNING, AGGIE kept busy. She prepared salads and vegetables for the barbecue. Henry helped her carry saw horses from the barn and set them up with boards stretching between them to create makeshift tables. Edith and Aggie spread sheets as tablecloths.

Busy hands, she thought. *Always keep your hands busy and your eyes alert.* That was her mantra for all those years at the Sullivan's kitchen.

Many of the drovers were indifferent to her, treating her like a kid sister. However, there were a handful who had tried to take liberties with her. Even when she was a young girl of 14 with barely any curves to tempt a man, they were after her, trying to reach under her skirt or touch her breasts as she served them meals. A few had attempted to corner her in the kitchen, coming in at odd times, saying they wanted a snack or a cup of coffee. Luckily, she was quick and smart and usually able to slip away.

However, on one occasion, she had been on her own in the kitchen, scrubbing the lunch dishes while the head cook had gone out to the kitchen garden to gather onions and potatoes for the stew they planned for supper.

With the water running, she hadn't heard Ross slip into the kitchen. He was on her before she knew what was happening, grabbing her from behind and pulling her against him. He was a big man, a shade over six feet tall, muscled from his work with the livestock. She squirmed to get away, but he was much larger and stronger than her. He squeezed her breast painfully. She was thrashing and yelling for him to get off her, to stop. Shouting she wasn't interested, but he paid her no mind.

He started pulling up the skirt of her work dress, and she kept screaming. She stomped down on his instep as hard as she could with her work boots. He gasped in pain and pulled back from her just enough that she could grab the knife she'd been washing in the sink. It was only a paring knife, small but sharp. When he tried to grab her again, she slashed at the arm he had around her waist. That made him let go and she whirled around, brandishing the knife.

"What did you do that for?" he demanded.

"I told you to stop. You didn't stop. I was screaming and kicking. I had to do something to make you stop."

"You're such a tease, flitting around in your dress, always bending over, showing off your bum when you serve us food. You can't say you didn't want it."

"That's exactly what I'm saying. I never wanted you to touch me. I don't want you to touch me ever again. Stay away from me. I don't want you anywhere near me. Am I making myself clear?"

That's when Mr. Sullivan stepped into the kitchen. He had heard Aggie's screaming and came to investigate. He stepped between Aggie and Ross.

"Ross, you are one of my best drovers, but I would suggest you leave Miss Ryan alone from now on. Get out of here."

He grabbed a dish towel off the counter and threw it at Ross.

"Wipe up that blood and go ask Doc if you're going to need stitches. Tell him you hurt yourself with the utility knife."

Ross stomped out, complaining that no one would believe the wound was from cutting himself with a utility knife. So what if nobody believed him? She hoped everyone could tell she had slashed him, so they'd stay away from her.

"Are you alright?" Mr. Sullivan asked her.

Aggie nodded, then began crying. She wiped her eyes and apologized to Mr. Sullivan.

"I'm sorry to cry. I was really scared. He snuck up on me and grabbed me. He started to..." Aggie couldn't imagine how she would explain to Mr. Sullivan how Ross had touched her.

"Is having you work here going to be a problem for me?" he asked.

"I beg your pardon?"

"I know you need this job, Aggie, and I know you're a hard worker. I'm asking if having you continue to work at Sullivan's is going to be an issue. I don't need my drovers being distracted and injured because you're working here."

She stared at him, slack jawed. He made it sound like this was her fault.

"I didn't do anything to draw attention to myself. I do my job and work hard. Ross wouldn't be injured if he hadn't..." She let out a small sob. "...if he hadn't attacked me. I wasn't looking for attention. I'm just here to help my family."

Mr. Sullivan looked at her sadly. "I know, Aggie. I see you doing your job and keeping your head down. But boys will be boys, they're going to make advances. You need to be better at avoiding their attention. I hope we won't need to have another conversation like this again."

With that, he left the kitchen. Aggie stood there with the knife in her hand hanging limply by her side. She had been washing the dishes, Ross forced himself on her, and Mr. Sullivan thought it was her responsibility to keep something like that from happening again or she would lose her job. She could not believe this was her fault.

When Chester collected her from the Sullivan's that Thursday night, she said nothing to him about what had happened. She didn't tell anyone from her family. Embarrassed and ashamed, she didn't want to cause any more trouble. If her brothers found out, they would go after Ross and likely get her fired. So, she said nothing.

That Sunday, as she packed her things to return to work, she left all her work dresses behind. She brought the work trousers that she wore around the homestead and a few of Chester's old work shirts that were so oversized on her she looked like she was wearing a feed sack. Mrs. Sullivan and Cook were not pleased with her new choice of wardrobe for working in the kitchen. When Mr. Sullivan saw her, he nodded solemnly and told his wife and Cook that she looked fine and these clothes were more practical.

Ross never touched her again. The incidents with other drovers trying to pinch her bottom or get her alone stopped as well, whether because she dressed like a boy or because they knew about the incident with the knife, she never knew. She was just happy their unwanted attention had diminished.

She had been so glad when she no longer had to work at Sullivan's. Moving away from those people and memories had been good for her as well. As much as she was enjoying her time with her family, being back at the homestead, the sights and sounds of the cattle and horses, brought back those terrible memories.

As neighbors arrived for the celebration, Aggie was glad that Henry never left her side. Several times her brothers had attempted to call him over to join a conversation with some of the other men, but he either brought Aggie with him into the conversation or demurred, stating that he wanted to stick close to his bride. He endured some good-natured ribbing from her brothers about being wrapped around her little finger, but Henry just laughed and waved them off.

When the truck arrived carrying the people from Sullivan's, Aggie felt herself tense. Mrs. Sullivan hurried over to congratulate her.

"Oh, Aggie, don't you look grown up! And your American pilot! So handsome. With that American accent, he sounds like a movie star!" Mrs. Sullivan was gushing.

"That's enough, dear," Mr. Sullivan said. He reached out to shake Aggie's hand. "Congratulations on your wedding, Aggie. We wish you well. We're glad you found yourself such a nice young man."

"I'm the lucky one," said Henry, introducing himself to the Sullivans. Aggie squeezed his hand in thanks.

Cook was next to greet them. "You look so pretty in that skirt and blouse. No wonder you captured this young fellow's heart. It's nice to see you dressed like a girl, Aggie, not some ragamuffin little boy."

Aggie ground out her thanks through gritted teeth.

Chester came over to chat with Mr. Sullivan about the latest issues in the cattle industry and Mrs. Sullivan joined Lily and Mary in admiring the littlest Ryans as the children raced around the door yard through the crowd of milling neighbors and friends. Joe and Casey came over with the pilot who had flown the green biplane all those years ago to talk aviation with Henry.

For a moment, Aggie stood alone.

"What have we here?"

Aggie heard the deep, familiar voice and tried to suppress a shudder. She turned to face Ross and his gang of minions, the four or five men who had most frequently tried to make advances. This group of men made her time at the cattle station kitchen awful. She recognized that now as she looked back.

"All grown up and looking like a woman," Ross observed with a sneer. "Not dressing like a boy anymore."

The other men laughed. Ross moved closer, towering over her.

"I heard you've been working for the RAAF and the US Navy. Another job where you're surrounded by men, huh? Are you still a tease? Or have you finally started putting out? Is that how you trapped this American pilot?"

The men circled around her and Aggie crossed her arms over her chest in defense. She held her head high and her back straight. Why did these men have to be here to spoil the day?

Suddenly, Henry was beside her, pulling her close to his side with his arm around her shoulder.

"Hiya, fellas," he greeted them, but she saw the menacing gleam in his blue eyes. "Joe and Casey mentioned you all used to work at that ranch with Aggie when she was a kid."

A few of the men backed off, but Ross stepped forward toward Henry. He was larger than Henry, but her husband stood tall and strong, not intimidated by the Aussie.

"Yeah, we knew her really well back then," Ross smirked. He looked at his buddies with a raised eyebrow and a knowing look. Aggie wished she had done more damage with that paring knife.

"Oh," Henry said. "So, you knew she was working there to support her brothers and sisters here at home? That every penny she earned went to them? That's good. You knew her well enough to know she was a good girl who was trying to help her family, right?"

To Aggie's amazement, Ross started to shrink a little.

"I've got to be the luckiest guy on the planet to have convinced Aggie to marry me. She's an absolute gem. The best and kindest girl I could ever hope to have met. Imagine finding her halfway around the world from my hometown of Chicago. You fellas have heard of Chicago, right?"

Ross gulped.

"Ah, sure, Chicago. Al Capone, right?"

"That's right!" Henry agreed enthusiastically. "Never met the man personally, but he was a legend. My gang? Not so established. But we know how to take care of business when needed. That's the Chicago way."

He looked Ross straight in the eye.

"Do I need to send Porky, Curly, and Skinny to take care of you?"

Ross paled visibly, and Aggie did her best not to giggle. She knew Henry hated when Al Capone was the first thing people mentioned when he said he was from Chicago, yet there he was, continuing the myth to scare off her nemesis from Sullivan's. He had told her about his 'gang,' a bunch of kids from his old neighborhood getting into mischief. Certainly nothing like the Chicago Mob.

Henry took a step closer to Ross, who took a step backward.

"We won't need to talk again for the rest of the day, will we?"

"No, sir," Ross replied.

"And you will not speak to Aggie ever again, right?"

"No, sir."

Henry gave him a wolfish smile. "Good. I'm glad we understand each other. Now, go enjoy the party somewhere else."

Ross and his friends scurried away. Aggie leaned into Henry's side with a sigh of relief. She wrapped her arms around him and gave him a kiss on the cheek.

"I love you."

He looked down at her with a smile. "Always here to slay your dragons."

"I'll say! Thank you. Thank you for looking out for me."

"Last night, you said you were dreading seeing some folks from the other ranch. I wanted to be sure I could help you if you needed it. And really, Aggie, I would say 'not pleasant' is the understatement of the century with that guy. What an ass."

She barked a laugh. "You have no idea."

"Do you want to tell me about it?"

"Not now. Someday, but not today. I don't want to spoil our wedding reception."

"Then let's go enjoy ourselves. I believe I've banished the dragon."

He took her hand and kissed her knuckles. Together, they made their way through the party, chatting with neighbors and family, enjoying their time together.

Chapter Twenty-Six

May 1945
Northern Territories, Australia

HENRY FOUND AGGIE SITTING on the porch, looking out toward the last of the light on the western horizon. There was a thin line of fiery red limning the distant hills as the sky darkened and the stars appeared in the heavens.

It had been quite a day. He felt like he understood Aggie better now, having seen her in this place that had shaped her. There was the good; her fierce love for her family, who had fed her interest in being mechanical and let her use those gifts. This place fostered such a strong work ethic. And there was the bad; working on the Sullivan's ranch, away from the family she loved. The men who had hurt her while she was trying to help her family.

He sat beside her on the porch steps and took her hand, looking out to the horizon with her. She had been happy and chatty today once the incident with Ross ended. Aggie caught up with neighbors she had not seen since she left to work for the WAAAF. He wondered if she was rethinking her decision to marry him and leave this place.

"Any regrets?" he asked quietly.

"I shouldn't have had that second piece of cake," she moaned. "I was so full from the barbecue, but Cook's cakes are so delicious. She must have used three months of sugar rations to make it. I couldn't say no when she offered me the last piece, even though I'd already had some. I'm stuffed!"

Henry chuckled. The cake was pretty spectacular.

"That's not what I meant."

"I know," she said quietly.

"Chicago is nothing like this. Really, NOTHING like this. We have parks along the lakefront. And the county was smart enough to create forest preserves around the city so people can go somewhere green with trees and see what the place looked like before they built up the city. But there aren't wide-open spaces like this. Are you going to miss it?"

"No," she said firmly. He looked at her in surprise; she sounded so certain.

"I will miss my family very much, but I will not miss this place. Life here is so hard, Henry. Even before my mum died and Da left us, it was always a struggle. We had each other, which was wonderful, but everything was so hard."

He looked at her silently, waiting for her to continue.

"I'm not afraid of hard work, Henry, you know that. I don't expect our lives to be free of struggle, but I want to be happy. For the past few days, I have been thinking about the last time I was happy when I lived here without constant worry, niggling at the back of my mind. The last time I remember being truly happy was the day we saw the biplane. That's a long time to not be truly happy."

He put his arm around her shoulders and pulled her in for a kiss.

"I will do my best to make you happy."

"I know, darling. You already do."

She kissed him back and then continued, "I think my life has gotten bigger than this place. I don't know that I ever pictured myself as a wife at home on the homestead, raising kids, gardening, and keeping house. After going to Sydney and seeing that there is a wider world that doesn't confine me to the life of a cattle station wife, I don't think I could live that life. I've met people from all over the country and all over the world. Meeting brilliant women like Betty, who's such a wiz with radios, and Jackie, who is studying engineering, I never knew women could do those things when I was living here. I never knew what I could dream of being. Now, I do. And I don't want to come back."

Henry felt the tension leave his shoulders at her words. He realized now that he secretly feared her time with her family would make her change her mind about marrying him.

"So, to answer your question, no, I have no regrets. Well, that's not true. I have one regret."

Henry braced himself. "What's that?"

"I regret that I won't be on that plane with you on Friday. That we won't be going back to the United States together."

He pulled her into his arms and kissed her.

"Me too, sweetheart. I wish you were coming with me. Sadly, I don't think I can smuggle you in my seabag."

They sat together on the porch as the stars filled the sky above them. They listened to the sounds of the house settling down for the evening; Lily putting away the last of the dishes from the party, Chester reading a story to the children, Edith reciting her vocabulary words at the kitchen table as she finished her homework.

Once the house grew quiet, they tiptoed to the bed they shared and quietly made love, knowing they would not have many more chances before he had to leave.

AGGIE HANDED HER SUITCASE to Henry to take out to the car. He touched her hand as he took it from her, then leaned forward to kiss her cheek.

"I'll wait for you outside," he murmured in her ear.

She gave him a small smile as he walked from the room and out of the house. Standing in her former bedroom, she turned in a circle, taking in the small room she'd shared with Mary and Edith for so many years. She knew Edith would be happy to have the room back once Henry and Aggie were gone. Aggie laughed to herself, thinking how luxurious it would have been to have her own bed at 14, much less an entire room to herself. She picked up her handbag and hat and walked out of the room for the last time.

The family gathered in the dooryard, waiting to say goodbye. There were hugs all around, laughing and joking. Before they got in the car, Mary asked for the attention of the crowd.

"We didn't want to say anything earlier and steal the spotlight from Aggie and Henry, but since everyone is together, we wanted to let you know that Louis and I are expecting again."

There were more hugs and congratulations. Aggie was happy for Mary and Louis; Mary had always wanted a home and family and to stay close to the land. She nodded to herself, knowing she was making the right decision. While she would always love her family and might miss Australia once she left, Henry was her home now. She knew if she returned to the Ryan's family homestead in the future, it would only be as a visitor.

Henry was checking his watch again, a sure sign they needed to get going. She made a final round of hugs and kisses with her siblings, nieces, and nephew and then let Henry help her into the car. Chester climbed behind the wheel, and they waved to the family as they drove away.

Chester and Henry chatted in the front seat as she watched the scenery pass by on the way back to Birdum. Aggie mentally said goodbye to the red earth and spreading blue sky.

"You're quiet back there, Aggie," her brother said.

"Just taking it all in. It's been quite a trip."

After they found a parking spot in front of the train station, Henry got out of the car to arrange their tickets and Chester turned around to face her.

"It's okay, Aggie. I know you won't be coming back."

"Of course, I'll come back."

"But not to stay," he clarified. "And that's okay. You were never meant for this life. You were always supposed to fly."

Tears welled up in her eyes as her big brother reached over the seat to take her hand.

"The boys always used to tease you about that time we saw the airplane. You talked about it non-stop, long after the rest of us would have forgotten about it. I knew you'd find a different life, Aggie. You put everything aside for us for a long time. I'm so glad you finally got your chance with the WAAAFs, and now with Henry. He's a good man and seems like he loves you an awful lot."

"He does," she sobbed. "I love him, too."

"You make a good team. That's half the battle in marriage. Having a good teammate to help shoulder the struggles and share the triumphs. We'll miss you, Aggie, but don't worry about us. Make a wonderful life in America."

She leaned forward to hug her brother. "Thank you, Chester. Thank you for everything."

She climbed out of the car and met Henry at the steps of the station. Chester waved as he backed out and drove away.

"You doing okay?" Henry asked. "You're kind of dripping there." He handed her his handkerchief.

"I'm fine," she said with a watery laugh. "Just saying goodbye to my big brother. He knows I won't be coming back to stay."

"Nope, you'll be coming home with me."

He threw his arm around her shoulder and led her up the station steps to the platform.

"By the way, I splurged on a sleeper compartment for us on the train."

"A sleeper compartment? But it's 9 o'clock in the morning, the train ride is eight hours. We'll be in Darwin before we even need a bed."

"That's what *you* think," he said with a cheeky wink and led her aboard the train.

UPON THEIR ARRIVAL, they returned to the Hotel Darwin, where they would spend the last night of their honeymoon. They met Conor and Katie in the Green Room for a leisurely supper and took a stroll along the Esplanade, looking at the boats in the harbor. The war seemed very far away.

They speculated about the future, such as where they would live when she came to America. Henry thought they might need to live with his mum for a while until they saved some money for a place of their own. Aggie thought that would be equal parts lovely – getting to know Henry's mum – and awkward, sharing a home with your mother-in-law after an extended separation.

Henry was also thinking ahead to what he might do for work one the war was over and he was no longer in the Navy.

"I still love flying and would like it even more if I wasn't dropping bombs on people while doing it. I'd like to keep flying if I can. When I was at Lewis, before the war started, they talked about the need for pilots for all kinds of flying, passenger planes, hauling mail and packages, crop dusting. What do you think?"

"Can you make a living flying like that?"

"I would think so. It's a pretty specific skill. Not everyone knows how to do it." He shrugged. "I guess I have plenty of time to figure it out. Who knows how much longer the Navy will need me? What do you think you will want to do after the war?"

"You mean for work?"

"Sure. Do you want to keep working on planes? Or try something else?"

"Do you think anyone will let me work on planes after the war ends?"

She felt certain that when the extraordinary needs of the war were at an end, most folks wouldn't want women repairing their airplanes.

"I don't see why not. You and Bill Lago are the best aviation mechanics I've ever seen."

She raised up on her toes to kiss him. Dear Henry, he had such faith in her.

When they returned to their hotel room, Henry pulled a stack of papers out of his bag.

"I know this isn't the most romantic way to spend our last night together, but I've been meaning to give these to you. These are copies of all my Navy paperwork. You already have a copy of our marriage certificate. You need to contact the US Consulate to start your paperwork to come to America. Unfortunately, there isn't a consulate in Darwin, but you can start writing."

He paused, a serious look on his face. "I also updated my Navy insurance policy. If something happens to me, you get half of the $10,000, Ma gets the other half. I wanted to be sure you would be okay."

Aggie felt like her stomach dropped to her feet. She sat down heavily on the bed. Henry dropped the papers and sat next to her.

"Nothing is likely to happen. We'll steam from Ulithi to Pearl, then onto Seattle. The Japanese are too busy protecting the home islands, they won't come after our busted-up carrier. I only wanted to be cautious."

She looked at him, stricken. "Oh, Henry, you really are leaving tomorrow!"

The past week had been like a dream. The surprise arrival, planning a wedding, getting married, traveling to see her family. It seemed impossible that a week ago she hadn't known if he was alive or dead. Now they were married and talking about life insurance policies.

"I know, sweetheart. I wish I could take you with me. But Admiral Nimitz is pretty strict about not having wives aboard aircraft carriers."

He squeezed her hands and gave her a little wink to show he was teasing.

"I wanted to be sure you had this paperwork so you can start working on getting to the US while you're here in Australia, while I work on getting you home on my end. The sooner we tackle this, the sooner we'll be back together."

She nodded in agreement. They reviewed the paperwork and the information Henry received from the chaplain until they felt certain they both knew the process to follow for Aggie to join him in the States.

Setting the papers aside, Henry pulled Aggie into his lap. They kissed passionately, Henry tracing soft kisses down her neck.

"What do you say you put on that pink number from our wedding night, for old time's sake?"

"Old time's sake?" she giggled. "That was three days ago."

"Well, I'd like to make as many memories as I can before my flight tomorrow morning."

"Wait right there," she said as she grabbed the pink nightgown and dashed into the bathroom.

IN THE MORNING, THEY woke in the pearl light of dawn and made love one more time.

Henry packed his bag and donned his khakis once again. They met Conor and Katie in the hotel lobby for a quiet breakfast. No one had very much to say. Henry kept running over a checklist in his mind, making sure he had discussed everything with Aggie and that she had all the paperwork she needed to show they were married, and she was eligible to emigrate to the US.

Henry and Aggie took a cab to the WAAAF barracks to drop off her things. The other women swarmed them, asking about their honeymoon. Aggie put on a brave face, telling them about their trip home to see her family, but he could tell she was sad and dreading their separation as much as he was.

Sergeant Maguire gave Aggie permission to drive Henry to the pier to catch the Catalina back to Ulithi. Henry thought the sergeant was all bark and no bite with the young ladies under his command. Henry heard Betty call him a softie, and he had to agree. Sergeant Maguire was a big teddy bear when it came to his girls.

It was a quiet drive to the pier. Henry was going to miss Aggie so much he couldn't put it into words, and even if he could, anything he would say would probably make them both cry. So, he kept his lips zipped.

Conor and Katie had arrived in a cab and the women discussed driving back to the base together in the jeep. Conor and Katie wandered away for a final, private goodbye.

Henry pulled Aggie into his arms and held her tight, savoring the feeling of her body pressed up against his. They fit together so well, her head tucked under his chin, her curves molding to his solid planes. He buried his nose in her hair, taking in the scent of her soap and shampoo, trying to lock the memory of her in his mind.

She looked up at him and he stared deeply into her eyes. He raised a hand and rested his palm against her cheek, tracing her eyebrows, cheeks, the straight line of her nose with his thumb. He bent to kiss her, wanting to taste her for a last time. They clung to each other, whispering "I love you" again and again into the other's ear.

There was the sound of someone clearing his throat behind them. They broke apart, and Henry turned to see the RAAF pilot standing there, looking sheepish.

"I hate to do this to you, mate, but we're about to cast off lines. We need to get you and your buddy aboard if you want that ride back to Ulithi."

Conor was leading Katie over to Aggie. Henry pulled her into a last embrace and kissed her again.

"I love you. More than anything."

Aggie nodded, blinking back her tears. "I love you, too."

"We'll be together as soon as we can. I promise."

With one more kiss, he turned and boarded the Catalina with Conor. He looked out the window to see the two women holding hands and wiping their eyes with handkerchiefs. Henry watched Aggie on the pier as long as he could, as the plane taxied out into the harbor for take-off then rose into the sky.

Chapter Twenty-Seven

May 1945-March 1946

MAY 1945

  Ulithi Atoll

  My Darling Aggie,

  Conor and I made it back to Ulithi with two days to spare! Not AWOL, so no troubles. Kowalski is still giving us plenty of grief that we "cut it too fine," but spending last week with you was more than worth any ribbing he doles out.

  I took Jeff Berek out for a beer at the O Club tonight. He's being reassigned here in the Pacific, so I wanted to take a chance to wish him well and good luck before we ship out. While we were at the club, the band was playing Moonlight Serenade, and I thought of dancing with you when you surprised me by being at Ulithi.

  I miss you so much, my Aggie. Really wish I had smuggled you aboard the Enterprise in my seabag. I'm counting the days until we can be together again. Be sure to write to the American Consulate to work on transportation to the States. I already sent a letter before we set off back to Hawaii. Hope we will be together soon.

  I love you very much,

  Henry

JUNE 1945

Waikiki, Hawaii

Dearest Aggie,

We arrived at Pearl Harbor without incident. I told you the Japanese would be too busy to mess with our battered aircraft carrier.

We received a heroes' welcome upon returning to Pearl. The Navy housed the whole ship's crew at the Royal Hawaiian on Waikiki, and it was a raucous night of celebration, I can tell you! There's a reason for the term "drunken sailor." Boy, the Shore Patrol was busy all night.

Conor and I passed on the drunken hijinks. We went out for our traditional steak dinner with Perry and Kowalski. They are both remaining in Hawaii to train the newest air group that just arrived. Perry mentioned he has plans to continue surfing while he's stationed here in Hawaii. Heaven knows, he can only get better. Remember how dreadful he was in Sydney?

Missing you terribly, my Aggie. I love you so much. I cannot wait to be together again.

I love you,

Henry

⎯⎯⎯⎯⎯⎯ ⟳ ⎯⎯⎯⎯⎯⎯

JUNE 1945

Bremerton, Washington

Sweet Aggie,

Back in the good old US of A! We arrived at Bremerton and the Puget Sound Naval Shipyard for our final stop and time for major repairs to the Big E.

When we arrived at Puget Sound, we hoisted a gigantic 578-foot pennant; one foot for every day since we left Bremerton in 1943. It's hard to believe I haven't been back on American soil in that long. Good to be back home in the US, but I'm missing you like crazy.

We have a few days here in Seattle before we board the Empire Builder back to Chicago. (That's the train that runs from Chicago to Seattle and back.) The train makes a stop in Minneapolis, so we're going to try to catch up with Sven as we pass through. It would be great to see him.

I hope you have been writing the US Consulate, Aggie. I made a stop at the Navy administrative offices as soon as we arrived at the base to see if there was anything the Navy could do to get you here to the States as soon as possible. It seems like they will not be moving anyone until hostilities have ended in the Pacific. One more reason to hope for a quick end to this war. I think we should keep trying. Maybe we can convince someone to change their mind.

I love you, Aggie. Thinking and dreaming of you all the time.
Love,
Henry

JUNE 1945
Darwin, Australia
My dearest Henry,
Received your letter and postcard from Waikiki. I'm so glad you arrived safely. The picture on the postcard was beautiful. Maybe someday we could go there together after the war is over.

I am enclosing several photographs from our wedding and honeymoon. Remember my brother Casey had his Kodak Brownie with him? He did a good job with the photos, don't you think? My favorite is the picture of the two of us standing on the steps of the church; I'm looking straight ahead at the camera with a wide, happy smile and you're looking at me with an equally happy smile. There's another photo from our honeymoon of us sitting on the porch steps back home, holding hands and my head resting on your shoulder. I don't remember Casey taking the picture, but I love it!

I have written to the American Consulate twice a week since you've gone. They have told me there will be no movement of foreign national spouses until "hostilities in the Pacific Theater have ceased." I will continue to write to them, anyway. Perhaps they will make an exception if I nag them enough. I'm very good at being persistent.

In exciting news here at the WAAAF squadron, Betty and Sergeant Maguire have eloped! Nobody saw that coming! They have been sniping at each other since the day we arrived in Sydney. I'm sure there's quite a story there.

Thinking of you day and night. I love you so much, darling.
All my love,
Aggie

— ❦ —

JULY 1945
> *Glenview, Illinois*
> *Darling Aggie,*
> *A month into my new assignment as a flight instructor and I find I'm enjoying my new position very much. Some of these kids are so young and green, though. I can't picture them battling in the Pacific. I imagine that's how Kowalski felt when he saw Conor and I that first day on the Enterprise.*
>
> *Ma is enjoying having me close by. I'm able to head home for Sunday dinner with her and she sends me back with enough leftovers to feed the entire air station! I brought Conor with me last Sunday and nearly had to roll him into the streetcar he'd eaten so many pierogies. Those are little Polish dumplings. My Ma's the best cook! Next Sunday I'll be going to have Sunday dinner with the McLeans.*
>
> *When I'm not flying, instructing, or stuffing myself with Ma's leftovers, I'm nagging the Navy to get you to the States. I'm writing letters at least twice a week. I know they say nothing can happen until the Japanese surrender, but who knows how long that will take?*

I will continue writing and wishing you were with me every day.
I love you,
Henry

AUGUST 14, 1945
Glenview, Illinois
My dearest Aggie,
I can't believe the war is over. The Japanese have surrendered and the war is over!

Everyone here is shocked and stunned and excited. It's been a long and costly four years with so many lost, but now it's over and we can try to rebuild our lives.

Conor and I have been discussing the devastating effect of the atomic bombs dropped on Japan. I dropped a lot of bombs in my time in the Pacific, usually on enemy ships and bases, but I can't imagine the power of those weapons. Conor wonders about the long-term effect they will have on the future of war. Mostly, though, our greatest feeling is one of relief that our boys don't have to face an invasion of Japan. Relief that the war is over, people can stop dying, and our wives can join us in the US.

I will redouble my efforts to get you here. I can't wait to see your smiling face next to me every day when I wake up. I love you, my darling Aggie, and miss you so much. Now that the war has ended, I want you beside me.

I love you,
Henry

AUGUST 14, 1945
Darwin, Australia
Darling Henry,

Can you believe the news? The war has ended!

I am so grateful and relieved. Now I can't wait to join you in America. I will start writing to the American Consulate every day to work on finding passage to the US.

We were discussing the atomic bombs in the mess hall. Jackie did her best to explain how she thought they might work, based on her understanding of physics and engineering. Most of it sailed right over my head. From the news, the effect of the bombs was such terrible devastation. Katie wondered if the Japanese had been working on such a weapon and if they might have used it in Australia. It's too horrible to contemplate.

Everyone is so relieved the war has ended and we can return to peace.

I'm glad you're enjoying your new flight instructor position. I knew you would be a good teacher. Remember, you taught me how to fly!

I love you, dearest Henry. I hope to be with you soon.

Your loving wife,

Aggie

SEPTEMBER 1945

Glenview, Illinois

Dearest Aggie,

Life at Glenview is oddly unchanged since the end of the war. We're still training the new pilots, though there is a decreased sense of urgency in the training. I think that has helped the safety and quality of the trainees flying, to be honest. They aren't pushing themselves to prove something so they can get into the war faster.

Bill Lago is back in Chicago. Conor and I met up with him for a Cubs game at Wrigley Field. It was a great day, even if the Cubs lost. Bill's mother fed us a gigantic Italian dinner after the game. I once again had to roll an overstuffed Conor onto the train back to Glenview.

I guess this is my new normal. Teaching kids to fly, overeating with Conor, and waiting for you to get passage to the States. I can't wait to see you, Aggie. There's so much I want to show you. And I just want to be together. I miss you so much.

I love you,

Henry

SEPTEMBER 1945

Ryan Homestead, NT

My darling Henry,

The WAAAFs are undergoing some changes. With so many men returning to Australia now that the fighting is over, the RAAF is looking to return them to their jobs, which means fewer positions for us women.

Some of the women who are married are leaving. Katie is heading back to Alice Springs to complete her training at the teachers's college. She wants to complete all her certifications before she moves to America. She and Conor are hoping she can work as a teacher in the US. Betty and Sergeant Maguire have moved to his newest posting near her family in Melbourne.

Jackie is returning to Perth to finish her engineering degree. She has a longtime friend, Elizabeth, and they plan to rent a house together as they finish their coursework. They're talking about setting up their own engineering firm when they are finished. Imagine that!

As for me, I wasn't entirely wrong when I questioned whether anyone would want a woman fixing their planes after the war. I looked around for a civilian position as an aircraft mechanic, but no one wanted to hire a woman. I was told the men coming home from the war needed these positions so they could support themselves and their families. As if I don't need to support myself also.

So, I will be staying in the WAAAFs for now. I was able to secure a part-time position at the RAAF air base in Larrimah, not far from our station. Remember we passed through Larrimah on our train trip from Darwin? It seems no RAAF mechanics wanted a position in such a remote location. I work at the air base Monday through Thursday, so I'm back to staying at the home place Friday through Saturday and returning on the train Monday morning. Edith and I are back to sharing a room when I'm at home, which doesn't make either of us very happy.

It's eerily reminiscent of my time working at the Sullivan's; working away from home part of the week and then coming home and keeping all of Chester's equipment working on the weekends. I thought I had moved past all that when I joined the WAAAFs and then got married!

I continue to write the American Consulate daily, trying to find passage to the US now that the war is over. They get almost as many letters from me as you do!

I miss you, my darling, and can't wait to be together. I love you so very much.

Your loving wife,

Aggie

OCTOBER 1945

Glenview, Illinois

Dearest Aggie,

Big news and I need your opinion. I received a letter from the Navy. I'm at the end of my commitment and they are giving me the option to resign my commission and return to civilian life or I can continue my career with the Navy.

Staying in the Navy means security and could help us find a way to get you to the States faster. If I resign my commission, I could probably find a civilian flying job, but it's less certain.

Ma has threatened to punch me in the head if I stay in the Navy. She said (and this is a direct quote), "No more flying planes off boats! You need to get a real job." Well, that's me told! Ha ha.

What are your thoughts, my darling? We are in this together. I don't want to make any big decisions about our future without your input.

I love you,
Henry

⸻ ❦ ⸻

TELEGRAM FROM AGGIE BOLANSKI, BIRDUM, AUSTRALIA <STOP>

OCTOBER 25 1945 <STOP>

DEAREST HENRY <STOP>

IF YOU AGREE TO STAY IN THE NAVY, YOUR MOTHER WILL HAVE TO STAND IN LINE BEHIND ME TO PUNCH YOU IN THE HEAD <STOP>

YOUR LOVING WIFE, AGGIE <STOP>

⸻ ❦ ⸻

NOVEMBER 1945
Chicago, Illinois
Darling Aggie,
Received your telegram. It seems the women in my life have made the decision that I will not be remaining in the Navy. Ha ha.

I've resigned my commission and moved back home with Ma. She's delighted to have me home and I will soon need to have all my trousers let out because she is feeding me like nobody's business!

On the work front, I'm casting around to see what I will do next. I received an invitation from the alumni group at Lewis for a 'Career Day' for former aviation students to discuss job opportunities in the aviation industry. Can you imagine? People seeking me out for jobs?

Who would have thought that would ever happen back in the Depression?

I asked Conor to go with me. I know he loves flying. He's attending classes at Loyola and thinks he could finish his history degree by spring, then get a job as a history teacher or professor at a small college. I told him he should come with me anyway. Maybe pilots would make more money than history professors.

I will let you know if anything comes of it. I'm still writing the US State Department and Australian embassy nearly every day to find a way to get you to Chicago. I miss you so much, my Aggie.

I love you,

Henry

—⇛—

DECEMBER 1945

Chicago, Illinois

My darling wife, Aggie,

Your husband is a newly minted pilot for American Airlines!

After the Career Day at Lewis, I had interviews with several airlines. They were impressed with my flying record with the Navy and especially liked my experience as a flight instructor. I think they thought someone who was trusted to train other pilots must be pretty safe! They offered Conor a position as well. It turns out pilots do make more money than history professors!

I had a few job offers, but took the position with American because they assured me I would fly out of the new O'Hare Field (named for legendary US Navy aviator and Medal of Honor recipient Butch O'Hare) just outside of Chicago. I can still live with Ma and take the bus out to the airfield for work. I was hoping if I worked for the airline, I could somehow get you to the States on a flight because they just started trans-Atlantic flights, so perhaps Pacific flights won't be far behind. So far, no luck.

I'm earning my type rating on the DC-3. It's very different from the Dauntless, needless to say! No breathtaking dives with a plane full of passengers. I'm enjoying the change, though. Enjoying being up in the blue over puffy cotton clouds without looking for an enemy or dropping bombs on people. We'll have to take you on another flight when you get here.

Hope you will be coming soon. I miss you so much, Aggie. It's been six months since we parted on that pier in Darwin. I long to hold you again. Sad that we won't be spending our first Christmas together.

I love you,

Henry

JANUARY 1946

Ryan Homestead, NT

Dearest Henry,

I have wonderful news!

The US Consulate notified me I'm selected for passage on the SS Lurline, the first ship carrying Australian war brides to the US! Can you believe it? Finally, I will be traveling to America and back to you! The ship sails from Brisbane on March first.

I had to laugh when I received the letter from the Consulate. They concluded the letter with their hope this arrangement would be satisfactory and to cease my constant inquiries regarding passage to the US. Ha! Sometimes the squeaky wheel gets the grease.

Oh, Henry! I'm so excited. Today Katie called, and she's been selected for passage on the Lurline as well, so I will have a travelling companion. We are writing the ship's company to request that we share a cabin for the voyage.

It's finally happening! Finally, I'm going to America. I'm so excited and happy that I will be seeing you again. I do feel sad for my family. Here I was, on top of the world with the news, and I could see that they were sad that I'd be leaving. It's a bittersweet moment, leaving my family so I can travel to my new family.

Oh, my darling! I can't wait to see you and have you hold me in your arms again. I miss you so much, but now there is light at the end of the tunnel.

Counting the days until I see you!

I love you,

Aggie

FEBRUARY 1946

> *Chicago, Illinois*
>
> *My dearest Aggie,*
>
> *One month until you depart for the States! I can't wait to see you. Ma is looking forward to meeting you so much.*
>
> *I won't be able to meet you when the ship arrives in San Francisco. Couldn't get the time away from the airlines since I've only been working there for a few months. So sorry, darling! Conor cannot make the trip either, he has midterms that week.*
>
> *We made arrangements with the Red Cross for you and Katie. Your hotel in San Francisco and your train tickets to Chicago are paid for. We were told you should find the Red Cross kiosk at the ship terminal, and they will provide you with everything we arranged. Conor and I are so glad you girls are traveling together and can look out for each other.*
>
> *I can't believe you're nearly here! I can't wait to see you again.*
>
> *Love you so much,*
>
> *Henry*

1 MARCH 1946

> *Brisbane, Australia*
>
> *My Darling Henry,*

I will drop this letter in the post box just before I board the ship to America. It will be a race to see which of us gets to you first!

It was a tearful goodbye when the family dropped me off at the train in Birdum. So different from when I left for the WAAAF, because they do not know when or if I will ever return. I will miss them very much, but you are my home now. I'm looking forward to building our life together.

Katie and I met in Brisbane on 27 February to have a day to finish any last preparations for the journey. There are so many women here who will be on the ship with us. And so many of them have babies! Leaving Australia and crossing the ocean will be hard enough; I can't imagine doing it with a baby in tow. I'm honestly a little relieved that I didn't get pregnant during our honeymoon.

Katie and I are looking forward to the journey. There will be all kinds of activities aboard the ship to keep us entertained; there are craft classes, concerts, movies. Even lectures on fitting into life in America. We plan to make the most of our time at sea.

I'm so anxious to see you and a little nervous. I hope I live up to your memories of me.

I love you, Henry. Just a little longer until we are together.
Your loving wife,
Aggie

Chapter Twenty-Eight

March 1946
Chicago, Illinois

AGGIE WAS NERVOUSLY pacing the compartment she shared with Katie on the train.

"Please sit down," Katie begged. "I'm getting dizzy watching you go 'round and 'round."

"Sorry."

Aggie flopped down beside her friend on the bench in their compartment. Katie began nervously drumming her fingers on the seat between them.

"Drumming again," Aggie said morosely.

"Sorry."

Aggie looked out the window as the train slowed to pull into Union Station in Chicago. The buildings surrounding the train tracks were so tall, much taller than even the buildings in Sydney. Henry had told her that Chicago was the birthplace of the skyscraper, so she supposed that made sense.

Aggie was nervous as the train rolled into the station. She thought back to when the ship pulled into San Francisco and the women aboard became quiet, worrying about what life would be like in their new adoptive country. Some had not really considered what it would be like to leave Australia. Now they were disembarking in a foreign land where they would know only a husband they may not have seen in months or years. Several women did not recognize their husbands when out of uniform. For two unhappy brides, their husbands did not appear to meet them.

Aggie and Katie knew their husbands couldn't make the trip to meet the ship in San Francisco. They stood in line at the Red Cross kiosk for their travel information. Henry and Conor had made all the arrangements and paid for the tickets and told the women the Red Cross would have their paperwork when they arrived in San Francisco. Stepping to the front of the line, Aggie smiled at the Red Cross lady behind the table.

"G'day. I'm Agnes Bolanski and this is my friend Catherine McLean. Our husbands have arranged for our trip to Chicago. We were told to come here to collect our tickets."

Aggie spoke slowly and carefully to the woman behind the table. She had noticed that some Americans struggled with her broad Australian accent.

The woman looked carefully through her files.

"Yes, here you are, Mrs. Bolanski. Let me find Mrs. McLean."

She paused, reaching for another accordion file.

"Here we go," she said cheerfully. She held out two envelopes with the women's names on them. "We have a hotel room booked near the train station and first-class tickets with a sleeping compartment on the California Zephyr, with an ending destination in Chicago. Does that sound correct?"

Aggie breathed a sigh of relief. After seeing a couple of brides abandoned at the pier, part of her had been fearing that Henry would have changed his mind, leaving her stranded in America. Now she knew for certain that Henry was waiting for her in Chicago. She smiled at the Red Cross lady.

"That's correct. Thank you so much for your help."

"Wonderful," the Red Cross lady looked down at her clipboard and ticked a few boxes on a form. "Please take this and follow the signs to the taxi stand. This voucher will cover your taxi to the hotel. Any other travel while in town will be made at your own expense."

Aggie took the proffered slip of paper.

"Thank you again," she said politely.

"My pleasure. Welcome to America," the Red Cross lady said before turning to help the next woman in line.

Aggie and Katie found their way through the crowd to the taxis and went straight to the hotel. They located the train station just down the street and then went to check in. They stayed at the hotel until it was time to get on the train, to avoid getting lost or having to deal with American money.

They spent the next three days marveling from the train window at the vast space of America and how varied the landscape was as they rolled through the heart of the country. Now, the train was slowing, pulling into the station, and she would see Henry in a matter of minutes.

She turned to look in the small mirror in their compartment. Aggie smoothed her hair and adjusted her hat atop her curls. She straightened her suit jacket and turned to Katie.

"How do I look?"

"You look lovely. Just like I told you the last three times you asked," Katie replied, then looked up at Aggie sheepishly. "How do I look?"

Aggie broke into a smile. "You look perfect. Conor won't know what hit him."

The women shared a hug.

"I'm so glad I had you with me on this trip, Katie. I don't know how I would have done it by myself."

"It was much easier to make this journey with a friend."

The train had pulled to a halt, and an announcement came on over the speakers.

"Chicago, Illinois. Last stop. Chicago."

Last stop, indeed, thought Aggie. She picked up her handbag and light trench coat, looking about the compartment to be sure she was leaving nothing behind. They had arranged for a porter to carry their suitcases off the train and would collect them in the station.

Katie looked over her shoulder at Aggie. Aggie stepped up and took Katie's hand to comfort them both.

"Let's go," she said as confidently as she could.

Time to go see her husband.

HENRY WAS PACING CIRCLES around the benches under the arching skylights of Union Station in Chicago.

"For the love of God, sit down. You're making me even more nervous with the pacing," Conor ground out.

Henry apologized and sat down next to his friend. Conor began drumming his fingers on the bench and bouncing his knee up and down like a jackhammer.

"Quit it with the drumming, Conor. It's driving me crazy."

Henry stood up again and resumed his pacing. He glanced at his watch and then at the clock over the ticket counter. Another ten minutes until the California Zephyr arrived with his wife.

It had been nine months since he had bid farewell to Aggie on that pier in Darwin. Nine months since he had kissed her goodbye.

Now, Aggie's train was arriving in moments and Henry was nervous as could be. Would she still love him? What if she didn't like Chicago? Or worse, what if she didn't get along with Ma? Henry continued pacing.

There was a distant chiming from the overhead system that announced the arrivals and departures of the trains.

"California Zephyr, arriving on Track 3. California Zephyr on Track 3," echoed the announcer's voice through the cavernous space of the station.

Henry and Conor shared a look. Henry took a deep breath and squared his shoulders. He straightened his suit coat and tie, then shot his cuffs. Time to go see his wife.

AS THEY DESCENDED FROM the train, the first thing that hit Aggie was the cold. Good heavens! She let go of Katie's hand and shrugged into her trench coat. It was still freezing. It was March. Wasn't that supposed to be springtime in Chicago?

Katie pulled on her jacket as well, then promptly grabbed Aggie's hand again. Aggie was grateful; she didn't want to be separated from her friend until they located their husbands. They followed the crowd and the sign reading "To Station."

Stepping through the doors from the platform, Aggie marveled at the size and space inside the station. There were huge pillars surrounding the Grand Hall, holding the high arching skylight overhead. There was a sweeping staircase with an intricate coffered ceiling and beautiful hanging light fixtures. Aggie did her best not to gawk, but the space was truly amazing.

Katie tugged her hand. "We're supposed to meet them by the clock."

As the women made their way to the clock at the center of the information desk, she heard someone shouting her name. She whirled around to see Henry racing toward her. She barely had time to take in his breathtaking smile before he barreled into her, sweeping her up in his arms and spinning her in a dizzying circle.

"You're here, you're here! You're finally here," he kept repeating as he held her tight. He paused, setting her on her feet, then took her face in his hands. He kissed her gently, then touched his forehead to hers.

"Oh my, it is so good to see you. I'm so glad you're finally home."

She reached up to touch his cheek as her eyes filled with tears. She was home. Wherever Henry was, that would be her home from now on. Whatever may come, she was with Henry. She was home.

Epilogue

May 1995
Western Caribbean Sea

WHAT A LOVELY WAY TO end the cruise, Henry thought as he stood on the Observation Deck of the ship looking out at the Caribbean sunset. He slid his arm around Aggie's shoulder and she slipped her arm around his waist. How many times had they stood together like this in the past 50 years?

The Bolanski and McLean families had celebrated the joint 50th anniversary of their marriages in style with a Caribbean cruise. All the kids, all the grandkids, everyone. They had done so many things together over the years; it made sense to celebrate this milestone together.

When Aggie first arrived in Chicago, they lived with his ma at her home to give themselves time to get reacquainted and decide what their next steps should be. Henry's worries that Aggie and Ma might not get along were unfounded. He discovered they'd written to each other while Aggie was waiting to come to America, so they knew each other well once Aggie arrived. Henry's status as the favorite child took a drubbing as Ma would take Aggie's side in disagreements, which Henry found most frustrating. Ma treated Aggie like a daughter and Aggie embraced her place in her new family.

Henry continued to work for American Airlines, flying out of O'Hare. After saving for a down payment, he and Aggie bought a home in Edison Park on the city's outskirts. Conor and Katie purchased a home a block away when they moved out of the McLean home. Conor had finished his last semester at Loyola, earning his history degree, but he continued to fly for American Airlines with Henry.

The children began arriving in short order. They named their first-born Ryan, using Aggie's maiden name to honor her family in Australia. In another two years, they welcomed a daughter, Karen. And two years after that, another daughter. They had planned to name her Linda, but Conor and Katie had named their daughter Lynda just months before, so little Amanda came home to join her siblings.

Aggie was busy with the children and keeping the household running, while Henry would be away for stretches of time for the airline. She enjoyed her time with the kids, teaching them and taking them on adventures around town as they explored the city she now called home. At times, though, she missed her time with the WAAAFs and working on planes.

Henry was still enjoying flying, but the airline schedule made it hard to spend time with his family. The Bolanski kids were starting grammar school and Henry hated missing out, not being around to help with homework and got to school plays and pee wee baseball games.

After a backyard barbecue with the McLean family, as the kids ran through the sprinkler on a hazy summer evening, Henry and Conor presented their wives with a proposal.

"We're thinking we could open a charter air service out of one of the small airports near the city," Henry explained.

"We would offer chartered flights for businessmen who want to get to and from business meetings without having to wait on a commercial flight or if their meeting wasn't accessible by a commercial flight," said Conor.

Aggie and Katie exchanged a glance. Henry mentioned the idea to Aggie, but this was the first time the two couples discussed it together.

"So, we would all be in business together?" Katie asked.

"Yes, Conor and I could alternate flights, giving each of us more time at home with our families."

After much discussion, they started their air service out of Palwaukee Airport, a small municipal airport in the northwest suburbs. They bought a used Beechcraft 18 to start the business and began building their clientele.

One problem plagued their fledgling company. They could not hire and keep competent maintenance staff. Henry reached out to his contacts at Lewis to recruit certified mechanics, but many of the young men in the program wanted to work for the airlines. He even contacted his old crew chief, Bill Lago, to see if they could lure him away from his job at United Airlines.

"Sorry, Hank, I'm a supervisor now. No way you boys could meet my pay. Plus, I'm getting too old for busting my knuckles fixing planes."

Henry sighed. He knew it was unlikely that Bill would take his job offer.

"Besides, I don't know why you're asking me," Bill said. "You already have the perfect candidate."

"I do?"

"One of the best mechanics I've ever seen is right under your nose. She's probably at home making you meatloaf and mashed potatoes."

Henry paused. Would Aggie even be interested in going to work? Ryan and Karen were in third and first grade. Little Amanda was just starting kindergarten. Would she want to be out of the house?

"Aggie, we need to talk."

Aggie and Henry were finishing the dinner dishes and Aggie turned to Henry, drying her hands on the dish towel.

"This sounds serious," she said with a smile.

"It is. I talked with Bill Lago today about the maintenance position."

"Will he take the job?" she asked hopefully.

"No, he's happy where he is. He did give me an idea, though, and I want to run it by you."

"Okay. I'm all ears."

"Bill said he didn't know why I was talking to him about the job when I already have the perfect candidate."

"Oh, yeah? Who's that?"

"You," Henry said.

"Me? You want me to be your head of maintenance?"

"Sure! You're one of the best mechanics I've ever seen. Bill said the same thing. You'd be perfect!"

Aggie thought for a moment. "I think I would like that. I love being with the children, but I do miss using that mechanical part of my mind."

"Then let's do it! We'll get you certified to work here in the US, and you can be our chief mechanic."

The next question was what to do with the children if she was working. Again, a simple solution presented itself. The old neighborhood where Ma lived was getting more dangerous. He had been discussing the situation with Aggie and his ma when Aggie suggested an idea.

"We need a home closer to Palwaukee. With the new business, it makes sense to be as close as possible. We could look in Glenview, near the air station, or Mount Prospect. They have excellent schools for the kids."

Clearly, she's been doing her research, Henry reflected.

"Why don't we find a home that has enough room for your mum to move in with us? Then you don't need to worry about her in the city and she could help us look after the children after school if needed."

The family agreed to this plan. They bought a larger home closer to the hangar and Waleria joined them in the suburbs. Aggie, of course, passed her A&P exams on the first attempt and became the new head of maintenance for Great Lakes Air Service.

She was happy to be working again. Because they owned the company and lived so close by, it was not uncommon for the kids to come to work with one of their parents, spending the day at the hangar with Mum or taking a flight with Dad. They even set up a small play area in the office for the kids.

As the years rolled by, the kids grew. Ryan followed his mom on the path to become an aviation mechanic. To Henry's unending surprise, Karen trained as a pilot and was one of the first female pilots at Delta Airlines. He couldn't have been prouder. Amanda followed the path of her mother's family, marrying a farmer and living a happy life as a farm wife, raising her children and chickens.

Here they were, after 50 years of love and life. What a life it had been. Sharing a family and a business. They had travelled the world and loved every minute together.

Henry pulled Aggie close as they gazed out at the sunset on the horizon. He kissed her temple and whispered he loved her.

Aggie turned to him, raising up on her toes to kiss his lips as she had done for 50 years.

"I love you too. Thank you for giving me this wonderful life."

"We're a team, remember?" he said, resting his forehead against hers and letting their noses touch. "We gave each other a wonderful life. I'm so glad I bumped into you on that street in Sydney." He shook his head, marveling at how a chance meeting had led to this full life and the family that surrounded them in the fading Caribbean sunlight.

AUTHOR'S NOTE

This story began on a summer's day under the spreading boughs of an oak tree at All Saint's Cemetery in Des Plaines, Illinois. We were at the cemetery for my younger son's Eagle Scout project, identifying and logging the location of veterans' graves. To complete the project, we needed to look at every one of the 36,000 headstones in the cemetery to determine if they had any sort of military designation. As I walked down a row, pushing away cut grass and fallen leaves, I found a headstone with the following inscription:

AGNES C BOLANOWSKI

AUSTRALIAN AIR FORCE WWII

DEEPLY LOVED

Well, that was interesting, I thought to myself. We had found very few female veterans, certainly no women from Australia. I stepped to the next grave and found:

HENRY F BOLANOWSKI

BM2 US NAVY

WORLD WAR II

Oh, I thought, a love story. I snapped a photo of each headstone and posted them to my Facebook page with a brief description about how I imagined them meeting in Melbourne while he was on leave and her coming to America to live happily ever after with Henry in Chicago. In response to the post, my niece Colette posted, "How awesome! You should write a novel about them."

Yeah, right, like I was ever going to write a novel.

I thought about them on and off over the years and what their story might look like. In 2023, when that original Facebook post popped up in my "Memories," I saw their headstones and read Colette's comment and thought, "What the hell? I'll write a novel."

Considering I didn't particularly enjoy my creative writing class in college, I decidedly did NOT have the goal of writing a novel on a bucket list, so I didn't know how to begin. Being a reader, I went to the library and took out a book called *No Plot? No Problem! Write a Novel in 30 Days* and got started. I actually wrote the first draft in a little over a month. Then came the revisions and the editing. Now, just shy of a year later, here we are.

This is a work of fiction. I have never been to Australia, so any errors are errors of my imagination. While this story is unrelated to the story of the real Henry and Agnes, I kept their names to honor their inspiration.

This story begins and ends with family.

My family, bless us, are nerds. History nerds. Aviation nerds. My son Ryan works in aviation maintenance. My younger son Connor is studying to be a pilot. Both attended Lewis University for their training (Of course Henry would train at Lewis!). A story around World War II aviation was tailor made for us.

Family on my mom's side will recognize my grandma, Mary, and the Wiskowski kids from central Wisconsin, whose father abandoned the family after his wife and their mother died. I used my grandma's real-life experience of leaving school in eighth grade to work in the kitchen at a logging camp for Aggie's backstory in Australia.

Those familiar with my father-in-law Chester Parks will recognize Chet's stories in Henry's youthful shenanigans in Chicago. Chet began writing in his 70's, starting with his memoirs and ending with three novels and a children's book before he passed away. Thanks for inspiration in more ways than one, Czesiu! I continued your tradition of using names of friends and family in my novel.

Thanks to my Mom and Dad, who always encouraged my love of reading. I was that kid who had to be shooed out of the house on summer days, to put my book down and go play. They never limited what I read, and I always enjoyed historical fiction whether World War II or the Plantagenets. Dad is strongly represented in this novel by the character of Bill Lago, a hard-working guy who can fix anything.

Thanks to my son Connor, who was the inspiration to put Henry on the Enterprise, his favorite ship from World War II. With the exception of the stops in Sydney so Henry could meet Aggie, I promise wherever Enterprise is in the book is where the ship was in real life. Connor also acted as my informal technical advisor for WW2 aviation. I would shoot him a text with some random question about planes flying off the Enterprise and he would respond without fail. Thanks, buddy!

Thanks to my son Ryan. Helping him study for his A&P exam gave me insights into aviation maintenance that proved helpful in writing about Aggie's job. He also shared his thoughts about the cover design.

Finally, a huge thank you to my husband, Jeff, who never questioned why I was writing a novel out of the blue. He didn't even bat an eye when I asked to postpone our 31st anniversary dinner because our local library was hosting a lecture about self-publishing on our anniversary. Thank you for your patience and opinions. I love you.

About the Author

Diane Shillington Parks can usually be found reading a book and that book will most likely be romance or historical fiction. A self-described history nerd, she has had a lifelong interest in World War II, but learned a great deal about the Pacific Theater while writing Austral Skies.

Diane is a Physical Therapist by profession and enjoys reading, cooking, and chocolate in her free time. She lives in the northwest suburbs of Chicago with her husband of 32 years and her children, one an aviation mechanic and the other a pilot.

Austral Skies is her first novel.